SCRIBBLERS ON THE ROOF

Scribblers

CONTEMPORARY AMERICAN

on the Roof

JEWISH FICTION

Edited by **MELVIN JULES BUKIET** and **DAVID G. ROSKIES**

A KAREN & MICHAEL BRAZILLER BOOK

PERSEA BOOKS / NEW YORK

For permission to reprint or for any other information,
write to the publisher:

Persea Books, Inc.
853 Broadway
New York, New York 10003

Library of Congress Cataloging-in-Publication Data

Scribblers on the roof : contemporary American Jewish fiction / edited
by Melvin Jules Bukiet and David G. Roskies.—1st ed.
p. cm.
"A Karen and Michael Braziller Book."
ISBN 0-89255-326-X (pbk. : alk. paper)
1. American fiction—Jewish authors. 2. Short stories, American. 3.
Short stories, Jewish. 4. American fiction—20th century.
5. Jews—United States—Fiction. 6. Jewish fiction. I. Bukiet, Melvin Jules.
II. Roskies, David G., 1948– III. Title.
PS647.J4S37 2006
813'.0108892409045—dc22
2006002819

Designed by Rita Lascaro
Manufactured in the United States of America

FIRST EDITION

Contents

An Introduction

Melvin Jules Bukiet

JEWS ARE GOOD AT TWO THINGS: being killed and writing about it. Indeed, our greatest story is, despite its conclusion in liberation, one of generations of enslavement and death in pharaohnic Egypt. All of our historical holidays—as opposed to the seasonal ones—are stories of suffering under larger empires, be they Roman, Persian or, in the case of Yom Hashoa, German. Even Yom Ha'atzma'ut, the Day of Independence celebrating the birth of Israel in 1948, is also a story of attack by the new nation's assembled Arab neighbors. As the joke goes: What's the definition of a Jewish holiday? They tried to kill us; they failed; let's eat. A less funny, more accurate sequence might be: They tried to kill us; they nearly succeeded; let's write.

Whatever cultural dynamic distinguishes between the ages and the continents, Jews have continued to suffer and to write in whatever native or diasaporic language we've had available. That writing has come to glorious fruition in the twentieth century's ultimate home of the Jews: America.

Not that all of us have suffered here. Just the opposite—witness Jewish success everywhere from Hollywood to corporate boardrooms to the Supreme Court—and yet something still whispers the imperative: "Write, for it may be all that you can take with you. Write, for it may be all that you leave behind. Write for those whom you love and in defiance of those who seek to kill you." Or, more philosophically: "Write to prove that you exist."

In retrospect, it seems like the first occupation the newly American Jews engaged in after landing at Castle Garden was the production of journalism and drama for the newspapers and theaters of the Lower East Side. That stewpot, the densest living quarter on the face of the earth, was the home for astonishing cultural activity. Of course, the neighborhood's very success doomed it, because once the immigrants prospered they immediately moved up in both lifestyle and geography to the haute bourgeois precincts of the Upper West Side—and with them went their writers.

Among the residents of the approximately three square miles that stretch between Central Park West and Riverside Drive from Lincoln Center at 64th Street to Columbia University at 116th Street have been novelists Philip Roth and I. B. Singer; critics Lionel and Diana Trilling and Alfred Kazin; editors of both magazines and publishing houses galore; and last as well as most enduring, fictional characters such as Saul Bellow's Mr. Sammler and Tommy Wilhelm and a host of Woody Allen's exotic fauna culminating in Gabe Roth, the novelist/professor of *Husbands and Wives,* whose celluloid home happened to be the real brick and mortar home of this writer.

Sure, there are outposts of Jewish life and imagination elsewhere, the 92nd Street Y eastward across Central Park and, for younger writers, the lettered streets of Alphabet City and, more recently, Brooklyn, but the cultural blend that emerged from cafeteria arguments and dinner parties in labyrinthine apartments with book-lined hallways is densest on the Upper West Side. Indeed, if any place can be said to be the epicenter of Jewish writing in the New World, this is it. For this reason it seemed entirely natural for Congregation Ansche Chesed, located in the center of the center of the Jewish universe, at 100th Street and West End Avenue, to establish a venue for such writers.

Seven years ago, thinking only of a little summer programming for its members, the adult education committee of Ansche Chesed came up with the notion of an al fresco reading series set atop the building on Monday nights from about the middle of June through the beginning of August. Scribblers on the Roof's first season of fourteen writers consisted almost entirely of those who lived within walking distance of the building. A few were even members. Nor did that list exhaust the local terrain. It's a testimony to the area that so many international cosmopolitans finally put down roots in the vicinity.

Cities are the natural habitat of Jews and among the ranks of urban metropoli none can hold a Shabbos candle to New York. Though Peter Stuyvesant did not wish to allow the first boatload of Jews to enter its harbor 350 years ago, he was wisely overruled by his Dutch masters, who knew that toleration, or as we presently call it pluralism, was the key to a city's cultural, spiritual, and financial prosperity. There's simply nowhere else in the world that can lay claim to such concentrated abundance.

The corollary to this abundance of scriveners is a similar plenitude of readers. On the debut evening of the Scribbler's series, a few dozen curious souls appeared to hear Steve Stern read about a flying rabbi. Gradually, however, word spread that something was going on and soon crowds of up to 150 people gathered on the roof to listen to the readings while basking in the view of adjacent water towers and elevator bulkheads. Who could have imagined that those first few haphazardly organized evenings might become the most successful program that the shul had ever embarked on and that more than half a decade later Scribblers would have evolved into a much-anticipated annual tradition? If initially people came to hear a particular writer, now they simply come because they expect the best. In gratitude to Ansche Chesed for providing such ears, my co-editor and I decided to put together a volume recollecting those first seasons for the benefit of the institution. We are editing *Scribblers on the Roof* pro bono so that the shul can receive every penny of advance and royalties from its sale. Similarly, the writers themselves have generously contributed their work on the same basis.

Ironically, the very success of the series provided its own difficulty when it came time to edit this book, because the first six years' lists included many times the number of writers that could fit between the covers. To begin the winnowing, we made a genre decision, leaving writers better known for nonfiction such as Nessa Rapoport and Daniel Asa Rose and poets like Alicia Ostriker and Gerald Stern for—we hope—another volume. But even then, there was still too much fiction to include, and so decisions had to be made.

Surely the easiest, but also the weirdest and most exciting request we made was to Cynthia Ozick: easy because Ozick may be the most significantly Jewish writer of our time; exciting because her story, "Stone," was the first fiction she ever published and has never been republished; and weird because it's about Mohammed—at least the statue of the prophet long since removed from atop the ornate Beaux Arts New York State Court of Appeals building on Madison Square. These days, the pedestal remains empty, yet the story lives.

One necessarily appended note to "Stone": we, the editors, thrilled with our find—unearthed from the de-acquisition room of the Columbia University library—requested its use in this book from Ms. Ozick, who generously agreed, though she had not read it in decades. Later in the publishing process, when she did read it, she regretted her acquiescence. The prose she finds "conventional, pedestrian, and tritely time-bound"; she considers the story overall to be "an act of ventriloquism in which my younger self lamely attempted, through false style, a WASP-y persona." These qualms may or may not be legitimate—a writer may not be the best judge of her own work—but we insist that the story also contains in incipient form a fascinating view of the theological concerns that have animated much of her subsequent work. Call us Max Brod.

Like "Stone," much of the work in *Scribblers* is set in New York City. Jonathan Rosen's "First Date," taken from his most recent novel, is a quirky tale of modern romance—she's a rabbi—that takes place during a funeral at Riverside Memorial Chapel on Amsterdam Avenue and 76th Street, from which, incidentally, many Ansche Chesed members make their last journey on earth, while in "Looking for the Answers," Jonathan Ames encounters a sensitive bag lady outside of Pennsylvania Station who turns viciously antisemitic.

Though mostly composed in New York, several of the stories here travel abroad to other loci of Jewish experience. Both Jon Papernick and Aryeh Lev Stollman set stories in Israel. Papernick's "An Unwelcome Guest" is an eerie take on the meaning of "home" within the context of Israeli / Arab conflict, and Stollman's "Mr. Mitochondria" involves a precocious young boy awaiting a biblically evocative swarm of locusts in the Negev Desert. In "Pu-239," Ken Kalfus posits a nuclear nightmare in present-day Russia. Note that "Pu-239" is not explicitly Jewish—whatever that means. Indeed, we did not insist that every story in this collection have a Jewish theme. We simply wanted the strongest work we could find from each of the authors. Besides, the notion of bad things happening in Eastern Europe feels Jewish.

Those bad things are faced head on in two Holocaust-related stories, by Sonia Pilcer and Jonathan Levi. Pilcer's "'Paskudnyak'" explores the dilemma of the so-called Second Generation, a term that she did much to popularize in an earlier essay that explicated the condition of children of Holocaust survivors. Levi's "The Scrimshaw Violin" follows one musical instrument from its evil origins in genocidal Europe to its uneasy resting place on Nantucket Island.

The stories also range in terms of age concerns from Max Apple's classic "'The Eighth Day,'" in which the protagonist hilariously seeks the true story of his circumcision to the tale of a lonely old woman in Lynne Sharon Schwartz's "Mrs. Saunders Writes to the World." Like "Pu-239," "Mrs. Saunders" has no overt Jewish content, yet its emphasis on the power of names evokes a Jewish mode of thought. Indeed, when God makes Jacob the father of the Jewish people, he seals the moment by changing Jacob's name to Israel.

Set between the extremes of infancy and senility are "Faith Is a Girl's Name," in which Binnie Kirshenbaum's protagonist recalls various young women in her life in a kind of mnemonic collage, and Mary Morris's "The Hall of the Meteorites," in which the main character thinks of the men in hers while affectionately pondering the cosmos in the Museum of Natural History on Central Park West.

Of course, other kinds of relationships are also explored. Myra Goldberg's "Gifts" focuses on the complicated interplay of a mother and her grown daughter who can never quite surmount the ties that bind, whereas "Solid Food" by Lucy Rosenthal and "What Must I Say to You?" by Norma Rosen respectively provide unique perspectives on individuals affected by international and racial politics. The former involves various forms of betrayal on the eve of the Second World War, whereas the latter depicts the connection between a Jewish woman and her child's black nanny.

In line with another longstanding Jewish literary tradition, several stories are fantastical. To start, we have Steve Stern's exuberant "Lazar Malkin Enters Heaven" about a kvetchy old man who negotiates with the Angel of Death. Just as giddy if more earthbound, Janice Eidus discovers the King of rock 'n' roll hiding among Orthodox Jews in the Bronx in "Elvis, Axl, and Me." Likewise falling within the realm of the unreal is Pearl Abraham's quasi-Hasidic parable, "The Seven Fat Brides," from her novel based on the work of Nachman of Bratslav, while a terrifyingly different parable of totalitarianism is executed to shocking effect in Lore Segal's "The Reverse Bug." Lastly, the youngest writer in the book, Dara Horn, travels the farthest literal and figurative distance from everyday concerns in "Readers Digest" when she ascends into the ethereum to visit heaven.

In short, we aimed for representation as well as excellence, matching up young and old, hip and straight, writers of political and personal concern, writers of social and magic realism, writers whose work takes place in New York itself and anywhere else the Jewish imagination lives or wanders.

Thus, we present a smorgasbord from glatt kosher to pure treyf, which can also be tasty. Frankly, we hope it's a feast. Let's eat.

SCRIBBLERS ON THE ROOF

The Seven Fat Brides

Pearl Abraham

IT CAME TO PASS that Joel's father stood waiting beside his son's bed, basin and pitcher in his hands. Joel gave his fingertips to the splash of cold water without lifting his head, one-two-three, and mouthed the "I admit before thee, O live and lasting king, who has returned to me my soul . . ."

Then he remembered what day it was. He would be meeting for a second time with Reb Mendel's seventh daughter. Before she would agree to marry him, there was a detail to work out, and she wanted to be sure it was acceptable to Joel. It was unusual for a young girl to make such a demand, and he wondered what she had in mind. He'd seen her once, and had decided right away that she was very acceptable to him.

The meeting was set for ten that morning which meant that he would miss his nine o'clock study session, and wouldn't have an opportunity to review yesterday's lecture. Which was why he'd asked his father to wake him early.

Traditionally the boy is expected to begin talking, Joel knew, but since this second meeting was arranged at the girl's request, he thought she might begin. When she didn't, he smiled, she smiled shyly in return, and he thought her smiling face immensely pleasing. He asked how she'd been.

The seventh daughter looked up into his eyes, nodded, and said fine, then looked down. Probably not so fine, Joel thought.

She hesitated, maybe it was just shyness, then spoke. I wanted to see you again because there is something I must explain to you. It was decided that such intimate information would be most acceptable to you coming from me.

Joel smiled encouragement. She seemed so serious, he thought the knowledge she was about to impart must be very intimate indeed. And who was it who had decided? Her parents?

You see, she said, you don't know my other sisters, but if you did, and God willing you soon will, you would see that I owe everything I have to them. When you see them it will become clear to you that every one of my parts that has been called beautiful is a copy of one of theirs, that I am altogether made up of my sisters' parts. I have my eldest sister's deep blue eyes, my second sister's shapely ears, my third sister's fluid voice, my fourth sister's slender long neck, my fifth sister's straight shoulders, and my sixth sister's pale long fingers. The best of each is in me, which is perhaps why I am fattest. So you see, in marrying me, you acquire also them, and therefore I must propose that you marry each of us separately, in the order in which we were born. You seem shocked. Perhaps you are thinking of the edict of Rabeinu Gershom against multiple wives. That shouldn't be a concern. Our father has received an allowance signed by forty elders. I have been told to advise you to think of this as Jacob's seven years of labor.

Joel nodded to acknowledge the reference. Although he was amazed at the request, he was conscious enough to register the girl's words and how well they'd been put together. She must have rehearsed them.

My sisters are here to meet you, she said, and stood.

He watched her walk to the door quickly, rather lightly, he thought, for someone carrying so much weight. Her six sisters came in and took seats at the table, leaving the chair on his immediate right for the youngest, and this too seemed significant.

The eldest sister cleared her throat and when Joel turned toward her, he felt himself transfixed. She spoke.

I have been blessed with what others agree are the most beautiful bluest eyes. Seeing through this deep blue makes everything appear more attractive and leaves me in a highly receptive state. Since I am always in this state, I will see you with utmost tenderness at all times. You will always be certain of the friendliest, kindest reception. Never will a harsh word pass between us. Never will you have to waste a moment thinking about what I said, or what I may have intended. Your mind will be free to think only of Torah, twelve hours a day. However, before I can agree to be your bride, there is something you must do. You must prove yourself worthy by fulfilling one of the seven tasks practiced by the great ascetics of Safed. The choice of the task is yours and I hope you will accomplish it with great joy.

Joel looked into her eyes as she spoke. It was true they were beautiful, deeply blue with a kind and deep black center. They held his own eyes. He couldn't turn away until she closed her eyes for a long blink, and then he was able to look into the seventh daughter's eyes for comparison. They were similar, but the younger eyes didn't hold him as her sister's had, didn't contain the same depths. About the girl's request that he perform an ascetic task, he didn't know what to think. Wasn't marrying all seven of them enough of a challenge?

The second sister shifted her weight and Joel turned toward her.

I have been blessed with the most intricately formed ears, which provide me with a level of hearing rarely attained by humans. I have the ability to detect the softest breaths and sighs. With such ears, I will be attuned to your every mood, your every discontent, however minor. I will understand what you are experiencing even before you are fully conscious of it. With every discomfort acknowledged and attended to, you will be free for only the highest thoughts. However, there is one thing you must do for me, and that is to take upon yourself the challenge of a daily recital of Psalms.

When Joel compared the ears of the youngest sister with those of her sister, he saw the difference and acquired a new appreciation for ears. These ears were livelier, attentive and expressive in a way other ears merely imitated. The challenge of a daily recital of Psalms, though not an impossible task, was unusual, the kind of burden a man ought to take upon himself only on personal impulse.

Joel heard the sound of a smooth clear voice, fluid and sweet as milk and honey, and he turned toward the third sister who was merely speaking but with so much melody it occurred to Joel that although a woman's voice is illicit to men only in song, this woman's plain speech was more beautiful than most singing. He was hearing the sound of her voice and not what she said, but it didn't matter. He knew that what she had to say was convincing, that her voice would inspire him to great prayer and song. And he was certain she had requested something difficult of him, too. He would have to ask about that later because already she was finished and the fourth sister had begun.

Joel turned toward her. Her neck was wrapped in a silk cloth spun of gold. Joel watched as she slowly untied it and looked into his eyes, but it was hard for him to take his own eyes from her pale, slender, and impossibly long neck, so delicate, you were afraid for it. He wanted to tell her to keep it wrapped, to protect it, but then he wouldn't see it. She was sitting down, but still he could see that the thinness of her neck was in great contrast to the rest of her, which made her appear more vulnerable.

She spoke softly and Joel had to crane his own neck to hear her.

The fragility of my exposed neck creates in men a great empathy for the weak and vulnerable. Seeing it on a daily basis will make of you a better person, a considerate being whose desire will be to help the weak. In helping others you will feel yourself most generous, and with such a feeling, every day of your life will be worthwhile. You will not experience a moment of despair, of wondering why you have been placed on earth. However, before I can become your bride, there is a difficult task I must ask of you, that you commit one day of every week to fasting for the first seven years of our married life.

Joel nodded. Fasting was a standard ascetic practice and he'd been expecting such a request from one of the sisters.

He turned toward the fifth sister whose posture was perfect. Without a trace of a slouch, she spoke.

I am blessedly noted for the straightest shoulders among women. These are shoulders that inspire men to take on the great burdens of the world, and such men, as you know, become eligible for a position among the thirty-six Just Men whose goodness maintains cosmic equilibrium. Much has been asked of you today, and therefore I will refrain from adding my own request. I choose rather merely to second those of the others.

Joel thought the girl's humility in the face of her sisters' demands quite fine and also clever. And he found much to admire in her shoulders, which were covered in a pretty, yellow, crocheted shawl whose loose stitches provided glimpses of the fine flesh beneath. He nodded to show his appreciation, and turned to the next sister.

The sixth sister put her hands, which were beautifully pale and slender, on the table, but before she could speak, the door opened and there was his mother, and behind her, the girls' mother, carrying the seven plates to be broken. He and the seven sisters watched as his mother broke the first plate and said mazel tov and then reached for the next plate, and the next. He tried to stop her, to make himself heard above the clattering sound of porcelain breaking. He tried to shout, Wait, but no sound emerged. His throat was dry and hoarse.

Moving his legs, he felt the dampness of his undergarments and his heart sank. He'd released spirits without bodies, demons who would work against man, and set back the redemption of the world. And these demons would attend his funeral, follow him to his grave, complaining of their bodiless state, and weigh in against him just as he entered the next world, with Judgment Day upon him.

He would have to attempt a correction, refrain from food and drink all day. He looked at his watch. It was late, he was tired, if only he could get to bed, but already his wedding to the eldest of the seven sisters was in full swing; he was sitting beside the bride, along with the wedding guests, waiting for Yankel Yankevitch, the first of the seven wedding rhymers to begin. The bride's father was talking to him, and Yankel nodded in agreement. Then, in the traditional *badkhn*'s chant, Yankel began, and Joel knew that whether he kept his eyes open or closed, whether conscious or not, the next six weddings would take place, the story would continue.

Yankel Yankevitch began with a preface, explaining that the father of the bride, R. Mendel, had begged him to keep the performance short, seeing as it was close to midnight and there were six more weddings scheduled to follow. And since he, Yankel, had always been a reasonable man, he had agreed, especially since there was good reason to keep things short: the family was tired, and marrying off one daughter required difficult and multitudinous preparations; multiplied seven times, the work would be without end, especially since each daughter had been promised a wedding unique to her. After all, Yankel pointed out, Reb Mendel's daughters are fine Jewish girls, they deserve proper Jewish weddings, no Sun Myung Moon orgy of sameness. To persuade the guests of the enormity of R. Mendel's burden, Yankel proposed to take a few moments to reflect on the preparations seven weddings might entail.

First the purchase of forty-five to fifty yards of heavy white satin, and plenty of yards of lace and several pounds of glistening pearls and other beads, and then some of that sheer fabric, what is it called, the women here ought to know—organza, thank you—and how many spools of thread, and packets of hooks and eyes, and don't forget the satin-covered buttons, and the stiff white tulle for the underlayers of the skirts. And I'm sure, being only a man and ignorant of such womanly things, I've managed to leave out some significant items.

Then the measuring, cutting, pinning, and stitching of seven bridal dresses must begin, each bride with her own style; and the question of whether to hire one seamstress for all the dresses, or seven different ones, has to be debated; however my wife informs me that good seamstresses aren't easy to come by, the name of a good seamstress is entered into the family vault of secrets.

Then the fittings. The seamstress finds that one daughter has gained five pounds (she runs out of the room crying), the other has shed a few (she tries and fails to hide her feeling of triumph), and you can't blame the girls, it's how things are before a wedding, some eat more when they're nervous, others don't eat at all; and so one dress is taken in, another let out, and the seamstress begs the girls to be certain there are no more changes in their figures. And then on the third fitting, it's discovered that the youngest daughter, who's still growing, has shot up two inches, and the dress has to be lengthened. After much discussion and debate, a band of lace is added. In the making of a bridal dress, every woman will inform you, traces of the miracles of Creation can be found. Since in this world every creative act features aspects of God's work, you have to agree that there's some truth in the claim. And if even God needed rest on the seventh day, how tired must this family be. Is it any wonder then that R. Mendel wants to keep things short. And I've only given you a taste of things. Listen further:

Of course every bride must have a pair of white shoes and even if R. Mendel's virtuous daughters wanted to save their dear father some hard-earned money, as fate would have it, the feet of these sisters happen to be like a set of Russian dolls, each pair a half size larger than the one before her. And so seven pairs of white shoes had to be purchased, and as we all know, in September, white shoes aren't easy to come by. The girls would have spent hours searching the sale racks of last season's shoes. In a dusty store on the Lower East Side, which has become a kind of open-air discount mall, the eldest sister found a pair of shoes made by Ralph Lauren, formerly Lipschutz, called a sling-back. The second sister purchased a pair that raised her off the floor several inches, and since she was already an inch or two taller than the others, she would stand out even more, which she didn't mind. Several more shopping trips, and a third shoe was found, this one so pointed and narrow that to wear it comfortably, a full size larger was necessary. The fourth sister came home one evening with a famous square-toed, square-heeled shoe. Her mother and sisters stared. The shoe was all corners, not a single note of grace. That's the whole point, the girl explained. It breaks out of the traditional ideas of what makes a shoe beautiful. That's what this designer is known for. Their mother shrugged. If you love it, I love it. The fifth sister decided to do what none of the others would: she purchased the traditional bridal pump from a traditional bridal shop, the renowned Kleinfeld's of Flatbush, and what brought amazed looks to the faces of her sisters: she paid more for this plain shoe than any of the others had. The sixth sister then broke all the rules and purchased an open toe, open heel, open everywhere shoe. The youngest sister went to her favorite shoe store, Buster Brown, and bought a pair of white patent-leather Mary-Janes that previously she'd owned only in black. The cost: a mere forty-five dollars, which meant that she hadn't cut so deeply into her bridal budget. The others fell in love with the innocence of the shoe, with the originality of the idea, and especially the cost, which had left their youngest sister with the most spending power. Also, she would be the only one who would dance comfortably at her own wedding.

The sisters decided that one bridal crown and veil could be used by all, which meant that all of them would have something to say about the design of this crown, the fabrics used, the length, the style, until their dear, exhausted mother put her foot down and said there will be seven different crowns and veils.

In the design and writing of the invitations, R. Mendel was consulted. A single invitation for all seven weddings was considered and ruled out. First the paper had to be selected, the stock and color, the shape and fold. Then the typeface, script or block type, traditional serif or modern sans-serif, raised or not, and in which color—black, brown, gold, or silver. One daughter insisted on white ink on linen white card stock, a style called white-on-white, and R. Mendel feared for the attendance at her wedding. Another decision he had to make: whether or not to feature an English-language version of the invitation on the facing side, as had become common even in Williamsburg. R. Mendel went back and forth on this, pointing out that each and every person on the guest list was perfectly fluent in Hebrew. In the end, though, he gave into what his daughters wanted, and English-language versions were featured on all seven invitations.

And when the printed invitations finally arrived, and were carefully examined and proofread for errors, the next seven evenings had to be spent addressing the envelopes, stuffing, stamping, and finally mailing them, and not all from the same mailbox since mailmen have been known to dump too-large batches of the same envelope in the trash.

In the addressing of the envelopes, more decisions had to be made. The color of the ink to be used. One daughter took great pride in her handwriting, she'd always excelled in penmanship, and so insisted on personally addressing all her invitations. Another daughter had studied calligraphy, and all her envelopes had to feature the flourishes of a fountain pen fitted with a half-inch nib. Not to be outdone, the other sisters devised their own solutions to the task of addressing invitations. The youngest sister, who worked on the computer at the office of the Beth Rachel School for Girls and had experience with mass mailings, entered the guest list into the computer and printed the addresses in Matura MT Script capitals on transparent labels. When R. Mendel saw the labels, he was inclined to grab and kiss his smartest of daughters, but not wanting to start something among the sisters—every father knows what Joseph's robe of many colors led to—satisfied himself with patting her on the back. Since the guest lists were identical for each sister, she offered to print several sets of labels. After showing samples of the various choices available, she brought home one set of labels in Brush Script, another in Arial Black, a third in Times New Roman, and a fourth in Bookman Old Style, and the remaining invitations were in the mail in a matter of hours.

Yankel held his hand up and counted off the next series of tasks on his fingers. There was the hiring of seven caterers, the planning of seven meals, the designing of seven centerpieces, the selecting of seven different wines, the writing of seven marriage contracts, the distributing of honors to the various rabbis and relatives of personage, seven per wedding, which adds up to forty-nine difficult decisions.

He paused to sip water and in the audience someone shouted, Enough is enough. You call yourself a wedding *badkhn*. Where are the promised rhymes, not one word you've uttered has rhymed with another. I've been doing this work for only a year and I can do better than that.

Yankel faced the man. You're obviously still wet behind the ears, he said. I haven't begun. This has all been a preface. But since you ask, I'll show you how an experienced *badkhn* works. Novices rhyme the last words, and that's fine, but child's play. In my work, every word rhymes with the one above it. In poetry this difficult technique is known as internal rhyming. If you and your colleagues agree to give up this evening's earnings to me, I'll show you how it's done.

The younger man looked to his five colleagues, and when he had a nod from each, shook hands on the agreement.

Listen closely and you'll learn a thing or two. He pressed the young man back into the throng, took three strides toward center stage, twirled his mustache, inhaled deeply, and delivered his first line

The holy groom, Reb Joel, son of Reb Moshe, is a heightened soul....

The audience filled in the missing notes: yaididai-didaidaidai...

Joel closed his eyes. When he opened them again, the second daughter was sitting beside him and Yankel Yankevitch was preparing to deliver the second internally rhyming line, as promised. Expectations were high. Various people had come up with various rhyming words for each of the words in the first line, but to conceive of the right combination of words and put them together in a meaningful sentence seemed impossible.

Yankel lifted his arms and there was silence. He twirled the ends of his mustache once again, put his hands behind his back, and delivered the second line:

The holy groom, Reb Joel, son of Reb Moshe, is a heightened soul....

The audience filled in the missing notes. After which there was a hush in the room of held breaths as they listened for the next line. But Yankel merely retired to his seat to wait for the next wedding.

Joel opened and closed his eyes, a reverse eyeblink, since in the scheme of cosmogonic time, everything in this world, including our dreams, is only as long as an eyeblink. And then his third bride was beside him, and Yankel Yankevitch was preparing to deliver his third line.

The room was silent; all eyes were on Yankel, who was in no hurry. He made a great show of putting his hands behind his back, of pacing to the right, then left. He paused at stage center, raised his hands as if in an appeal to the muses, and chanted.

The holy groom Reb Joel son of Reb Moshe is a heightened soul....

The audience roared.

Before Joel opened and closed his eyes again, he saw the six rivals surround Yankel.

Looking for the Answers

Jonathan Ames

IT WAS ONE OF THOSE DAYS when every time I went to go out the door, something grabbed me in the back of the brain and said, lie down and masturbate one more time. So I spent the whole day moving in and out of consciousness between naps and reveries, counting the hours until the free phone-sex message would change. It changes three times a day. Finally around midnight when the paper bag to my right was filled with tissue paper I pushed myself out the door with a surge of will and courage.

Once on the street the cold air braced me and I judged myself guilty of murdering a perfectly good day off and so sentenced myself to walk as far as I could to make up for the terrible sloth I had just endured. I didn't stop, except for an onion roll at an all-night deli, until one A.M., when I arrived at Penn Station. I was not alone in the great train cave under Thirty-fourth Street as there were hundreds of homeless snuggled into corners to sleep or grow ill. I walked around and all was yellow down there because of the lights, except for some drunk sports fans who seemed green and waited for trains to New Jersey. An occasional cop patrolled with his modern-handled billy club to keep all of us in order and I always think cops are fat, until I remember the bulletproof vests under their blue shirts.

I sat down on the escalator stairs and perched above me, beside me, and below me, like so many birds in a tree were old bag ladies cooing and chirping to themselves and shaking their saggy, gray faces in imaginary conversations. Some of them drifted in and out of sleep and their heads fell to their chests, until they would snap them back, afraid and alert. They muttered to themselves to stay awake to protect their bags. They're known to carry money or something of value in those sacks, and to fall asleep might mean a kick to the ribs (and their bones heal no more) and the loss of another possession. So they sit alone fighting sleep and they are all loners, for unlike the fellowship that exists among male bums, the bag ladies don't even trust one another.

I offered the old lady next to me half the roll I had bought at the deli. She accepted it, gummed half of it, then wrapped the rest in some old sandwich paper and hid it somewhere in her many layers of clothes. I watched her closely, because over the years I've had this off and on fantasy that someone out there is carrying a pearl of knowledge that is meant just for me. It's something of a wise man search and I don't take it too seriously, but I have made a point of talking to lots of people, whores, bums, countermen, relatives, yet no one has told me, as far as I can tell, the thing I need to hear. So having given this bag lady something to eat, I thought that perhaps she wouldn't mind giving me some advice. Maybe she was the one.

"Excuse me, ma'am. I was wondering, if you don't mind, if you could tell me.... See I'm cracking up," I blurted out, "I mean I am very unhappy, I spent the whole day in my room, and I don't know what to do. Do you have any idea?" As with every time I ask this question I experience this wonderful eternal moment of hope that the answer is coming forth. She was a fiery one and went right into it, almost yelling at me.

"What do you expect. Of course you're unhappy. I'm unhappy, we're all unhappy because the god damn Jews killed our Christ. You know that, everyone knows that, and not only did they kill Christ but they're still out here doing evil because they took all my money, took all my clothes, turned my children against me and put me on the street. They'd have me sell myself, but I will not sell my body. And they're starving us and feeding their god damn Jewselves. Just look at all these Christians starving and sleeping on cardboard. You don't see any Jews down here. And a Jew owns Penn Station, you better believe it! I hate the bastards."

She stopped a second, took a breath, and her eyes got a little less wild. She ran her hands over the gray, dirty clump of weed that was her hair just like a genteel lady. She smiled with her gums at me and the gray skin of her face creased and shifted upward. She was calm.

"I can see you're a good boy," she said, "you must have fine parents. I can tell these things. They must have told you, to be happy you've got to have a position. With a position you can do anything, have food, money, a house. You see," she smiled again and explained, "I don't have a position. I'm trying to get one, but I don't have it yet. But you're young, get yourself a position and the money hungry Jews won't put you on the street."

"I'm a Jew," I said.

She turned her head quickly in shock to look at me and said, "And you don't have a position?"

"The Eighth Day"

Max Apple

1

I WAS ALWAYS INTERESTED IN MYSELF, but I never thought I went back so far. Joan and I talked about birth almost as soon as we met. I told her I believed in the importance of early experience.

"What do you mean by early?" she asked. "Before puberty, before loss of innocence?"

"Before age five," I said.

She sized me up. I could tell it was the right answer.

She had light-blond hair that fell over one eye. I liked the way she moved her hair away to look at me with two eyes when she got serious.

"How soon before age five?" She took a deep breath before she asked me that. I decided to go the limit.

"The instant of birth," I said, though I didn't mean it and had no idea where it would lead me.

She gave me the kind of look then that men would dream about if being men didn't rush us so.

With that look Joan and I became lovers. We were in a crowded restaurant watching four large goldfish flick their tails at each other in a display across from the cash register. There was also another couple, who had introduced us.

Joan's hand snuck behind the napkin holder to rub my right index finger. With us chronology went backwards. Birth led us to love.

2

Joan was twenty-six and had devoted her adult life to knowing herself.

"Getting to know another person, especially one from the opposite gender, is fairly easy." She said this after our first night together. "Apart from reproduction, it's the main function of sex. The biblical word 'to know' someone is exactly right. But nature didn't give us any such easy and direct ways to know ourselves. In fact, it's almost perverse how difficult it is to find out anything about the self."

She propped herself up on an elbow to look at me, still doing all the talking.

"You probably know more about my essential nature from this simple biological act than I learned from two years of psychoanalysis."

Joan had been through Jung, Freud, LSD, philosophy, and primitive religion. A few months before we met, she had re-experienced her own birth in primal therapy. She encouraged me to do the same. I tried and was amazed at how much early experience I seemed able to remember, with Joan and the therapist to help me. But there was a great stumbling block, one that Joan did not have. On the eighth day after my birth, according to the ancient Hebrew tradition, I had been circumcised. The circumcision and its pain seemed to have replaced in my consciousness the birth trauma. No matter how much I tried, I couldn't get back any earlier than the eighth day.

"Don't be afraid," Joan said. "Go back to birth. Think of all experience as an arch."

I thought of the golden arches of McDonald's. I focused. I howled. The therapist immersed me in warm water. Joan, already many weeks past her mother's postpartum depression, watched and coaxed. She meant well. She wanted me to share pain like an orgasm, like lovers in poems who slit their wrists together. She wanted us to be as content as trees in the rain forest. She wanted our mingling to begin in utero.

"Try," she said.

The therapist rubbed Vaseline on my temples and gripped me gently with Teflon-coated kitchen tongs. Joan shut off all the lights and played in stereo the heartbeat of a laboring mother.

For thirty seconds I held my face under water. Two rooms away a tiny flashlight glowed. The therapist squeezed my ribs until I bruised. The kitchen tongs hung from my head like antennae. But I could go back no farther than the hairs beneath the chin of the man with the blade who pulled at and then slit my tiny penis, the man who prayed and drank wine over my foreskin. I howled and I gagged.

"The birth canal," Joan and the therapist said.

"The knife," I screamed, "the blood, the tube, the pain between my legs."

Finally we gave up.

"You Hebrews," Joan said. "Your ancient totems cut you off from the centers of your being. It must explain the high density of neurosis among Jewish males."

The therapist said that the subject ought to be studied, but she didn't think anyone would give her a grant.

I was a newcomer to things like primal therapy, but Joan had been born for the speculative. She was the Einstein of pseudo-science. She knew tarot, phrenology, and metaposcopy the way other people knew about baseball or cooking. All her time was spare time except when she didn't believe in time.

When Joan could not break down those eight days between my birth and my birthright, she became, for a while, seriously anti-Semitic. She used surgical tape to hunch my penis over into a facsimile of precircumcision. She told me that smegma was probably a healthy secretion. For a week she cooked nothing but pork. I didn't mind, but I worried a little about trichinosis because she liked everything rare.

Joan had an incredible grip. Her older brother gave her a set of Charles Atlas Squeezers when she was eight. While she read, she still did twenty minutes a day with each hand. If she wanted to show off, she could close the grip exerciser with just her thumb and middle finger. The power went right up into her shoulders. She could squeeze your hand until her nipples stood upright. She won spending money arm wrestling with men in bars. She had broken bones in the hands of two people, though she tried to be careful and gentle with everyone.

I met Joan just when people were starting to bore her, all people, and she had no patience for pets either. She put up with me, at least at the beginning, because of the primal therapy. Getting me back to my birth gave her a project. When the project failed and she also tired of lacing me with pork, she told me one night to go make love to dark Jewesses named Esther or Rebecca and leave her alone.

I hit her.

"Uncharacteristic for a neurotic Jewish male," she said.

It was my first fight since grade school. Her hands were much stronger than mine. In wrestling she could have killed me, but I stayed on the balls of my feet and kept my left in her face. My reach was longer so she couldn't get me in her grip.

"I'll pull your cock off!" she screamed and rushed at me. When my jab didn't slow her, I hit her a right cross to the nose. Blood spurted down her chin. She got one hand on my shirt and ripped it so hard she sprained my neck. I hit her in the midsection and then a hard but openhanded punch to the head.

"Christ killer, cocksucker," she called me, "wife beater." She was crying. The blood and tears mingled on her madras shirt. It matched the pattern of the fabric. I dropped my arms. She rushed me and got her hands around my neck.

"I must love you," I said, "to risk my life this way."

She loosened her grip but kept her thumbs on my jugular. Her face came down on mine, making us both a bloody mess. We kissed amid the carnage. She let go, but my neck kept her fingerprints for a week.

"I'd never kill anyone I didn't love," she said. We washed each other's faces. Later she said she was glad she hadn't pulled my cock off.

After the fight we decided, mutually, to respect one another more. We agreed that the circumcision was a genuine issue. Neither of us wanted it to come between us.

"Getting to the bottom of anything is one of the great pleasures of life," Joan said. She also believed a fresh start ought to be just that, not one eight days old.

So we started fresh and I began to research my circumcision. Since my father had been dead for ten years, my mother was my only source of information. She was very reluctant to talk about it. She refused to remember the time of day or even whether it happened in the house or the hospital or the synagogue.

"All I know," she said, "is that Reb Berkowitz did it. He was the only one in town. Leave me alone with this craziness. Go swallow dope with all your friends. It's her, isn't it? To marry her in a church you need to know about your circumcision? Do what you want; at least the circumcision is one thing she can't change."

Listening in on the other line, Joan said, "They can even change sex now. To change the circumcision would be minor surgery, but that's not the point."

"Go to hell," my mother said and hung up. My mother and I had not been on good terms since I quit college. She is closer to my two brothers, who are CPAs and have an office together in New Jersey. But, to be fair to my mother, she probably wouldn't want to talk about their circumcisions either.

From the *United Synagogue Yearbook* which I found in the library of Temple Beth-El only a few blocks from my apartment I located three Berkowitzes. Two were clearly too young to have done me, so mine was Hyman J., listed at Congregation Adath Israel, South Bend, Indiana. "They all have such funny names," Joan said. "If he's the one, we'll have to go to him. It may be the breakthrough you need."

"Why?" my mother begged, when I told her we were going to South Bend to investigate. "For God's sake, why?"

"Love," I said. "I love her, and we both believe it's important to know this. Love happens to you through bodies."

"I wish," my mother said, "that after eight days they could cut the love off too and then maybe you'd act normal."

South Bend was a three-hundred-mile drive. I made an appointment with the synagogue secretary to meet Hyman Berkowitz late in the afternoon. Joan and I left before dawn. She packed peanut butter sandwiches and apples: She also took along the portable tape recorder so we could get everything down exactly as Berkowitz remembered it.

"I'm not all that into primal therapy anymore," she said as we started down the interstate. "You know that this is for your sake, that even if you don't get back to the birth canal this circumcision thing is no small matter. I mean, it's almost accidental that it popped up in primal; it probably would have affected you in psychoanalysis as well. I wonder if they started circumcising before or after astrology was a very well-developed Egyptian science. Imagine taking infants and mutilating them with crude instruments."

"The instruments weren't so crude," I reminded her. "The ancient Egyptians used to do brain surgery. They invented eye shadow and embalming. How hard was it to get a knife sharp, even in the Bronze Age?"

"Don't be such a defensive Jewish boy," she said. "After all, it's your pecker they sliced, and at eight days too, some definition of the age of reason."

For people who are not especially sexual, Joan and I talk about it a lot. She has friends who are orgiasts. She has watched though never participated in group sex.

"Still," she says, "nothing shocks me like the thought of cutting the foreskin of a newborn."

3

"It's no big deal," Berkowitz tells us late that afternoon. His office is a converted lavatory. The frosted glass windows block what little daylight there still is. His desk is slightly recessed in the cavity where once a four-legged tub stood. His synagogue is a converted Victorian house. Paint is peeling from all the walls. Just off the interstate we passed an ultramodern temple.

"Ritual isn't in style these days," he tells Joan when she asks about his surroundings. "The clothing store owners and scrap dealers have put their money into the Reformed. They want to be more like the goyim."

"I'm a goy," Joan says. She raises her head proudly to display a short straight nose. Her blond hair is shoulder length.

"So what else is new?" Berkowitz laughs. "Somehow, by

accident, I learned how to talk to goyim too." She asks to see his tools.

From his desk drawer he withdraws two flannel-wrapped packets. They look like place settings of sterling silver. It takes him a minute or two to undo the knots. Before us lies a long thin pearl-handled jackknife.

"It looks like a switchblade," Joan says. "Can I touch it?" He nods. She holds the knife and examines the pearl handle for inscriptions.

"No writing?"

"Nothing," says Berkowitz. "We don't read knives."

He takes it from her and opens it. The blade is as long as a Bic pen. Even in his dark office the sharpness glows.

"All that power," she says, "just to snip at a tiny penis."

"Wrong," says Berkowitz. "For the shmekel I got another knife. This one kills chickens."

Joan looks puzzled and nauseated.

"You think a person can make a living in South Bend, Indiana, on newborn Jewish boys? You saw the temple. I've got to compete with a half dozen Jewish pediatricians who for the extra fifty bucks will say a prayer too. When I kill a chicken, there's not two cousins who are surgeons watching every move. Chickens are my livelihood. Circumcising is a hobby."

"You're cute," Joan tells him.

H. Berkowitz blushes. "Shiksas always like me. My wife worries that someday I'll run off with a convert. You came all this way to see my knife?" He is a little embarrassed by his question.

I try to explain my primal therapy, my failure to scream before the eighth day.

"In my bones, in my body, all I can remember is you, the knife, the blood."

"It's funny," Berkowitz says, "I don't remember you at all. Did your parents make a big party, or did they pay me a little extra or something? I don't keep records, and believe me, foreskins are nothing to remember."

"I know you did mine."

"I'm not denying. I'm just telling you it's not so special to me to remember it."

"Reverend," Joan says, "you may think this is all silly, but here is a man who wants to clear his mind by reliving his birth. Circumcision is standing in the way. Won't you help him?"

"I can't put it back."

"Don't joke with us, Reverend. We came a long way. Will you do it again?"

"Also impossible," he says. "I never leave a long enough piece of foreskin. Maybe some of the doctors do that, but I always do a nice clean job. Look."

He motions for me to pull out my penis. Joan also instructs me to do so. It seems oddly appropriate in this converted bathroom.

"There," he says, admiringly. "I recognize my work. Clean, tight, no flab."

"We don't really want you to cut it," Joan says. "He just wants to relive the experience so that he can travel back beyond it to the suffering of his birth. Right now your circumcision is a block in his memory."

Berkowitz shakes his head. I zip my fly.

"You're sure you want to go back so far?"

"Not completely," I admit, but Joan gives me a look.

"Well," Berkowitz says, "in this business you get used to people making jokes, but if you want it, I'll try. It's not like you're asking me to commit a crime. There's not even a rabbinic law against pretending to circumcise someone a second time."

4

The recircumcision takes place that night at Hyman Berkowitz's house. His wife and two children are already asleep. He asks me to try to be quiet. I am lying on his dining room table under a bright chandelier.

"I'd just as soon my wife not see this," Berkowitz says. "She's not as up to date as I am."

I am naked beneath a sheet on the hard table.

Berkowitz takes a small double-edged knife out of a torn and stained case. I can make out the remnants of his initials on the case. The instrument is nondescript stainless steel. If not for his initials, it might be mistaken for an industrial tool. I close my eyes.

"The babies," he says, "always keep their eyes open. You'd be surprised how alert they are. At eight days they already know when something's happening."

Joan puts a throw pillow from the sofa under my head.

"I'm proud of you," she whispers. "Most other men would never dare to do this. My instincts were right about you." She kisses my cheek.

Berkowitz lays down his razor.

"With babies," he says, "there's always a crowd around, at least the family. The little fellow wrapped in a blanket looks around or screams. You take off the diaper and one-two it's over." He hesitates. "With you it's like I'm a doctor. It's making me nervous, all this talking about it. I've been a mohel thirty-four years and I started slaughtering chickens four years before that. I'm almost ready for Social Security. Just baby boys, chickens, turkeys, occasionally a duck. Once someone brought me a captured deer. He was so beautiful. I looked in his eyes. I couldn't do it. The man understood. He put the deer back in his truck, drove him to the woods, and let him go. He came back later to thank me."

"You're not really going to have to do much," Joan says, "just relive the thing. Draw a drop of blood, that will be enough: one symbolic drop."

"Down there there's no drops," Berkowitz says. "It's close to arteries; the heart wants blood there. It's the way the Almighty wanted it to be."

As Berkowitz hesitates, I begin to be afraid. Not primal fear but very contemporary panic. Fear about what's happening right now, right before my eyes.

Berkowitz drinks a little of the Manischewitz wine he has poured for the blessing. He loosens his necktie. He sits down.

"I didn't have the voice to be a cantor," he says, "and for sure I wasn't smart enough to become a rabbi. Still, I wanted the religious life. I wanted some type of religious work. I'm not an immigrant, you know. I graduated from high school and junior college. I could have done lots of things. My brother is a dentist. He's almost assimilated in White Plains. He doesn't like to tell people what his older brother does.

"In English I sound like the Mafia, 'a ritual slaughterer.'" Berkowitz laughs nervously. "Every time on the forms when it says Job Description, I write 'ritual slaughterer.' I hate how it sounds."

"You've probably had second thoughts about your career right from the start," Joan says.

"Yes, I have. God's work, I tell myself, but why does God want me to slit the throats of chickens and slice the foreskins of babies? When Abraham did it, it mattered; now, why not let the pediatricians mumble the blessing, why not electrocute the chickens?"

"Do you think God wanted you to be a dentist," Joan asks, "or an insurance agent? Don't be ashamed of your work. What you do is holiness. A pediatrician is not a man of God. An electrocuted chicken is not an animal whose life has been taken seriously."

Hyman Berkowitz looks in amazement at my Joan, a twenty-six-year-old gentile woman who has already relived her own birth.

"Not everyone understands this," Berkowitz says. "Most people when they eat chicken think of the crust, the flavor, maybe Colonel Sanders. They don't consider the life of the bird that flows through my fingers."

"You are indeed a holy man," Joan says.

Berkowitz holds my penis in his left hand. The breeze from the air conditioner makes the chandelier above me sway.

"Do it," I say.

His knife, my first memory, I suddenly think, may be the last thing I'll ever see. I feel a lot like a chicken. I already imagine that he'll hang me upside down and run off with Joan.

She'll break your hands, I struggle to tell him. You'll be out of a job. Your wife was right about you.

The words clot in my throat. I keep my eyes shut tightly.

"I can't do it," Berkowitz says. "I can't do this, even symbolically, to a full-grown male. It may not be against the law; still I consider it an abomination."

I am so relieved I want to kiss his fingertips.

Joan looks disappointed but she, too, understands.

"A man," Hyman Berkowitz says, "is not a chicken."

I pull on my trousers and give him gladly the fifty-dollar check that was to have been his professional fee. Joan kisses his pale cheek.

The holy man, clutching his check, waves to us from his front porch. My past remains as secret, as mysterious, as my father's baldness. My mother in the throes of labor is a stranger I never knew. It will always be so. She is as lost to me as my foreskin. My penis feels like a blindfolded man standing before the executioner who has been saved at the last second.

"Well," Joan says, "we tried."

On the long drive home Joan falls asleep before we're out of South Bend. I cruise the turnpike, not sure of whether I'm a failure at knowing myself. At a roadside rest stop to the east of

Indiana beneath a full moon, I wake Joan. Fitfully, imperfectly, we know each other.

"A man," I whisper, "is not a chicken." On the eighth day I did learn something.

Elvis, Axl, and Me

Janice Eidus

I MET ELVIS FOR THE FIRST TIME in the deli across the street from the elevated line on White Plains Road and Pelham Parkway in the Bronx. Elvis was the only customer besides me. He was sitting at the next table. I could tell it was him right away, even though he was dressed up as a Hasidic Jew. He was wearing a *yarmulke* on top of his head, and a lopsided, shiny black wig with long peyes on the sides that drooped past his chin, a fake-looking beard to his collarbone, and a shapeless black coat, which didn't hide his paunch, even sitting down. His skin was as white as flour, and his eyes looked glazed, as though he spent far too much time indoors.

"I'll have that soup there, with the round balls floatin' in it," he said to the elderly waiter. He pointed at a large vat of matzoh ball soup. Elvis's Yiddish accent was so bad he might as well have held up a sign saying, "Hey, it's me, Elvis Presley, the Hillbilly Hassid, and I ain't dead at all!" But the waiter, who was wearing a huge hearing aid, just nodded, not appearing to notice anything unusual about his customer.

Sipping my coffee, I stared surreptitiously at Elvis, amazed that he was alive and pretending to be a Hasidic Jew on Pelham Parkway. Unlike all those Elvis-obsessed women who made annual pilgrimages to Graceland and who'd voted on the Elvis postage stamp, I'd never particularly had a thing for Elvis. Elvis just wasn't my type. He was too goody-goody for me. Even back when I was a little girl and I'd watched him swiveling his hips on *The Ed Sullivan Show,* I could tell that, underneath, he was just an All American Kid.

My type is Axl Rose, the tattooed bad boy lead singer of the heavy metal band Guns n' Roses, whom I'd recently had a *very* minor nervous breakdown over. Although I've never met Axl Rose in the flesh, and although he's *very* immature and *very* politically incorrect, I know that, somehow, somewhere, I *will* meet him one day, because I know that he's destined to be the great love of my life.

Still, even though Elvis is a lot older, tamer, and fatter than Axl, he *is* the King of Rock 'n' Roll, and that's nothing to scoff at. Even Axl himself would have to be impressed by Elvis.

I waited until Elvis's soup had arrived before going over to him. Boldly, I sat right down at his table. "Hey, Elvis," I said, "it's nice to see you."

He looked at me with surprise, nervously twirling one of his fake peyes. And then he blushed, a long, slow blush, and I could tell two things: one, he liked my looks, and two, he wasn't at all sorry that I'd recognized him.

"Why, hon," he said, in his charming, sleepy-sounding voice, "you're the prettiest darn thing I've seen here on Pelham Parkway in a hound dog's age. You're also the first person who's ever really spotted me. All those other Elvis sightings, at Disneyland and shopping malls in New Jersey, you know, they're all bogus as three-dollar bills. I've been right here on Pelham Parkway the whole darned time."

"Tell me *all* about it, Elvis." I leaned forward on my elbows, feeling very flirtatious, the way I used to when I was still living downtown in the East Village. That was before I'd moved back here to Pelham Parkway, where I grew up. The reason I moved back was because, the year before, I inherited my parents' two-bedroom apartment on Holland Avenue, after their tragic death when the chartered bus taking them to Atlantic City had crashed into a Mack truck. During my East Village days, though, I'd had lots of flirtations, as well as lots and lots of dramatic and tortured affairs with angry-looking, spike-haired poets and painters. But all that was before I discovered Axl Rose, of course, and before I had my *very* minor nervous breakdown over him. I mean, my breakdown was so minor I didn't do anything crazy at all. I didn't stand in the middle of the street directing traffic, or jump off the Brooklyn Bridge, or anything like that. Mostly I just had a wonderful time fantasizing about what it would be like to make love to him, what it would be like to bite his sexy pierced nipple, to run my fingers through his long, sleek, red hair and all over his many tattoos, and to stick my hand inside his skintight, nearly see-through, white Lycra biking shorts. In the meantime, though, since I had happily bid good-riddance to the spike-haired poets and painters, and since Axl Rose wasn't anywhere around, I figured I might as well do some heavy flirting with Elvis.

"Okay," Elvis smiled, almost shyly, "I'll tell you the truth." His teeth were glistening white and perfectly capped, definitely not the teeth of a Hasidic Jew. "And the truth, little girl, is that I'd gotten mighty burned out."

I liked hearing him call me that—*little girl.* Mindy, the

social worker assigned to my case at the hospital after my breakdown, used to say, "Nancy, you're not a little girl any longer, and rock stars like their women really young. Do you truly believe—I'll be brutal and honest here, it's for your own good—that if, somehow, you actually were to run into Axl Rose on the street, he would even look your way?" Mindy was a big believer in a branch of therapy called "Reality Therapy," which I'd overheard some of the other social workers calling "Pseudo-Reality Therapy" behind her back. Mindy was only twenty three, and she'd actually had the nerve to laugh in my face when I tried to explain to her that ultimately it would be my womanly, sophisticated, and knowing mind that would make Axl go wild with uncontrollable lust, the kind of lust no vacuous twenty-three-year-old bimbo could ever evoke in a man. Axl and I were destined for each other precisely *because* we were so different, and together we would create a kind of magic sensuality unequaled in the history of the world, and, in addition, I would educate him, change him, and help him to grow into a sensitive, mature, and socially-concerned male. But Mindy had stopped listening to me. So after that, I changed my strategy. I kept agreeing with her, instead. "You're right, Mindy," I would declare emphatically, "Axl Rose is a spoiled rock 'n' roll superstar and a sexist pig who probably likes jailbait, and there's no way our paths are ever going to cross. I'm not obsessed with him any more. You can sign my release papers now."

"Little girl," Elvis repeated that first day in the deli, maybe sensing how much I liked hearing him say those words, "I ain't gonna go into all the grizzly details about myself. You've read the newspapers and seen those soppy TV movies, right?"

I nodded.

"I figured you had," he sighed, stirring his soup. "Everyone has. There ain't been no stone left unturned—even the way I had to wear diapers after a while," he blushed again, "and the way I used my gun to shoot out the TV set, and all that other stuff I did, and how the pressures of being The King, the greatest rock 'n' roll singer in the world, led me to booze, drugs, compulsive overeatin', and impotence. . . . "

I nodded again, charmed by the way he pronounced it im*po*tence with the accent in the middle. My heart went out to him, because he looked so sad and yet so proud of himself at the same time. And I really, really liked that he'd called me *little girl* twice.

"Want some of this here soup?" he offered. "I ain't never had none better."

I shook my head. "Go on, Elvis," I said. "Tell me more." I was really enjoying myself. True, he wasn't Axl, but he *was* The King.

"Well," he said, taking a big bite out of the larger of the two matzoh balls left in his bowl, "what I decided to do, see, was to fake my own death and then spend the rest of my life hiding out, somewhere where nobody would ever think to look, somewhere where I could lead a clean, sober, and pious life." He flirtatiously wiggled his fake peyes at me. "And little girl, that's when I remembered an article I'd read, about how the Bronx is called `The Forgotten Borough,' because nobody, but *nobody*, with any power or money, ever comes up here."

"I can vouch for that," I agreed, sadly. "I grew up here."

"And, hon, I did it. I cleaned myself up. I ain't a drug and booze addict no more. As for the overeatin', well, even the Good Lord must have one or two vices, is the way I see it." He smiled.

I smiled back, reminding myself that, after all, not everyone can be as wiry and trim as a tattooed rock 'n' roll singer at the height of his career.

"And I ain't im*po*tent no more," Elvis added, leering suggestively at me.

Of course, he had completely won me over. I invited him home with me after he'd finished his soup and the two slices of honey cake he'd ordered for dessert. When we got back to my parents' apartment, he grew hungry again. I went into the kitchen and cooked some kreplach for him. My obese Bubba Sadie had taught me how to make kreplach when I was ten years old, although, before meeting Elvis, I hadn't ever made it on my own.

"Little girl, I just love Jewish food," Elvis told me sincerely, spearing a kreplach with his fork. "I'm so honored that you whipped this up on my humble account."

Elvis ate three servings of my kreplach. He smacked his lips. "Better than my own momma's fried chicken," he said, which I knew was a heapful of praise coming from him, since, according to the newspapers and TV movies, Elvis had an unresolved thing for his mother. It was my turn to blush. And then he stood up and, looking deeply and romantically into my eyes, sang, "Love Me Tender." And although his voice showed the signs of age, and the wear and tear of booze and drugs, it was still a beautiful voice, and tears came to my eyes.

After that, we cleared the table, and we went to bed. He wasn't a bad lover, despite his girth. "One thing I do know," he said, again sounding simultaneously humble and proud, "is how to pleasure a woman."

I didn't tell him that night about my obsessive love for Axl Rose, and I'm very glad that I didn't. Because since then I've learned that Elvis has no respect at all for contemporary rock 'n' roll singers. "Pretty boy wussies with hair," he describes them. He always grabs the TV remote away from me and changes the channel when I'm going around the stations and happen to land on MTV. Once, before he was able to change the channel, we caught a quick glimpse together of Axl, strutting in front of the mike in his sexy black leather kilt and singing his pretty heart out about some cruel woman who'd hurt him and who he intended to hurt back. I held my breath, hoping that Elvis, sitting next to me on my mother's pink brocade sofa, wouldn't hear how rapidly my heart was beating, wouldn't see that my skin was turning almost as pink as the sofa.

"What a momma's boy and wussey *that* skinny li'l wannabe rock 'n' roller is," Elvis merely sneered, exaggerating his own drawl and grabbing the remote out of my hand. He switched to HBO, which was showing an old Burt Reynolds movie. "Hot dawg," Elvis said, settling back on the sofa, "a Burt flick!"

Still, sometimes when we're in bed, I make a mistake and call him Axl. And he blinks and looks at me and says, "Huh? What'd you say, little girl?" "Oh, Elvis, darling," I always answer without missing a beat, "I just said *Ask. Ask* me to do anything for you, anything at all, and I'll do it. Just *ask.*" And really, I've grown so fond of him, and we have such fun together, that I mean it. I *would* do anything for Elvis. It isn't his fault that Axl Rose, who captured my heart first, is my destiny.

Elvis and I lead a simple, sweet life together. He comes over three or four times every week in his disguise—the yarmulke, the fake beard and peyes, the shapeless black coat—and we take little strolls together through Bronx Park. Then, when he grows tired, we head back to my parents' apartment, and I cook dinner for him. In addition to my kreplach, he's crazy about my blintzes and noodle kugel.

After dinner, we go to bed, where he pleasures me, and I fantasize about Axl. Later, we put our clothes back on, and we sit side by side on my mother's sofa and watch Burt Reynolds movies. Sometimes we watch Elvis's old movies, too. His favorites are *Jailhouse Rock* and *Viva Las Vegas*. But they always make him weepy and sad, which breaks my heart, so I prefer to watch Burt Reynolds.

And Elvis is content just to keep on dating. He never pressures me to move in with him, or to get married, which—as much as I care for him—is fine with me. "Little girl," Elvis always says, "I love you with all my country boy's heart and soul, more than I ever loved Priscilla, I swear I do, and there ain't a selfish bone in my body, but my rent-controlled apartment on a tree-lined block, well, it's a once-in-a-lifetime deal, so I just can't give it up and move in to your parents' apartment with you."

"Hey, Elvis, no sweat," I reply, sweetly. And I tell him that, much as I love him, I can't move in with him, either, because *his* apartment—a studio with kitchenette—is just too small for both of us. "I understand, little girl," he says, hugging me. "I really do. You've got some of that feisty women's libber inside of you, and you need your own space."

But the truth is, it's not my space I care about so much. The truth is that I've got long range plans, which don't include Elvis. Here's how I figure it: down the road, when Axl, like Elvis before him, burns out—and it's inevitable that he will, given the way that boy is going—when he's finally driven, like Elvis, to fake his own death in order to escape the pressures of rock 'n' roll superstardom, and when he goes into hiding under an assumed identity, well, then, I think the odds are pretty good he'll end up living right here on Pelham Parkway. After all, Axl and I are *bound* to meet up some day—destiny is destiny, and there's no way around it.

I'm not saying it *will* happen just that way, mind you. All I'm saying is that, if Elvis Presley is alive and well and masquerading as a Hasidic Jew in the Bronx, well, then, anything is possible, and I do mean *anything*. And anything includes me and Axl, right here on Pelham Parkway, pleasuring each other night and day. It's not that I want to hurt Elvis, believe me. But I figure he probably won't last long enough to see it happen, anyway, considering how out of shape he is, and all.

The way I picture it is this: Axl holding me in his tattooed, wiry arms and telling me that all his life he's been waiting to find me, even though he hardly dared dream that I existed in the flesh, the perfect woman, an experienced woman who can make kreplach and blintzes and noodle kugel, a woman who was the last—and best—lover of Elvis Presley, the King of Rock 'n' Roll himself. It *could* happen. That's all I'm saying.

Gifts

❧

Myra Goldberg

MY MOTHER TELLS ME that a gift will arrive for me by mail, from Macy's. I try to thank her, but can't, because I've asked her not to send me gifts anymore, clothes especially. I'm thirty. I've got a closet full of gifts from her, have never really dressed myself. My mother is sixty-five. We're in the dressing room of the municipal pool together. Her back is to me. She's squatting. Piling clothes into her locker. She turns around, stands, looks up at me. Her small pointed face is hopeful. Her breasts droop. She's naked.

"It's a shirt," she says.

So you asked her not to send you gifts, I think. She wants to send you a shirt from Macy's. Let her send you a shirt from Macy's.

"You can always return it," she says, after a while.

"Okay. I'll return it if it isn't right."

"Fine," she says. "I'll return it for you. It's easier for me to get to Macy's. I'm not so busy." She pulls her bathing suit up, settles her breasts inside. "I would have gotten it for myself," she adds," if they had it in my size or in a different color."

I put one foot into the leg of my leotard.

"You're not taking a shower before you go in?"

"I never do. Look, Ma, I probably won't want to return it. You have wonderful taste, usually."

"It looked like you," she says. "Simple. Not severe. But I could be wrong."

We start for the pool. The water is warm, chlorinated. She breaststrokes. I crawl. She favors her right side, because her left hip was broken in a car accident and never mended. I favor my left, because my bad basketball knee won't kick. We swim back and forth, lose each other. I look around. She's holding on to the ladder, dangling. I swim up to her.

"Are you okay?"

"Fine. I was watching you. You're a strong swimmer."

"So are you."

"Grandma was stronger."

We used to watch from the beach. Grandma at the water's edge. Mrs. Handelman on one side, Mrs. Scheineman on the other. Black woolen tank suits wrinkling around their old ladies' thighs, the three women chatting, bending, scooping water from the lake, sprinkling water on their bosoms, rubbing water into their wrists, elbows, shoulder blades, like perfume, then crack— Grandma was gone, wading into the lake, thighs carrying her out, past the rope, past the lifeguard's whistling objections, breaststroking across the lake, then back to us again, bunioned feet covered with sand, water dripping on our blanket as she reached for the bathrobe that my mother held out to her, wrapped it around her, waited like a wrestler for the lifeguard to approach: "What's he so afraid of, that boy in the high chair? I'll be drowned? I can't go out alone? An old lady like me?"

"I loved her," says my mother." But I could never talk to her." She lets go of the ladder. Her legs stir up the waters behind her. Her freckled arms part the waters in front of her. She detours around a group of splashing children, swims swiftly down the center of the pool, then lifts herself to the concrete edge at the other end, dangles her legs in the water, kicks, smiles.

I wave.

We meet in the dressing room.

I admire her haircut. She likes the way I wrap my towel around my head. We start for the subway. She's tired now. Her hip hurts her. At the turnstile, she takes two tokens out of her pocketbook. "Here. For you."

"Never mind. I can get one."

"You'll have to stand in line. "She points to the token booth.

I take the token. Offer her fifty cents.

She shakes her head. "The price is terrible," she says, slipping her token into the turnstile. The machine clanks and turns, noisy, but functional. Then it's my turn.

Inside the subway car, I find an empty seat for her. She holds the pole. "Save the seat for someone who needs it," she says. I hold the same pole, thinking longingly of France, where subway sitting is regulated by the state, where the *mutilés de guerre* go first, then *les personnes âgés, les femmes enceintes, multilés ordinaries.*

"For my sake," I say, pointing to the seat.

She sits down.

I grab the strap above her. She wipes her eyes. I lean down to see what the matter is. She says the chlorine in the pool makes her eyes hurt. It's not right, what they do to the waters, the elements.

I'm sorry about her eyes, I say, but the pool is better than nothing, better than what most people have.

She's grateful, she supposes.

My stop is next.

At home, there's a package from Macy's waiting.

Unwrapped, it's the same shirt I bought four years ago, got tired of, hung on the tree outside, watched my neighbor take home with her.

No, it's not the same shirt, I see, unpinning it, unfolding it, slipping the cardboard out, holding it against me. Same material. Different cut. Softer. Not so severe.

I call my mother to thank her.

She says, "I thought it looked like you, but I wasn't sure. I worried."

"Don't worry, Ma," I say.

She's quiet.

"I love it," I say.

"I did okay?"

"You did fine, believe me. "

"I'm surprised," she says. "I didn't expect it to arrive so soon."

Now we're both quiet. I follow the telephone wires across town and back." I don't want to run up your phone bill," she says. "I'm getting off."

She gets off. The line is free again. I stand, listening to nothing. A few minutes later, I'm dialing my brother in California. I want to hear his voice. See what he sounds like.

"Hello," he says." Is that you?"

Readers Digest

Dara Horn

THE DRINKING AGE in the world to come is twenty-one. Twenty-one days, that is—three weeks until one's time has come to be born. At that point, the not-yets are allowed into the famous bars of the world to come, where they must choose for themselves whether to remain sober, to let themselves get a bit tipsy, or to drink themselves to birth. But the drinks in these bars aren't like the poor, dark, dingy ones in the world below. Instead, the vast wine cellars of the world to come are filled with bottled books.

They are arranged, the wine cellars, like libraries, by vineyard, varietal, vintage—author, genre, date. The librarian-sommeliers bring up the requested bottles carefully. Some are meant to be drunk warm, heated with love; others are plunged into icy buckets of hatred or chilled slightly in anger before drinking. Most are served at room temperature, objectively tasted; while some (cheap titles, usually, avoided at least in public by the smarter not-yets) are served lust-hot. Wary drinkers usually ask to see the label before opening the bottle, inspecting the title and the author's name to make sure it matches what they ordered. ("*Deuteronomy,*" Daniel cried once when a drowsy bartender brought out a flinty screw-capped carafe. "I asked for *Deuteronomy,* not for *The New Economy.*") The true bibliophiles are also offered a drop to sample first, to swivel under their tongues, testing for basic quality. ("Tfu!" Daniel once spat. "Plagiarism!") After that, it is simply a matter of taste, and of how long one takes to get drunk.

Most of the visitors to the paradise bar drink cheap pints of newspapers and magazines, microbrewed advertising copy and, lately, internet screeds on tap. Some like fancy anthology cocktails, readers' digests of different works that make them seem more sophisticated than they are. Others prefer the hard stuff that needs no particular vintage, tossing back murder mystery shots and swilling down romances and thrillers that leave them plastered on the floor for days. Of course, many of the not-yets take one look into the bars of paradise, at the frightening effects of stories on the soul, and vow to stay sober until the day they are born. They hold themselves back for twenty-one days, and then they are born contented, living their entire lives on earth without ever thirsting to read. But others—the thirsty ones, the ones who aren't satisfied with the meals at the museum and long to wash them down with something bigger, bolder—are drawn to the bar, believing that behind the crowds swallowing cheap words, there might be something worthy of their not-yet lips. And those are the ones who meet the librarian-sommeliers.

It wasn't long after his twenty-first prebirthday that Daniel met Rosalie, an already-was who worked as a sommelier at his local paradise bar. Turned off by the crowd of natals at the counter—one of whom had just vomited the plot of an entire soap opera onto his celestial barstool—Daniel had wandered off into a corner, a shady nook of the kind many paradise bars make available to the most antisocial bibliophiles, though he didn't know that he was one yet. Rosalie found him there, sulking, his head in his wings.

"Would you like to see the wine list?" she asked.

"Wine list?" he repeated, confused. He was, after all, new.

"Let me show you," she said, and landed softly at his side. He watched her fluttering beside him. The presence of this mortal felt different from the other bartenders, he noticed. It reminded him of the attendant at the bath house: stern, stirring, somehow slightly too close. His wings tingled beside hers as she unfurled a long scroll before him.

"You're one lucky guy," she said. "We've got the best wine list this side of paradise."

Daniel looked over her shoulder, squinting to see the long list of names in the bar's low light. "Don't tell me you've never had a drink before," she scolded. Daniel shook his head, shyly, but something told him that she already knew the answer. For a moment, she held his wing and looked him in the eye. "You're going to want something sophisticated, I can tell," she said. "I would recommend this one, for starters." He followed her fingertips along the scroll until she pointed at a name that he couldn't read in the dark. "Sound good to you?"

"Sure," he shrugged, feigning nonchalance. But a fire had entered him. A thirst.

"I'll bring it right up," she said, and flew away.

A few moments later—moments that felt to Daniel like eons, and perhaps they were—she returned from the cellar, landing in his nook with a bottle in one hand. "Here it is," she said, and brandished the bottle's glowing label in his face: *Genesis*.

Clueless, Daniel nodded as she poured a few drops into his glass. "You have to drink it slowly to appreciate it," she said. "A lot of people just chug it down and miss the whole point."

He raised the glass to his lips and sipped the liquid carefully, holding it under his tongue, unsure of what to expect. At first it was sickly sweet, reminding him of some of the more cloying paintings at the museum—darkness, water, light, earth, sun, moon, stars. Typical. But then it heated up, then burned with spices, then turned creamy, then grassy, then suddenly flattened into a bitter tannin. Just before he swallowed, it reared itself up into a final burst of flavor, fruit from the tree of knowledge, which fruitfully multiplied before flowing down his throat.

"This is *very good*," he muttered a moment later, and poured himself a full glass.

"This whole vintage is exceptional," Rosalie told him as he slurped it down, swallowing a vast flood of pure rainwater and the chalky remnants of a collapsing tower before bracing his stomach against the flinty tannin of a man holding a knife to his son's throat. "You'd be surprised, though. There are people who take one sip and spit the whole thing out." Daniel kept drinking, relishing the spicy hints of jealous siblings on his tongue. "Would you like to try some of the other varietals? Same vintage, different mouth-feel?"

"Mm," Daniel murmured. He had begun drinking directly from the bottle, curling up with it like the baby he was about to become, dreaming sweet drunken dreams of eleven stars and sheaves of grain bowing down before him. A hint of flint again as jealous siblings attacked on his tongue; then a soft note, later, of sour grapes.

"Great, I'll go bring up some more." Rosalie flew down to the cellar and then back up, carrying several bottles with her that she put down on the table in front of him—*Exodus, Isaiah, Ezekiel*. "Watch out for this one," she said, holding up a bottle of

Ecclesiastes. "It's kind of a downer. But still worth a taste. Eat, drink, and be merry."

Daniel popped the cork and poured himself a glass, spilling sour vanities into his mouth, one vain sip after another until all was vanity. As his eyes grew dim, he agreed with Rosalie. A downer. What really made him dizzy, though, was the peculiarly balanced sweet-and-sour flavor, the time to be born and the time to die, the time to weep and the time to laugh, the time to mourn and the time to dance. And the residue at the bottom of the bottle was particularly hard to swallow, when he tasted the hint that of the making of many books there is no end, and that much study is wearying of the flesh. It was a little too heavy, and made him thirsty for something simpler. He reached for the bottle of *Psalms.*

"Want a new glass?" Rosalie asked.

"Renew it as in days of old," he said, and hiccupped.

Before he knew it, his cup had runneth over.

It wasn't long before Daniel became a regular at Rosalie's bar. There were some bottles he would request again and again—he was fond, for instance, of certain appellations of Talmudic vintage pertaining to life before birth (they had a comforting, familiar flavor)—but it was mostly Rosalie's tastes that guided his literary binges. She had a particular fondness for Hebrew and Yiddish vineyards, which was convenient, since few other patrons at the bar chose to sample those languages. Even the true bibliophiles usually stuck to the products of presses from the larger, more standard book-growing regions: English, Russian, French, Spanish, German, Arabic, Chinese. The Yiddish vintages in particular Daniel could count on having all to himself. It wasn't long before his reading habit became the only thing on his mind, turning into an addiction. He would sit in school waiting for the day to end, then race to the paradise bar.

Rosalie was almost always waiting for him, ready with a glass of poetry on the house.

Sometimes they would get together for a few comedies, and he would become so drunk that he would stumble out the door still laughing. Other times, she would pour out tales of lost love and tragedy until he was crying into his glass. More often, sweet laughter and bitter tannins would blend in the same cup, and each alternating sip made him thirsty for more. She never provided a bottle without commentary or at least an opinion—a sommelier's note on the vintage, or a suggestion on how to enjoy it. One day she stood beside his table as he sipped a fresh, fruit-tinged poem from a bottle by Itsik Manger:

> Eve stands before the apple tree
> The sunset sky is red.
> What do you know, mother Eve,
> What do you know of death?
>
> Adam is gone for the day
> In the wild wood alone.
> Adam says, "The wood is wild,
> And beauty is all that's unknown."
>
> But Eve is afraid of the wild wood.
> She is drawn to the apple tree.
> And when she doesn't go to it,
> It comes to her in dreams.

"This is just the kind of thing that everyone gulps down wrong, if they bother tasting it at all," Rosalie told him as she sampled a sip from the copper cup around her neck. "People taste the apple flavor and think they're drinking juice. They say, 'Oh, it's about sex.' No one ever understands what happened with Adam and Eve. That story isn't about sex. It's about death. The forbidden desire isn't love or lust—you can get that stuff any time down at the public bath, even on earth. The forbidden desire is immortality."

"Hm," Daniel murmured. Intellectual discussions, he had noticed, tended to sound more profound when he was drunk. He took another swig and finished off his glass, then poured himself a refreshing sip of *Psalms*. "Yet mine is the faith," he slurred, "that I shall behold the goodness of God in the land of the living." He belched, then snored.

Rosalie laughed. "Don't count on it," she said, and carried him out.

Becoming a biblioholic changed Daniel's eating habits. Prior to that, he had loved to eat, but now he lost his appetite. Long periods passed when he wouldn't even taste a work of art. Every painting, no matter how delicately seasoned, soured in comparison to the drunken rapture of reading. Instead he would drink himself into a stupor and then wander into the bath, where he would try to loosen his hangover by throwing himself into a chilled sulfur tub of loneliness. One morning, after drinking a particularly disturbing bottle whose town full of dead people left him feeling wasted and worthless, he skulked off to the sulfur tub and soaked there for a long time, sunken and shivering. But then Boris discovered him, and slapped him across the face.

"Daniel, what are you doing? Get out of that bath," he shouted.

Daniel lolled in the cold, smelly water. The slap barely registered; he was still drunk. "Why?" he muttered.

Boris leaned over him, his wings folded at his sides. "Because if you stay in there, your skin will soak up the stench, and then when you're born, no one will want to go near you."

Daniel slouched down further into the pool. "I don't care," he said.

Boris watched him for a moment, then snorted. "That's your problem," he snapped. "You don't care. I haven't seen such a stupid not-yet since your uncle was born. Now get out of that bath."

Daniel still didn't budge. Boris stood for a moment, sighed, and then reached down and hauled him out of the water, carrying him over his shoulder to a warm steam room. He sat Daniel down on a bench near the vent that billowed white clouds of trust, leaving a faithful film of dewdrops on Daniel's wings.

Boris sat down and leaned toward him, then pinched his own nose. "Ugh, that explains it. I can smell *Lamentations* on your breath." Daniel's face began turning red, though perhaps it was only from the steam. "Don't tell me Rosalie has been getting you drunk."

Daniel looked up, his surprise dulled by the roar of words between his temples. "You know Rosalie?" he asked.

Boris snorted, then evaded. "It's not healthy to drink all those books. It's like all the not-yets who sit in the warm pool and never try the other ones. You're going to be born addicted to those stories. And then you're going to go through life thirsty for things that don't exist."

Daniel inhaled the clean, pure mist, and wailed. "Trust me," he sighed, "if you knew what those books were like—"

Boris sighed, a deep sigh that sucked in some of Daniel's trust, making him wonder what Boris really knew, whether he might not have had a few drinks himself, long ago, before he was born and died. "What I know is that you haven't been eating," Boris said.

Trust seeped back up into Daniel's nostrils. "There's nothing worth eating anymore," he cried. "Once you've had those books, all the landscapes and portraits and photographs in the whole world to come just seem like—nothing. Even the photographs.

Even the abstract ones. Even the surreal ones. Especially the post-modern ones. Nothing *happens* in them. They're just—" Daniel began, and choked.

"But don't you see?" Boris demanded over Daniel's sobs. "That's the whole point: *You are* what's going to happen in them. After you're born, you're going to be hungry for those things, those people and places, and then you're going to look for them, and see them and find them and put yourself into them. The artwork is just the settings, or the other characters. You have to make the plot yourself."

Daniel sobbed even more. "But how can anyone make a new plot?" he sputtered. His breath reeked of *Ecclesiastes*. "One generation goes, another comes," he rattled. "Whatever already was, will always be, and whatever has already been done will be done again. There's—there's just nothing new under the sun."

Boris sighed. "You need to eat," he said.

Daniel groaned over the rumbling of his own stomach. "But it's all just—I don't know, vanity."

Boris put his wing around Daniel. "How about this," he suggested. "Why don't you ask your curator to bring you something to eat that will complement what you've been drinking?"

Daniel lifted his head, feeling his hangover subside. "Do you think it would help?"

Boris looked at him, his eyes gleaming under his bald forehead. He embraced Daniel around the neck until Daniel leaned toward him, closer to the steam vent. "You won't know if you don't try," he said.

Under other circumstances, Daniel might have noticed that something was up. But at that moment his nostrils were clouded with deep breaths of trust, and he could see nothing but the brightest corners of paradise.

Pu-239

Ken Kalfus

SOMEONE COMMITTED A SIMPLE ERROR THAT, according to the plant's blueprints, should have been impossible, and a valve was left open, a pipe ruptured, a technician was trapped in a crawlspace, and a small fire destroyed several workstations. At first the alarm was discounted: false alarms commonly rang and flashed through the plant like birds in a tropical rain forest. Once the seriousness of the accident was appreciated, the rescue crew discovered that a soft drink dispenser waiting to be sent out for repair blocked the room in which the radiation suits were kept. After moving it and entering the storage room, they learned that several of the oxygen tanks had been left uncharged. By the time they reached the lab the fire was nearly out, but smoke laced with elements from the actinide series filled the unit. Lying on his back above the ceiling, staring at the wormlike pattern of surface corrosion on the tin duct a few centimeters from his face, Timofey had inhaled the fumes for an hour and forty minutes. In that time he had tried to imagine that he was inhaling dollar bills and that once they lodged in his lungs and bone marrow they would bombard his body tissue with high-energy dimes, nickels, and quarters.

Timofey had worked in 16 nearly his entire adult life, entrusted with the bounteous, transfiguring secrets of the atom. For most of that life, he had been exhilarated by the reactor's song of nuclear fission, the hiss of particle capture and loss. Highly valued for his ingenuity, Timofey carried in his head not only a detailed knowledge of the plant's design, but also a precise recollection of its every repair and improvised alteration. He knew where the patches were and how well they had been executed. He knew which stated tolerances could be exceeded and by how much, which gauges ran hot, which ran slow, and which could be completely ignored. The plant managers and scientists were often forced to defer to his judgment. On these occasions a glitter of derision showed in his voice, as he tapped a finger significantly against a sheet of engineering designs and explained why there was only a single correct answer to the question.

After Timofey's death, his colleagues recalled a dressing down he had received a few years earlier at the hands of a visiting scientist. No one remembered the details, except that she had proposed slightly altering the reaction process in order to produce a somewhat greater quantity of a certain isotope that she employed in her own research. Hovering in his stained and wrinkled white coat behind the half dozen plant officials whom she had been addressing, Timofey objected to the proposal. He said that greater quantities of the isotope would not be produced in the way she suggested and, in fact, could not be produced at all, according to well established principles of nuclear physics. Blood rushed to the woman's square, fleshy, bulldog face. "Idiot!" she spat. "I'm Nuclear Section Secretary of the Academy of Sciences. I fucking *own* the established principles of nuclear physics. You're a *technician!*" Those who were there recalled that Timofey tried to stand his ground, but as he began to explain the flaw in her reasoning his voice lost its resonance and he began to mumble, straying away from the main point. She cut him off, asking her audience, "Are there any other questions, any educated questions?" As it turned out, neither Timofey nor the scientist was ever proved right. The Defense Ministry rejected the proposal for reasons of economy.

Timofey's relations with his co-workers were more comfortable, if distant, and he usually joined the others in his unit at lunch in the plant's low-ceilinged, windowless buffet. The room rustled with murmured complaint. Timofey could hardly be counted among the most embittered of the technical workers— a point sagely observed later. All joked with stale irony about the lapses in safety and the precipitous decline in their salaries caused by inflation; these comments had become almost entirely humorless three months earlier, when management followed a flurry of assuring memos, beseeching directives, and unambiguous promises with a failure to pay them at all. No one had been paid since.

Every afternoon at four Timofey fled the compromises and incompetence of his workplace in an old Zhiguli that he had purchased precisely so that he could arrive home a half hour earlier than if he had taken the tram. Against the odds set by personality and circumstance, he had married, late in his fourth decade, an electrical engineer assigned to another unit. Now, with the attentiveness he had once offered the reactor, Timofey often sat across the kitchen table from his wife with his head cocked, listening to their spindly, asthmatic eight-year-old son, Tolya, in the next room give ruinous commands to his toy soldiers. A serious respiratory ailment similar to the boy's kept

Marina from working; disability leave had brought a pretty bloom to her soft cheeks.

The family lived on the eighth floor of a weather stained concrete apartment tower with crumbling front steps and unlit hallways. In this rotted box lay a jewel of a two-bedroom apartment that smelled of fresh bread and meat dumplings and overlooked a birch forest. Laced with ski tracks in the winter and fragranced by grilled shashlik in the summer, home to deer, rabbits, and even gray wolves, the forest stretched well beyond their sight, all the way to the city's double-fenced perimeter.

His colleagues thought of Marina and the boy as Timofey was pulled from the crawlspace. He was conscious, but dazed, his eyes unfocused and his face slack. Surrounded by phantoms in radiation suits, Timofey saw the unit as if for the first time: the cracked walls, the electrical cords snaking underfoot, the scratched and fogged glass over the gauges, the mold-spattered valves and pipes, the disabled equipment piled in an unused workstation, and the frayed tubing that bypassed sections of missing pipe and was kept in place by electrical tape. He staggered from the lab, took a shower, vomited twice, disposed of his clothes, and was briefly examined by a medic, who took his pulse and temperature. No one looked him in the eye. Timofey was sent home. His colleagues were surprised when he returned the next day, shrugging off the accident and saying that he had a few things to take care of before going on the "rest leave" he had been granted as a matter of course. But his smile was as wan as the moon on a midsummer night, and his hands trembled. In any case, his colleagues were too busy to chat. The clean-up was chaotically underway and the normal activities of the plant had been suspended.

Early one evening a week after the "event," as it was known in the plant and within the appropriate ministries (it was not known anywhere else), Timofey was sitting at a café table in the bar off

the lobby of a towering Brezhnev-era hotel on one of the boule-
vards that radiated from Moscow's nucleus. A domestically-
made, double-breasted sports jacket the color of milk chocolate
hung from his frame like wash left to dry. He was only fifty years
old but, lank and stooped, his face lined by a spiderwork of
dilated veins, he looked at least fifteen years older, almost a vet-
eran of the war. His skin was as gray as wet concrete, except for
the radiation erythema inflaming the skin around his eyes and
nose. Coarse white hair bristled from his skull. Set close beneath
white caterpillar eyebrows, his blue eyes blazed.

He was not by nature impressed by attempts to suggest lux-
ury and comfort, and the gypsies and touts milling outside the
entrance had in any case already mitigated the hotel's grandeur.
He recognized that the lounge area was meant to approximate
the soaring glass and marble atria of the West, but the girders of
the greenhouse roof impended two stories above his head, supported by walls of chipped concrete blocks. A line of shuttered
windows ran the perimeter above the lounge, looking down
upon it as if it were a factory floor. The single appealing amenity
was the set of flourishing potted plants and ferns in the center of
the room. As Timofey watched over a glass of unsipped vodka
that had cost him a third of his remaining rubles, a fat security
guard in a maroon suit flicked a cigarette butt into the plant
beds, and stalked away.

Timofey strained to detect the aspirates and dental fricatives
of a foreign language, but the other patrons were all either
Russian or "black"-that is, Caucasian. Overweight, unshaven
men in lurid track suits and cheap leather jackets huddled over
the stained plastic tables, blowing smoke into each other's faces.
Occasionally they looked up from their drinks and eyed the people around them. Then they fell back into negotiation. At
another table, a rectangular woman in a low-cut, short, black
dress and black leggings scowled at a newspaper.

Directly behind Timofey, sitting alone, a young man with dark, bony features decided that this hick would be incapable of getting a girl on his own. Not that there would be too many girls around this early. He wondered if Timofey had any money and whether he could make him part with it. Certainly the mark would have enough for one of the kids in ski parkas waving down cars on the boulevard. The young man, called Shiv by his Moscow acquaintances (he had no friends), got up from his table, leaving his drink.

"First time in Moscow, my friend?"

Timofey was not taken off guard. He slowly raised his head and studied the young man standing before him. Either the man's nose had once been broken, or his nose had never been touched and the rest of his face had been broken many times, leaving his cheeks and the arches beneath his eyes jutted askew. The youth wore a foreign blazer and a black shirt, and what looked like foreign shoes as well, a pair of black loafers. His dark, curly hair was cut long, lapping neatly against the top of his collar. Jewelry glinted from his fingers and wrists. It was impossible to imagine the existence of such a creature in 16.

Shiv didn't care for the fearlessness in Timofey's eyes; it suggested a profound ignorance of the world. But he pulled a chair underneath him, sat down heavily, and said in a low. voice, "It's lonely here. Would you like to meet someone?"

The mark didn't reply, nor make any sign that he had even heard him. His jaw was clenched shut, his face blank. Shiv wondered whether he spoke Russian. He himself spoke no foreign languages and detested the capriciousness with which foreigners chose to speak their own. He added, "You've come to the right place. I'd be pleased to make an introduction."

Timofey continued to stare at Shiv in a way that he should have known, if he had any sense at all, was extremely dangerous. A crazy, Shiv thought, a waste of time. But then the mark abruptly rasped, in educated, unaccented Russian, "I have something to sell."

Shiv grinned, showing large white canines. He congratulated him, "You're a businessman. Well, you've come to the right place for that, too. I'm also a businessman. What is it you want to sell?"

"I can't discuss it here."

"All right."

Shiv stood and Timofey tentatively followed him to a little alcove stuffed with video poker machines. They whined and yelped, devouring gambling tokens. Incandescent images of kings, queens, and knaves flickered across the young man's face.

"No, this isn't private enough."

"Sure it is," Shiv said. "More business is done here than on the Moscow Stock Exchange."

"No."

Shiv shrugged and headed back to his table, which the girl, in a rare display of zeal, had already cleared. His drink was gone. Shiv frowned, but knew he could make her apologize and give him another drink on the house, which would taste much better for it. He had that kind of respect, he thought.

"You're making the biggest mistake of your life," Timofey whispered behind him. "I'll make you rich."

What changed Shiv's mind was not the promise, which these days was laden in nearly every commercial advertisement, political manifesto, and murmur of love. Rather, he discerned two vigorously competing elements within the mark's voice. One of them was desperation, in itself an augury of profit. Yet as desperate as he was, Timofey had spoken just barely within range of Shiv's hearing. Shiv was impressed by the guy's self-control. Perhaps he was serious after all.

He turned back toward Timofey, who continued to stare at him in appraisal. With a barely perceptible flick of his head, Shiv motioned him toward a row of elevators bedecked with posters for travel agencies and masseuses. Timofey remained in the alcove for a long moment, trying to decide whether to follow. Shiv looked away and punched the call button. After a minute or so the elevator arrived. Timofey stepped in just as the doors were closing.

Shiv said, "If you're jerking me around . . ."

The usually reliable fourth-floor *dezhurnaya,* the suppurating wart who watched the floor's rooms, decided to be difficult. Shiv slipped her a five-dollar bill, and she said, "More." She returned the second fiver because it had a crease down the middle, dispelling its notional value. Shiv had been trying to pass it off for weeks and now conceded that he would be stuck with it until the day he died. The crone accepted the next bill, scowling, and even then gazed a long time into her drawer of keys, as if undecided about giving him one.

As they entered the room, Shiv pulled out a pack of Marlboros and a gold-plated lighter and leaned against a beige chipboard dresser. The room's ponderous velvet curtains smelled of insecticide; unperturbed, a bloated fly did lazy eights around the naked bulb on the ceiling. Shiv didn't offer the mark a cigarette. "All right," he said, flame billowing from the lighter before he brought it to his face. "This better be worth my while."

Timofey reached into his jacket, almost too abruptly: he didn't notice Shiv tense and go for the dirk in his back pocket. The mark pulled out a green cardboard folder and proffered it. "Look at this."

Shiv returned the blade. He carried four knives of varying sizes, grades, and means of employment.

"Why?

"Just look at it."

Shiv opened the folder. Inside was Timofey's internal passport, plus some other documents. Shiv was not accustomed to strangers shoving their papers in his face; indeed, he knew the family names of very few people in Moscow. This guy, then, had to be a nut case, and Shiv rued the ten bucks he had given the *dezhurnaya*. The mark stared up through the stamped black-and-white photograph as if from under water. "Timofey Fyodorovich, pleased to meet you. So what?"

"Look at where I live: Skotoprigonyevsk-16."

Shiv made no sign of being impressed, but for Timofey the words had the force of an incantation. The existence of the city, a scientific complex established by the military, had once been so secret that it was left undocumented on the Red Army's own field maps. Even its name, which was meant to indicate that it lay sixteen kilometers from the original Skotoprigonyevsk, was a deception: the two cities were nearly two hundred kilometers apart. Without permission from the KGB, it had been impossible to enter or leave 16. Until two years earlier, Timofey had never been outside, not once in twenty-three years. He now realized, as he would have realized if he hadn't been so distracted by the events of the past week, that it wasn't enough to find a criminal. He needed someone with brains, someone who had read a newspaper in the last five years.

"Now look at the other papers. See, this is my pass to the Strategic Production Facility."

"Comrade," Shiv said sarcastically, "if you think I'm buying some fancy documents—"

"Listen to me. My unit's principal task is the supply of the strategic weapons force. Our reactor produces Pu-239 as a fission by-product for manufacture into warheads. These operations have been curtailed, but the reactors must be kept functioning. Decommissioning them would be even more costly than maintaining them—and we can't even do that properly." Timofey's voice fell to an angry whisper. "There have been many lapses in the administration of safety procedure."

Timofey looked intently at Shiv, to see if he understood. But Shiv wasn't listening; he didn't like to be lectured and especially didn't like to be told to read things, even identity papers. The world was full of men who knew more than Shiv did, and he hated each one of them. A murderous black cloud rose from the stained orange carpeting at his feet and occulted his vision. The more Timofey talked, the more Shiv wanted to hurt him. But at the same time, starting from the moment he heard the name Skotoprigonyevsk-16, Shiv gradually became aware that he was onto something big, bigger than anything he had ever done before. He was nudged by an incipient awareness that perhaps it was even too big for him.

In flat, clipped sentences, Timofey spoke: "There was an accident. I was contaminated. I have a wife and child, and nothing to leave them. This is why I'm here."

"Don't tell me about your wife and child. You can fuck them both to hell. I'm a businessman."

For a moment, Timofey was shocked by the violence in the young man's voice. But then he reminded himself that, in coming to Moscow for the first time in twenty-five years, he had entered a country where violence was the most stable and valuable currency. Maybe this was the right guy for the deal after all. There was no room for sentimentality.

He braced himself. "All right then. Here's what you need to know. I have diverted a small quantity of fissile material. I'm here to sell it."

Shiv removed his handkerchief again and savagely wiped his nose. He had a cold, Timofey observed. Acute radiation exposure severely compromised the immune system, commonly leading to fatal bacterial infection. He wondered if the hoodlum's germs were the ones fated to kill him.

Timofey said, "Well, are you interested?"

To counteract any impression of weakness given by the handkerchief, Shiv tugged a mouthful of smoke from his cigarette.

"In what?"

"Are you listening to anything I'm saying? I have a little more than three hundred grams of weapons-grade plutonium. It can be used to make an atomic bomb. I want thirty thousand dollars for it."

As a matter of principle, Shiv laughed. He always laughed when a mark named a price. But a chill seeped through him as far down as his testicles.

"It will fetch many times that on the market. Iraq, Iran, Libya, North Korea all have nuclear weapons programs, but they don't have the technology to produce enriched fissile material. They're desperate for it; there's no price Saddam Hussein wouldn't pay for an atomic bomb."

"I don't know anything about selling this stuff..."

"Don't be a fool," Timofey rasped. "Neither do I. That's why I've come here. But you say you're a businessman. You must have contacts, people with money, people who can get it out of the country."

Shiv grunted. He was just playing for time now, to assemble his thoughts and devise a strategy. The word *fool* remained lodged in his gut like a spoiled piece of meat.

"Maybe I do, maybe I don't."

"Make up your mind."

"Where's the stuff?"

"With me."

A predatory light flicked on in the hoodlum's eyes. But Timofey had expected that. He slowly unbuttoned his jacket. It fell away to reveal an invention of several hours' work that, he realized only when he assembled it in the kitchen the day after the accident, he had been planning for years. At that moment of realization, his entire body had been flooded with a searing wonder at the dark soul that inhabited it. Now, under his arm, a steel canister no bigger than a coffee tin was attached to his left side by an impenetrably complex arrangement of belts, straps, hooks, and buckles.

"Do you see how I rigged the container?" he said. "There's a right way of taking it off my body and many wrong ways. Take it off one of the wrong ways and the container opens and the material spills out. Are you aware of the radiological properties of plutonium and their effect on living organisms?"

Shiv almost laughed. He once knew a girl who wore something like this.

"Let me see it."

"It's *plutonium*. It has to be examined under controlled laboratory conditions. If even a microscopic amount of it lodges within your body, ionizing radiation will irreversibly damage body tissue and your cells' nucleic material. A thousandth of a gram is fatal...I'll put it to you more simply. Anything it touches dies. It's like in a fairy tale."

Shiv did indeed have business contacts, but he'd been burned about six months earlier, helping to move some Uzbek heroin that must have been worth more than a half million dollars. He had actually held the bags in his hands and pinched the powder through the plastic, marveling at the physics that transmuted such a trivial quantity of something into so much money. But once he made the arrangements and the businessmen had the stuff in *their* hands, they gave him only two thousand dollars for his trouble, little more than a tip. Across a table covered by a freshly stained tablecloth, the Don—his name was Voronenko, and he was from Tambov, but he insisted on being called the Don anyway, and being served spaghetti and meatballs for lunch—had grinned at the shattering disappointment on Shiv's face. Shiv had wanted to protest, but he was frightened. Afterwards he was so angry that he gambled and whored the two grand away in a single night.

He said, "So, there was an accident. How do I know the stuff's still good?"

"Do you know what a half-life is? The half-life of plutonium two-thirty-nine is twenty-four thousand years."

"That's what you're telling me . . ."

"You can look it up."

"What am I, a fucking librarian? Listen, I know this game. It's mixed with something."

Timofey's whole body was burning; he could feel each of his vital organs being singed by alpha radiation. For a moment he wished he could lie on one of the narrow beds in the room and nap. When he woke, perhaps he would be home. But he dared not imagine that he would wake to find that the accident had never happened. He said, "Yes, of course. The sample contains significant amounts of uranium and other plutonium isotopes, plus trace quantities of americium and gallium. But the Pu-239 content is ninety-four-point-seven percent."

"So you admit it's not the first-quality stuff."

"Anything greater than ninety-three percent is considered weapons-grade. Look, do you have somebody you can bring this to? Otherwise, we're wasting my time."

Shiv took out another cigarette from his jacket and tapped it against the back of his hand. Igniting the lighter, he kept his finger lingering on the gas feed. He passed the flame in front of his face so that it appeared to completely immolate the mark.

"Yeah, I do, but he's in Perkhuskovo. It's a forty-minute drive. I'll take you to him."

"I have a car. I'll follow you.".

Shiv shook his head. "That won't work. His dacha's protected. You can't go through the gate alone."

"Forget it then. I'll take the material someplace else."

Shiv's shrug of indifference was nearly sincere. The guy was too weird, the stuff was too weird. His conscience told him he was better off pimping for schoolgirls. But he said, "If you like. But for a deal like this, you'll need to go to one godfather or another. On your own you're not going to find someone walking around with thirty thousand dollars in his pocket. This businessman knows me, his staff knows me. I'll go with you in your car. You can drive."

Timofey said, "No, we each drive separately."

The mark was unmovable. Shiv offered him a conciliatory smile.

"All right," he said. "Maybe. I'll call him from the lobby and try to set it up. I'm not even sure he can see us tonight."

"It has to be tonight or there's no deal."

"Don't be in such a hurry. You said the stuff lasts twenty-four thousand years, right?"

"Tell him I'm from Skotoprigonyevsk 16. Tell him it's weapons-grade. That's all he needs to know. Do you understand the very least bit of what I'm saying?"

The pale solar disc had dissolved in the horizontal haze long ago, but the autumn evening was still in its adolescent hours, alive to possibility. As the two cars lurched into the swirl of traffic on the Garden Ring road, Timofey could taste the unburned gasoline in the hoodlum's exhaust. He had never before driven in so much traffic or seen so many foreign cars, or guessed that they would ever be driven so recklessly. Their rear lights flitted and spun like fireflies. At his every hesitation or deceleration the cars behind him flashed their headlights. Their drivers navigated their vehicles as if from the edges of their seats, peering over their dashboards, white-knuckled and grim, and as if they all carried three hundred grams of weapons-grade plutonium strapped to their chests. Driving among Audis and Mercedeses would have thrilled Tolya, who cut pictures of them from magazines and cherished his small collection of mismatched models. The thought of his son, a sweet and cheerful boy with orthodontic braces, and utterly, utterly innocent, stabbed at him.

The road passed beneath what Timofey recognized as Mayakovsky Square from television broadcasts of holiday marches. He knew that the vengeful, lustrating revision of Moscow's street names in the last few years had renamed the square Triumfalnaya, though there was nothing triumphant about it, except for its big Philips billboard advertisement. Were all the advertisements on the Garden Ring posted in the Latin alphabet? Was Cyrillic no longer anything more than a folk custom? It was as if he had traveled to the capital of a country in which he had never lived.

Of course hardly any commercial advertising could be seen in 16. Since Gorbachev's fall a halfhearted attempt had been made to obscure most of the Soviet agitprop, but it was still a Soviet city untouched by foreign retailing and foreign advertising. The few foreign goods that found their way into the city's state-owned shops arrived dented and tattered, as if produced in Asian, European, and North American factories by demoralized Russian workers. Well, these days 16 was much less of a city. It was not uncommon to see chickens and other small livestock grazing in the gravel between the high-rises, where pensioners and unpaid workers had taken up subsistence farming. Resentment of Moscow burned in Timofey's chest, alongside the Pu-239.

Plutonium. There was no exit for the stuff. It was as permanent and universal as original sin. Since its first synthesis in 1941 (what did Seaborg do with that magical, primeval stone of his own creation? put it in his vault? was it still there?) more than a thousand metric tons of the element had been produced. It was still being manufactured, not only in Russia, but in France and Britain as well, and it remained stockpiled in America. Nearly all of it was locked in steel containers, buried in mines, or sealed in glass—safe, safe, safe. But the very minimal fraction that wasn't secured, the few flakes that had escaped in nuclear tests, reactor accidents, transport mishaps, thefts, and leakages, veiled the entire planet. Sometime within the next three months Timofey would die with plutonium in his body, joined in the same year by thousands of other victims in Russia and around the world. His body would be brought directly to the city crematorium, abstractly designed in jaggedly cut, pale yellow concrete so as to be vaguely "life-affirming," where the chemistry of his skin and lungs, heart and head, would be transformed by fire and wind. In the rendering oven, the Pu-239 would oxidize and engage in wanton couplings with other substances, but it would always stay faithful to its radioactive, elemental properties. Some of it would remain in the ash plowed back to the earth; the rest would be borne aloft into the vast white skies arching above the frozen plain. Dust to dust.

Yet it would remain intangible, completely invisible, hovering elusively before us like a floater in our eyes' vitreous humor. People get cancer all the time and almost never know why. A nucleic acid on a DNA site is knocked out of place, a chromosome sequence is deleted, an oncogene is activated. It would show up only in statistics, where it remained divorced from the lives and deaths of individuals. It was just as well, Timofey thought, that we couldn't take in the enormity of the threat; if we did, we would be paralyzed with fear—not for ourselves, but for our children. We couldn't wrap our minds around it; we could think of it only for a few moments and then have to turn away from it. But the accident had liberated Timofey. He could now contemplate plutonium without any difficulty at all.

And it was not only plutonium. Timofey was now exquisitely aware of the ethereal solution that washed over him every day like a warm bath: the insidiously subatomic, the swarmingly microscopic, and the multi-syllabically chemical. His body was soaked in pesticides, the liquefied remains of electrical batteries, leaded gasoline exhaust, dioxin, nitrates, toxic waste metals, dyes, and deadly viral organisms generated in untreated sewage—the entire carcinogenic and otherwise malevolent slough of the great Soviet industrial empire. Like Homo Sovieticus himself, Timofey was ending his life as a melange of damaged chromosomes, metal-laden tissue, crumbling bone, fragmented membranes, and oxygen-deprived blood. Perhaps his nation's casual regard for the biological consequences of environmental degradation was the result of some quasi-Hegelian conviction that man lived in history, not nature. It was no wonder everyone smoked.

For a moment, as the hoodlum swung into the turning lane at the Novy Arbat, Timofey considered passing the turnoff and driving on through the night and the following day back to 16's familiar embrace. But there was only one hundred and twenty dollars hidden in the bookcase in his apartment. It was the sum total of his family's savings.

Now Shiv saw Timofey's shudder of indecision in his rearview mirror; he had suspected that the mark might turn tail. If he had, Shiv would have broken from the turning lane with a shriek of tire (he savored the image) and chased him down.

In tandem the two cars crossed the bridge over the Moscow River, the brilliantly lit White House on their right nearly effervescing in the haze off the water. It was as white and polished as a tooth, having been capped recently by a squadron of Turkish workers after Yeltsin's troops had shelled and nearly gutted it. Shiv and Timofey passed the Pizza Hut and the arch commemorating the battle against Napoleon at Borodino. They were leaving the city. Now Timofey knew he was committed. The hoodlum wouldn't let him go. He knew this as surely as if he were sitting in the car beside him. If the world of the atom were controlled by random quantum events, then the macroscopic universe through which the two Zhigulis were piloted was purely deterministic. The canister was heavy and the straps that supported it were beginning to cut into Timofey's back.

He could have even more easily evaded Shiv at the exit off Kutuzovsky Prospekt; then on the next road there was another turnoff, then another and another. Timofey lost count of the turns. It was like driving down a rabbit hole: he'd never find his way back. Soon they were kicking up stones on a dark country road, the only traffic. Every once in a while the Moscow River or one of its tributaries showed itself through the naked, snowless birches. A pocked and torn slice of moon bobbed and weaved across his windshield. Shiv paused, looking for the way, and then abruptly pivoted his car into a lane hardly wider than the Zhiguli itself.

Timofey followed, taking care to stay on the path. He could hear himself breathing: the sound from his lungs was muffled and wet. Gravel crunched beneath his tires and bushes scraped their nails against the car's doors. The hood slowed even further, crossing a small bridge made of a few planks. They clattered like bones.

Timofey's rearview mirror incandesced. Annoyed, he pushed it from his line of sight. Shiv slowed to a stop, blinked a pair of white lights in reverse, and backed up just short of Timofey's front bumper. At the same time, Timofey felt a hard tap at his rear.

Shiv stepped from his car. Pinned against the night by the glare of headlights, the boy appeared vulnerable and very young, almost untouched by life. Timofey detected a measure of gentleness in his face, despite the lunar shadows cast across it. Shiv grimaced at the driver of the third automobile, signaling him to close his lights. He walked in front of his own car and squeezed alongside the brush to Timofey's passenger door.

"We have to talk," he said. "Open it."

Timofey hesitated for a moment, but the lengthy drive had softened his resolve and confused his plan. And there was a car pressed against his rear bumper. He reached over and unlocked the door.

Shiv slid into the seat and stretched his legs. Even for short people, the Zhigulis were too goddamned small.

"We're here?"

"Where else could we be?"

Timofey turned his head and peered into the dark, looking for the businessman's dacha. There was nothing to see at all.

"All right, now hand over the stuff."

"Look, let's do this right—" Timofey began, but then comprehension darkened his face. He didn't need to consider an escape: he understood the whole setup. Perhaps he had chosen the coward's way out. "I see. You're as foolish as a peasant in a fairy tale."

Shiv opened his coat and removed from a holster in his sport jacket an oiled straight blade nearly twenty centimeters long. He turned it so that the moonlight ran its length. He looked into the mark's face for fear. Instead he found ridicule.

Timofey said, "You're threatening me with a knife? I have enough plutonium in my lungs to power a small city for a year, and you're threatening me with a *knife?*"

Shiv placed the shaft against Timofey's side, hard enough to leave a mark even if it were removed. Timofey acted as if he didn't feel it. Again something dark passed before Shiv's eyes.

"Look, this is a high-carbon steel Premium Gessl manufactured by Imperial Gessl in Frankfurt, Germany. I paid eighty bucks for it. It passes through flesh like water. Just give me the goddamned stuff."

"No. I won't do that," Timofey said primly. "I want thirty thousand dollars. It's a fair price, I think, and I won't settle for anything less. I drove here in good faith."

Timofey was the first man Shiv had ever killed, though he had cut a dozen others, plus two women. He wondered if it got easier each time; that's what he had heard. In any case, this was easy enough. There wasn't even much blood, though he was glad the mark had driven his own car after all.

Now Shiv sat alone, aware of the hiss of his lungs, and also that his armpits were wet. Well, it wasn't every day you killed a man. But Timofey hadn't resisted, it hadn't been like killing a man. The knife had passed through him not as if he were water, but as if he were a ghost. Shiv sensed that he had been cheated again.

He opened and pushed *away* Timofey's brown sports jacket, which even in the soundless dark nearly screamed Era of Stagnation. The canister was there, still strapped to his chest. The configuration of straps, hooks, and buckles that kept it in place taunted Shiv with its intricacy. He couldn't follow where each strap went, or what was being buckled or snapped. To Shiv it was a labyrinth, a rat's nest, a knot. To Timofey it had been a topographical equation, clockworks, a flowchart. "Fuck it," Shiv said aloud. He took the Gessl and cut the thin strap above the cylinder with two quick strokes.

Already the mark's body was cool; perhaps time was passing more quickly than Shiv realized. Or maybe it was passing much more slowly: in a single dilated instant he discerned the two cut pieces of the strap hovering at each other's torn edge, longing to be one again. But then they flew away with a robust *snap!* and the entire assembly lost the tension that had kept it wrapped around Timofey's body. The effect was so dramatic he fancied that Timofey had come alive and that he would have the opportunity to kill him again. The canister popped open—he now apprehended which two hooks and which three straps had kept it closed-and fell against the gearshift.

Powder spilled out, but not much. Shiv grabbed the canister and shoveled back some of what was on the seat, at least a few thousand dollars' worth. He couldn't really see the stuff, but it was warm and gritty between his fingers. He scooped in as much as he could, screwed the cylinder shut, and then dusted off his hands against his trousers. He cut away the rest of the straps, leaving them draped on Timofey's body. He climbed from the car.

"Good work, lads."

The two brothers, Andrei and Yegor, each stood nearly two meters tall on either side of their car, which was still parked flush against Timofey's bumper. They were not twins, though it was often difficult to recall which was which, they were so empty of personality. Shiv, who had called them from the hotel lobby, thought of them as pure muscle. By most standards of measurement, they were of equally deficient intelligence. They spoke slowly, reasoned even more slowly, and became steadily more unreliable the further they traveled from their last glass of vodka. Nevertheless, they were useful, and they could do what they were told, or a satisfactory approximation of it.

"What do you got there?" said Yegor.

"You wouldn't understand, believe me."

It was then that he saw that Andrei was holding a gun at his hip, leveling it directly at him. It was some kind of pistol, and it looked ridiculously small in Andrei's hands. Still, it was a gun. In the old days, no one had a gun, everyone fought it out with knives and brass knuckles and solid, honest fists, and pieces of lead pipe. You couldn't get firearms. They never reached the market, and the mere possession of one made the cops dangerously angry. But this was democracy: now every moron had a gun.

"Put it away. What did you think, I was going to cut you out?"

Yegor stepped toward him, his arm outstretched. "Hand it over."

Shiv nodded his head, as if in agreement, but he kept the canister clutched to his stomach. "All right, you've got the drop on me. I admit it. I'll put it in writing if you like. They'll be talking about this for years. But you're not going to be able to move it on your own."

"Why not?" said Andrei. He raised the gun with both hands. The hands trembled. For a moment, Shiv thought he could see straight down the barrel. "You think we're stupid."

"If you want to show me how smart you are, you'll put down the fucking gun."

"I don't have to show you anything."

"Listen, this is plutonium. Do you know what it is?"

"Yeah, I know."

"Do you know what's it's used for?"

"I don't got to know. All I got to know is that people will buy it. That's the free market."

"Idiot! Who are you going to sell it to?"

"Private enterprise. They'll buy it from us just like they'd buy it from you. And did you call me an idiot?"

"Listen, I'm just trying to explain to you"—Shiv thought for a moment—" the material's radiological properties."

Shiv was too close to be surprised, it happened too quickly. In one moment he was trying to reason with Andrei, intimidate him, and was only beginning to appreciate the seriousness of the problem, and had just observed, in a casual way, that the entire time of his life up to the moment he had stepped out of Timofey's car seemed equal in length to the time since then, and in the next moment he was unconscious, bleeding from a large wound in his head.

"Well, fuck you," said Andrei, or, more literally, "go to a fucked mother." He had never shot a man before, and he was surprised and frightened by the blood, which had splattered all over Shiv's clothes, and even on himself. He had expected that the impact of the shot would have propelled Shiv off the bridge, but it hadn't. Shiv lay there at his feet, bleeding against the rear tire. The sound of the little gun was tremendous; it continued roaring through the woods long after Andrei had brought the weapon to his side.

Neither brother said anything for awhile. In fact, they weren't brothers, as everyone believed, but were stepbrothers, as well as in-laws, in some kind of complicated way that neither had ever figured out. From Yegor's silence, Andrei guessed that he was angry with him for shooting Shiv. They hadn't agreed to shoot him beforehand. But Yegor had allowed him to carry the gun, which meant Andrei had the right to make the decision. Yegor couldn't second-guess him, Andrei resolved, his nostrils flaring.

But Yegor broke the long silence with a gasped guffaw. In the bark of his surprise lay a tremor of anxiety. "Look at this mess," he said. "You fucking near tore off his head."

Andrei could tell his brother was proud of him, at least a bit. He felt a surge of love.

"Well, fuck," said Yegor, shaking his head in wonder. "It's really a mess. How are we going to clean it up? It's all over the car. Shit, it's on my pants."

"Let's just take the stuff and leave."

Yegor said, "Go through his pockets. He always carries a roll. I'll check the other guy."

"No, it's too much blood. I'll go through the other guy's pockets."

"Look, it's like I've been telling you, that's what's wrong with this country. People don't accept the consequences of their actions. Now; *you* put a hole in the guy's head, *you* go through his pockets."

Andrei scowled but quickly ran his hands through Shiv's trousers, jacket, and coat anyway. The body stirred and some-thing like a groan bubbled from Shiv's blood-filled mouth. Some of the blood trickled onto Andrei's hand. It was disgust-ingly warm and viscid. He snatched his hand away and wiped it on Shiv's jacket. Taking more care now, he reached into the inside jacket pocket and pulled out a gold-colored money clip with some rubles, about ten twenty-dollar bills, a few tens, and a creased five. He slipped the clip and four or five of the twenties into his pocket and, stacking the rest on the car's trunk, announced, "Not much, just some cash."

Yegor emerged from the car. "There's nothing at all on this guy, only rubles."

Andrei doubted that. He should have pocketed all of Shiv's money.

"I wonder what the stuff's like," said Yegor, taking the closed canister from Shiv's lap.

He placed it next to the money and pulled off the top, revealing inside a coarse, silvery gray powder. Yegor grimaced. It was nothing like he had ever seen. He wet his finger, poked it into the container, and removed a fingerprint's worth. The stuff tasted chalky.

"What did he call it?" he asked.

"Plutonium. From Bolivia, he said."

Andrei reached in, took a pinch of the powder, and placed it on the back of his left hand. He then closed his right nostril with a finger and brought the stuff up to his face. He loved doing this. From the moment he had pulled the gun on Shiv he had felt as if he were in Chicago or Miami. He sniffed up the powder.

It burned, but not in the right way. It was as if someone—Yegor—had grabbed his nostril with a pair of hot pliers. The pain shot through his head like a nail, and he saw stars. Then he saw atoms, their nuclei surrounded by hairy penumbrae of indeterminately placed electrons. The nuclei themselves pulsed with indeterminacy, their masses slightly less than the sum of their parts. Bombarded by neutrons, the nuclei were drastically deformed. Some burst. The repulsion of two highly charged nuclear fragments released Promethean, adamantine energy, as well as excess neutrons that bounced among the other nuclei, a cascade of excitation and transformation.

"It's crap. It's complete crap. Crap, crap, *crap!*"

Enraged, Andrei hoisted the open container, brought it behind his head, and, with a grunt and a cry, hurled it far into the night sky. The canister sailed. For a moment, as it reached the top of its ascent beyond the bridge, it caught a piece of moonlight along its sides. It looked like a little crescent moon itself, in an eternal orbit above the earth, the stuff forever pluming behind it. And then it very swiftly vanished. Everything was quiet for a moment, and then there was a distant, voluptuous sound as the container plunged into the river. As the two brothers turned toward each other, one of them with a gun, everything was quiet again.

Faith Is a Girl's Name

Binnie Kirshenbaum

I)

SHE SHOWED ME HOW TO PAINT LIGHT. Imagine. Painting light. A dab of white dotting the clown's nose and presto! a reflection. A streak of yellow breaking up a cloud, and I got light like God coming to Moses in my book, *Bible Stories*. Light. This was no small accomplishment. Painting light. Then she said to me, "I'm sure the other children are very nice, but they are inferior to you. Remember that."

Aside from how to create light, aside from the fact that I was superior to the other kids, she instructed I keep a good address. "She's *meshugge*," my father said. "Sleeps on an army cot. No food in the cupboards. But on Riverside Drive, yet."

There was food, though. She ate sardines and crackers. Sardines packed neatly in their cans. Clever little fish fitting together just so. Like a puzzle. Or an illusion. A single fish reflected twelve times.

Oh, there was one other thing she said. "Never, ever disturb a bird's nest," she told me, "because if you do, the birds will abandon it."

II)

Drop dead gorgeous. Exotic in junior furs. Sweaters by Jones. Add-A-Pearl necklaces by Tiffany's completed for Sweet Sixteens. Ambitions by mothers, and if not graced by God's light touch, then by Dr. Diamond's scalpel. Dr. Diamond, the nose-job king. Pink frosted lipstick. Frosted hair. Frosted nails. Frost like a fine layer of ice. Such glamorous dolls, we were Social Darwinism in action. The mean-spiritedness was nothing more than acts of omission.

Once, a short and plump boy threw an egg at Marcia. It landed squarely on her chest. Splatted on off-white Jones' cashmere, and it made Marcia cry. When the rest of us confronted him, demanding to know what the fuck his problem was, he went red with rage. "All of you. You look at me like I'm not there."

"So what?" Bev said. "We look at everyone like they're not there."

Even each other. Even ourselves. And I considered myself blessed to be included, to break bread at their lunch table.

III)

Before Yeltsin, before Gorbachev, before sporting Cyrillic T-shirts was all the rage, Nancy shaved off her eyebrows. She dyed her white cat red, and took up smoking cigarettes through an amber holder. Next, she said, "I'm to be called Natasha now," and she joined the Russian Orthodox Church, the one on the Upper East Side.

After the Easter service, an all-night affair without so much as a bathroom break, they rejoiced over breakfast, a buffet of treats imported from the Motherland. Employing the natural sensuality of fish eggs, Natasha made a sexual suggestion to a bearded and brooding priest. Tongues wagged Russian style, and so Natasha converted.

This time she became an Episcopalian. Read Barbara Pym novels and asked the vicar in for tea. Over Earl Grey, scones with jam, and cucumber sandwiches, the vicar described for her his collection of Fiestaware. He had the complete set in red. Nancy would've blown the Pope for a full set of red Fiestaware. She set her sights on this vicar, on becoming his wife, on joint custody of the dishes. She talked much of this, and of the good work she'd do with the gentlewomen—which is English for bag ladies—as the clergyman's wife.

The vicar came to tea again, and the two of them waxed ecstatic over cobalt glass, ruby glass, crystal cut so all colors of the spectrum reflect, refract, onto a white linen tablecloth.

On his third afternoon to tea, the vicar left Nancy's apartment not long before dawn. When he stepped out onto the street to hail a cab back to the rectory, hoping to get there before the others awoke, he was knocked down, killed, by a garbage truck making early morning rounds.

For Nancy, there were no churches left. She'd been through them all.

IV)

Ann's ancestors were Plain. Not Amish, although something like that. They wore somber colors. No buttons or jewelry. Laughter was the devil's voice. They didn't dance either.

But Ann was not at all like her grandmothers. Ann was self-indulgent. She wore makeup, bracelets, hair ribbons, the works. She considered herself to be wild even though she was thirty years old and still lived, along with four brothers, at home with her parents. Theirs was a square house on a tree-lined block in a part of Brooklyn like no other part of Brooklyn, an enclave cut off from mass transit. With her family lived three dogs and a cat. One dog was deaf, another blinded by glaucoma. The third dog had only two legs. The cat, too, was blind. Its eyes were missing. Each animal's story ended with Ann's family offering refuge, an act of charity.

It was that sort of thing, an act of charity, which prompted me to offer Ann my apartment for the summer I was away. Privacy was a gift she could use. "Make yourself at home," I said.

She made herself very much at home. When I returned, I found my furniture rearranged. My paintings were taken down and stacked in a closet. Only the nails jutting out from the walls remained as testimony that something had once hung there. A pair of silver earrings had vanished along with my Add-A-Pearl necklace, two silk camisoles, a garter belt, and a pair of fishnet stockings.

But the baffling question remains: Why did she cut out the elastic from the fitted sheets?

When I asked, she went mute. Rocked in her high-backed chair like Norman Bates as his mother, denying it all.

V)

There are no coincidences. That Bev and I should meet while waiting for the light to change at Third Avenue and 46th Street was a miracle. But troubling. I hadn't seen her in ten or eleven years, and there she was, wearing a floral print dress with a white scalloped collar. She had Reeboks on her feet and one of those papoose thingies strapped to her back. There was a baby in it. Its head and arms and legs stuck out like a pithed frog. It drooled on her Lord & Taylor dress, and I couldn't fathom how it got there.

Prior to this meeting, the last time I'd seen her was the night before we went off to college, our separate ways. We'd dropped Quaaludes and, consequently, everything was funny. We got so silly that we even talked about our lives, about what we wanted, what we'd get. "I know I'm supposed to grow as a person," Bev said, "but honestly, I can't see it happening." We stretched our legs out on her blue shag carpet, and I told her I didn't think I'd ever get married because I couldn't imagine being faithful. This we thought so hilarious that Bev peed. Perhaps it was sitting in the puddle that sobered her. "You are so fucking weird," she said.

Now, she talked about her new name, which was Shapiro, and about her co-op, and about her upcoming vacation to Puerto Rico. Finally I said, "Is that yours?" meaning the baby. Only it came out like I was referring to something that had fallen to the ground, a piece of paper or a scarf, maybe.

"Don't you have children?" she asked.

At first, I didn't understand the question. Then, I shook my head and explained, "I'm very immature for my age."

VI)

As if I could be a band of Israeli commandos, and the Entebbe airport were a mobile home someplace awful, I wanted to swoop down and rescue her. Save her from yet another stupid mistake.

The last time I tried saving her, I couldn't. And she hit bottom from which she did not bounce back like the clean and swift rebound on a trampoline. Rather, she crawled her way out, grabbing hold of dirt and twigs. Afterwards, she said to me, "I appreciated your effort, but you can't stop a natural disaster. It's not possible. Don't even try."

I did learn one other thing. One she does not know about: Just because she is gone, I do not also disappear.

This past February, she came back to town to collect the rest of her stuff from storage. Nice Jewish Boys Moving and Storage

Company. She always put her things in safekeeping with Nice Jewish Boys. "Your people," she'd say to me.

I helped her load up, and then we went for dinner to one of those Cuban-Chinese joints on Eighth Avenue. We ate pollo frito and plantains. Sweet plantains. It was snowing when I walked her to her car. Under a streetlamp we stood, snowflakes landing on her eyelashes, lingering for only an instant before melting away. "Please," she said, "don't abandon me."

The Scrimshaw Violin

Jonathan Levi

MADELEINE GORDON was not much of a Jew. She was a Starbuck, the daughter of whalers, pirates, and other not-so-genteel Semitophobes of Nantucket. But she had married David Gordon (who was the genuine article) and, in the innocence that calls itself love, had created her own cultural revolution, shocking not only her mother and several generations of Starbucks, but all the Jews of Nantucket by becoming more knowledgeable, more spiritual, more legalistic (and a better cook of gefilte fish—not to mention she caught her own pike) than any of the genetic Jewesses on the island. She hung a Chagall print above the headboard of her great-grandfather's four-poster, taught herself Biblical Hebrew from CD-ROM, and read every word ever written by Elie Wiesel. She subscribed to the *Jerusalem Post* and the *Forward*, and had the *New York Times* delivered to the mansion on Orange Street, where she lived with David and her mother, scanning them religiously for the latest news on what it meant to be a Jew. And so it came to pass that Madeleine saw an Op-Ed piece by the Rabbi Doctor Alexander Abba Lincoln on the discovery of the Jew Gene—she was not entirely sure whether he was serious—and sent the invitation.

Sandy Lincoln was not much of a rabbi, at least not down in that secret place of superstition and fear that people call the soul. He had spent too much time in civil service, and worse yet, in the Talmudic details of forensics, to believe that humanity was much more than a hank of hair and a piece of bone.

But Sandy had discovered over the years—especially over the years after the communes and the jug bands and the solar-powered yurts, when the beads and batik gave way to a tight layer of fat around the belly and a halo of white hair around the jowls that made him seem perpetually open for business—that people, like Madeleine Gordon, flocked to him as if he were, God forbid, a practicing rabbi. They wrote him letters, stopped him on the street, woke him at two o'clock in the morning. Every Friday night they invited him—a synagogue here, a Jewish Community Center there—to speak to them, as a rabbi and a coroner, to instruct them on the Dahmer, the Anastasia, the O. J. of the day. And after the talks, in the hallway after the kiddush, by the swingset after the dinner, people sought him out, pressed his hand, looked into his eyes, not for his expert opinion on DNA or carbon dating (or even on their private concerns about stray hairs or semen stains), but for the kind of deep advice that only someone who knew both the Midrash and the Dead could provide. Within a three-hundred-dollar round-trip radius of New York, the word spread—Rabbi Sandy Lincoln, he's a mensch, he's got a soul.

Normally, Sandy would have scribbled a brief note to his assistant, Indira, to include a polite, but firm apology to

Madeleine, as he did with the many invitations he received that read more like the personal memoirs of the Chairwoman of the Speakers Committee of this synagogue or that JCC, lonely women in search of a little safe, spiritual recognition in the form of a traveling rabbi.

But Madeleine's invitation included a unique postscript. "Rabbi," it read, "I hope you will find in my Nantucket what I have found in your religion." Sandy was less moved by the chutzpah of the comparison, than by the mystery of what it was he might discover. Besides, the invitation arrived in the depression of February, when he was having trouble with Indira, and the Medical Examiner's Office was the warmest spot in Manhattan. Madeleine Gordon wanted him in the middle of July. There was the promise of a barbecue, the hint of a yacht. Sandy accepted.

Nevertheless, now that he was on the island, he found himself feeling less enthusiastic at half-past-seven than he'd expected. David Gordon, not Madeleine, had met the three-forty flight from LaGuardia in an open-sided Willys Jeep that made all conversation impossible on the way from the airport into town. He had deposited Sandy, without much more than a nod, at the entrance of the Unitarian sailors' chapel on Orange Street that served as a temple for the dozen Sabbaths between Memorial Day and Labor Day, before disappearing with Sandy's overnighter.

The talk had gone well, that wasn't the problem. He had rambled around intermarriage (Madeleine had specifically requested the topic in her invitation) in mock forensic terms. He had dissected the current phobia—that the Jews were intermarrying themselves into extinction. The Jews of Nantucket sat at the edge of their Unitarian pews. Of course they were worried, all of them, no matter how many lobsters they allowed themselves between Shavuoth and Tisha b'Av. They worried that every time a David Gordon married a Madeleine Starbuck, he was finishing off what Hitler had begun. That ten years from now, you'd be more likely to run into a blue whale on Orange Street than a nice, Jewish doctor for your daughter.

His advice had been greeted with the usual rush of applause by the seventy-five assorted Jews who had bought into the lighthouse baskets and lobster pants of the Gentiles but still wanted to maintain some semblance of Otherness. There had been the usual wilding afterwards by the local bridge ladies and their unmarried daughters. But Madeleine Gordon, if she was there, had failed to introduce herself. And while some might interpret her invisibility and the silence of her husband as mystery, Sandy felt only annoyance and a need, despite the rush of the momentary celebrity, for air and a moment of tranquility. He pled a weak bladder and stepped out the back door.

Orange was a one-way street of cobblestones. The Unitarian Church was no larger, just more exposed than many of the white, clapboard mansions hidden behind generations of hedge and rose. To the right was the airport—Sandy guessed the town was in the other direction. There was to be a dinner at eight—that much David had communicated. With a half-hour to regain some kind of enthusiasm, Sandy walked left.

The problem—if Sandy wanted to get to the root of it—had begun in the morning. The number three train had shut down between Twenty-third and Fourteenth Street for thirty minutes, and Indira was still out with a summer flu. Which meant that Sandy lacked the ten minutes tranquility at the beginning of the day, that moment with a cardboard cup of Colombian roast and two Danish, that can seal you against the daily pain. Selwyn, his other assistant, Selwyn of the hunched shoulders and nicotine hair, was in the office already, of course, as Sandy entered.

"What's in today?" The room was kept at forty-two degrees exactly. He missed his coffee.

"NYPD, Rabbi," Selwyn said. He was standing at the examination table, waiting for Sandy, hunched over a police body bag. It smelled like smoke, even through the chill of the room and the polyurethene of the bag. "Third Avenue, restaurant up in the Eighties, kitchen fire. Owner says bad wires, Fire Department says arson. Some poor Jew found his Auschwitz."

And so it began. All morning, as Sandy and Selwyn diluted powdered chemicals, ran local tests and bagged parts for further analysis, Selwyn worked to keep the conversation within the perimeter of the death camps and the crematoria even as Sandy struggled to push it out. Selwyn was a survivor—his mother had died in Sobibor—and the Holocaust was never far from Selwyn's petri dishes and beakers. For Selwyn, this is what it meant to be a Jew. He wore his mother on his sleeve and the Holocaust around his neck like a Phi Beta Kappa key. All fire victims led to Auschwitz, all gold teeth to Switzerland.

Sandy felt great sympathy for Selwyn and had learned to accept this tic along with the shoulders and yellowed hair. For Sandy, the Holocaust, the fires, the teeth, the bones—these were human tragedies, human triumphs. There was nothing particularly Jewish about them. He was a Jew, he wouldn't deny it. But he was no more proud of being a Jew than he was proud of having two arms, a spleen, ten metatarsals, and eighteen ribs. Sandy knew Selwyn, and Selwyn knew his boss. There was nothing new about this back and forth—Selwyn had worked for him for twelve years. Sandy wasn't going to jeopardize a good assistant by saying anything new.

It was after one when Sandy announced that he had finished whatever it was he could do with the polybag. "Write out the report, Selwyn, will you?" He grabbed his overnighter. "I've gotta run."

"Rabbi," Selwyn said, "I've figured it out."

"Yes, Selwyn?" Maybe his tone was patronizing, but Sandy

was in a hurry to make his plane and would have to make do with whatever lunch he could find at LaGuardia. He had no time for more Jews.

"Rabbi," Selwyn said, "you have no soul."

"Rabbi," a voice called. Sandy looked up. For a moment, he felt the chill of the examination room. "Rabbi," the voice called again.

A woman was standing across the street. More exactly, she was standing on the raised portico of what looked, from Sandy's vantage, to be the grandest mansion on the block. Doric columns, iron lanterns, a curved driveway of crushed scallop shells. And this woman. Even at the distance of a couple of dozen cobblestones, Sandy guessed she was six feet tall. She wasn't beautiful in the breath-catching sense of the word. She was too tall, her blonde hair too frizzy and pulled back too tightly in a too colorful ponytail. But Sandy recognized the confidence of her letter's postscript and allowed himself to be lured across the street.

"Mrs. Gordon."

"Madeleine."

"Sandy."

"I'm sorry," Madeleine began, but Sandy waved her off, "there was a last-minute hitch." She stepped down from the portico. "My mother—I wrote you."

"Of course." Sandy remembered the reference to old Mrs. Starbuck who, if her late husband, in his wisdom and knowledge of inheritance law, hadn't bequeathed this mansion to his only daughter, would have banned poor, silent David, Sandy himself, and the rest of their tribe from the island.

"The talk?"

"Everyone was very kind." Sandy looked down. Now that she was standing next to him, he began to feel an attraction, partially an awe—not just her height, but the straw of her hair, the pebbled beauty of her cheeks, the Nantucket she'd promised of sand and heath.

"Good," she said, but Sandy felt she was looking down into his face in search of something else.

"I thought—"

"I'm sorry, Sandy." Madeleine must have seen something in his face below the beard. "You wanted to take a walk." He stood there, realizing that some kind of response was expected of him. But something had caught Sandy as Madeleine spoke. It was a fragrance, something like wisteria, a breeze that came as much from the house as from Madeleine herself. Sandy pulled his head back, retreated one step. But the fragrance followed him with a gentle urgency.

"No, no," Sandy answered quickly, with a shy speed that convinced Madeleine of his sincerity.

"I'm glad," she said, holding out her hand. "Before the others come, I want to show you something." The postscript, the promise of a discovery. Sandy forgot about his escape, forgot about Selwyn and the fire on Third Avenue. With the faint scent of wisteria in his nose, Sandy followed Madeleine across the threshold.

Inside, the Starbuck mansion was magnificent, a mid-nineteenth-century collage of exotic woods and veneers carefully chosen by homesick Starbucks on the distant shores of the whaling grounds. Although she seemed to have a specific destination in mind, there was a method to Madeleine's tour. She was determined to show Sandy every mahogany panel, every teak louvre, the priceless screens of bamboo and Javanese balsa. She led Sandy through the bedrooms, the dressing rooms, up into the attic, out onto the widow's walk where he could see the masts of the rich and famous two hundred yards down the bluff in the marina. She led him back down again into the body of the house, linking each room to a tale of this captain or that shipowner who had left this piece of furniture or that bit of history. It was a treasury, a genealogy, each room a branch of a family tradition that fanned across the seas in search of another leviathan to bring home to this tiny island.

But Sandy found that, despite the melody of her voice, the obvious life she put into her description of these ancient histories, his mind had latched onto something else. It was that breeze again, that wisteria-laden breath, stronger in some rooms than in others, as if the house itself were teasing him with a secret. It came to him as the ebb and flow of a presence—he wasn't ready yet to call it anything more metaphysical.

He thought about asking Madeleine, but what would he ask her? Excuse me, but what is that perfume you're wearing? Sandy's greatest fear, almost a certainty, was that the presence he felt had little to do with smells, with something that Madeleine could recognize and share. It had to do with him. Maybe, despite Selwyn's barb, with his soul.

Was it love? It was a nonsense of a question, but one that he always felt compelled to ask himself—in a clinical way, of course—on these weekend road trips and these easy talks. Not that he was seeking a wife in the rabbinical sense of a woman to bear children and keep the accounts, nor was he looking for a fleshy bed-warmer, although both types were plentiful along the Friday night circuit, and Indira, despite her summer flu and polytheism, was always a possibility.

One day, long ago—it was his last year in the Seminary, but he'd long since forgotten who was teaching the seminar—he heard a story out of the *Pirke of Rabbi Eliezer*, or the *Alphabet of Ben Sira*, or some other lost fairy tale, about the creation of the first woman. Early on the sixth day, the apocrypha ran, before the birth of Eve, God let Adam watch while he fashioned Woman. He began with a toe bone and then added a metatarsal, an ankle bone, one leg, then the other. Once he had the skeleton, God threaded it with muscle and sinew, vein and artery, organ and flesh. He covered the whole with a layer of the smoothest skin, topped it off with the richest head of the darkest hair. When God was finished, this first woman stood before Adam, this proto-Eve, more beautiful than her successor, more beautiful than any woman since. God smiled in delight at his own creation. He'd wanted Adam to understand completely, in the same way he did, just what it meant to be a woman.

But beautiful as this woman was, all Adam could see were the toe bones and the ligaments, the capillaries and the intestines. He clenched his eyes shut and then opened them. God saw he'd been wrong. Mystery was needed. To create the woman of Adam's dreams, God had to put Adam to sleep.

So what happened to the first woman?—Sandy remembered some bright fellow student's question. Did God send her away, did God destroy her? Did He dismantle her like a used car, recycle her liver and kidneys and corneas? Sandy knew, at least he knew now, after years in the morgues and the cutting rooms. She was there, before him, the first woman, on every table. She might be missing half her head from a gunshot wound, or bloated and peeling beyond mere formal recognition from a month or two in the East River, but there she was, nevertheless, the first woman, bones and stuff and nothing else.

What happened to Eve? That was the question, or maybe just the corner of the Talmud that Sandy was given to dissect. It was Eve who was missing, Eve, the woman God gave more than just a body, the woman God gave breath, gave a soul. Eve was the woman he'd never found no matter how many times he'd dragged the river. But this presence, this ebb and flow that he felt, following Madeleine from room to room. Maybe here, Nantucket, this Eden, this Eve, leading him on, down some garden path, maybe here was the discovery Madeleine had promised in her invitation, far more confusing than love.

"Wait!" Madeleine stopped Sandy with a touch on his elbow. "This is what I wanted you to see." They were in a windowless anteroom, more of a passageway or a closet, with only a border of mirrored lozenges below the lowered ceiling to reflect the dim electric light. Had she felt something, too, Sandy wondered, a presence? She reached forward with two long arms to open a set of double doors concealed in the wall. "Do you know about scrimshaw, Rabbi?"

At first, Sandy couldn't tell what he was looking at. He had expected that the double doors opened up into a glass case or a china cabinet of heirlooms, a shallow closet at the most, something flat, a recess in what he'd thought was the exterior wall of the house. Instead, he saw before him a hollow, ten, twenty feet deep, a cave lit at the roof and floor with tiny Christmas bulbs. The double doors must have opened into some hidden tower, a round space in the four-square symmetry of the Starbuck mansion, a secret grotto within the Quaker simplicity of Nantucket. The presence was so strong here, the feeling that this room was the besomim box, the censer, of the wisteria fragrance, that Sandy was unable, for a moment, to answer.

"Whalebone," Madeleine said. "One hundred and fifty years of whalebone." She took his hand again, and he felt the pressure of her fingers as she led him into the room. "A hundred and fifty years of Starbuck men going to sea, carving their lives on whalebone with knives and ink." She pointed to the lights—not lights at all, but shining whale teeth, lit from below so that the India ink of their engravings, their whaling ships and sea monsters, glowed with an underwater incandescence. It wasn't just a tower, Sandy could see that, not just a blue grotto she had led him into, but the very jaw of a whale, fully open, the palate raised high enough for the tallest Jonah. The full skull, top and bottom, had been fitted into the cave, the room carved around it. Row upon row of teeth—Madeleine showed him each unique design and date, the signature and whereabouts of its Starbuck artist.

"A harpoon boat off Iceland," she said. "C. G. Starbuck, my grandfather's grandfather, 1843. Palm trees and hula girls,"—she pointed to another—"Pitcairn Island, T. Coffin Starbuck, his nephew, 1874." Behind the teeth, along the curved wall of the room, a hanging garden of other artifacts—scrimshaw bowls, scrimshaw clocks, scrimshaw pipes—led down to the back of the throat.

Sandy followed the curve with Madeleine, her head bent as much in reverence as from the lowering ceiling. He was impressed—it would be a good story to file away for after-dinner conversation, maybe even insert into some other Friday night sermon, in an Iowa or an Illinois that knew not from whales. But this wasn't it, not yet. There was something else Madeleine wanted him to see. She led him deeper into the room, to the very gullet of the whale, where a thicket of walking sticks was wedged as a screen against future Jonahs.

Madeleine lifted her free hand. "Here." Very simply. Here. The fragrance was overwhelming, and Sandy understood. This is what she had meant in her postscript, this is what she wanted him to see. Here, in the center of the thicket, its scrimshaw fingerboard shining like a ripe fruit, floated a violin.

Long before forensics and Seminary, the violin—not *this* violin, but the violin as a way of life—had once been the cornerstone of Sandy's faith. In his thinner youth, with his bar mitzvah passed, when he spent every vacant minute with his hands wrapped around a violin, Sandy believed in a soul—not the human soul, perhaps, but the soul of the violin, a conjunction of fingers and wood and string that was greater than the sum of its parts. It was a transcendence that didn't add up, an experience he couldn't explain. It gave him a power over people very different from the one that later made the telephone ring in the small hours of the night. It frightened others and it frightened him, the soul of the violin. Even after it became clear that this soul would only take him as far as the first violin section of a third-rate orchestra and he began playing with long-haired guitarists and barefoot girls, Sandy continued to believe in that ineffable something called Music.

Then, in the doldrums of the Seventies, when it looked like disco was on its way to annihilating everything he found beautiful and potentially profitable about his way of playing music, Sandy found himself slouching toward the Seminary. While he had always gravitated toward displaced persons, he had never had much to do with Jews and Jewishness, at least not in the self-congratulatory, secret handshake kind of a way. But he found the Seminary compatible, a distant, intellectual place that left him alone, by and large, and provided him with a free dorm room when he made the decision to seek his explanations of the world in the study of medicine over at Mt. Sinai Hospital.

He had planned on finishing his rabbinical courses and entering a graduate program in medical research. But his Talmud classes gave him basic tools of investigation that seemed more suited to criminology than the study of origins, and the little bit of preaching he had to do to fulfill his rabbinical requirements gave him a view of the human heart that set him apart from the corpse-cutters in forensics. He found he had a gift of recognition, solving mysteries with a single bone the way dowsers find water with a single willow branch. So he switched to forensics, and he continued, albeit with the irregularity forced by circumstance, to play the violin.

He couldn't say when it happened, but with every autopsy, with every dissection into parts, his desire, his will to play the violin grew weaker and weaker. His fingers, once so adept at jumping positions, at finding the pitch, the exact timbre and vibrato for the music, grew more accustomed to weighing livers and reading femurs. First the violin, then music disappeared, leaving only the scattered ashes of notes.

"How?" Sandy began.

"It's my mother's," Madeleine whispered. "She brought it with her from France after the War."

Sandy stepped closer, squatted down so that the bridge of the scrimshaw violin was level with his chin. It was a strange-looking beast, the violin, one of those freaks of nature, a calcium-white scrimshaw fingerboard—in place of the usual ebony—standing out like an albino against the varnished maple of the body. The carving on the fingerboard was exquisite. It was the figure of a mermaid, her hair spreading down from the scroll, her tail flowing down to the spumy sea, down where the rosin of the bow leaves white caps on the strings. In the distance, behind the mermaid's left shoulder, Leviathan spouted a carnivorous threat, a whale boat already protruding like an after-dinner toothpick—unrealistically, if Sandy remembered his Melville—from his enormous jaws. It was a carving of a certain beauty, Sandy had enough intermediate aesthetics to recognize that. But there was a menace in the whale and, now that he looked more closely, in the mermaid too—not the next victim, but a co-conspirator, the lure, the bait that drew the men to the sea, into their boats and ultimately to their biblical deaths. Strange as it looked, the violin meant she knew. Madeleine knew about him and music and the violin, as if she, twenty years younger though she was, had been there at his own creation.

"It is the only scrimshaw violin in the world." Sandy turned. The voice came full, with the husky depth of a Jeanne Moreau, from a tiny shadow in the far light of the hallway.

"Sandy," Madeleine said, leading him over to the shadow, "my mother, Françoise. Mama, Rabbi Lincoln." Sandy followed Madeleine out of the mouth of the whale. The old lady was standing just far enough away from the light for a halo of shadow to blind him to her details.

"Mrs. Starbuck," he took the old lady's hand, "I am overwhelmed." He pointed into the grotto, and most specifically toward the deep distance where the violin floated like an extra rib in its own light.

"Yes," she said, letting her hand go limp. "My violin. A gift from a soldier." Sandy tried to imagine old Mrs. Starbuck dancing in the street of some French seaport—where would French whalers have sailed from? Brest?—with a laughing GI.

"Do you play?" Sandy asked. Looking down into her eyes for the first time, Sandy saw a deep yellow within the sockets that, despite the hatred that fired out from the pupils, spoke of a death imminent enough—the pulse, the general torpor of the palm he could feel in his practiced hand, Sandy guessed a year, a little more, a little less—to excuse all behavior.

"Once," she said. "My late husband, alas, he had no ear for music. But once I played." She withdrew her hand and turned down the hallway. "Like you." Had she been able to read his eyes, his palm? "But now it is time for dinner."

There must have been fifty people in the ballroom. They stood and applauded Sandy as he entered between the two Starbuck women and took his seat at the head table. Candles, the dim light of the harbor filtering in through a full wall of French windows opening out into a garden, flowers—Sandy had been fêted by a number of congregations, but this was something well out of the ordinary. Even David smiled over to him from the second table, to which he had been happily banished, Sandy guessed, to talk real estate.

Sandy felt—well, he had never been married, but he felt in the daze of a bridegroom being led to the altar. And why not? If intermarriage wasn't a sin, as he had explained in his talk, then why not this? Why not be celebrated by all these Jews, all these Jews whom he had taught, through the miracle of forensics, that morality, the commandment to treat all people as equal under the skin, was more important than survival? All these Jews whom he had forgiven for renting condos during the school vacations, for giving their children sailing lessons, for generally letting them sow their wild oats among alien corn and chowder?

What was it to be a Jew, after all? Wasn't the connection, the connection he'd felt once upon a time with the violin, the connection a violin now made between him and Madeleine, and, yes, even her tiny, French mother, wasn't all this beyond sects? Sandy felt—even as he blessed the wine and made the motzi over the sourdough challah—no more a Jew than old Mrs. Starbuck. The joys of the Jewish people, their accomplishments, their Einsteins and Heifetzes and Hillels and Maimonideses, their Israels and their Sinais and their Holocausts with their bones and their teeth—Sandy didn't, he couldn't share these canine attachments. Teeth were teeth. And some teeth—he looked over to Madeleine, smiling at him about their secret scrimshaw upstairs—were works of art.

Wouldn't this be something, he thought—Madeleine's mezzo-soprano leading the grace after the meal, holier and faster and more lovely than the rest—to leave the laboratory and civil service and death and make a life up here on the island with this woman? Madeleine could stay with her silent David, have children with him, the whole nuptial package. He would counsel these people, why not, the bridge ladies, the debutantes, loosen his belt and listen to their issues over iced tea and Planter's Punch. Maybe he'd even find a violin. All Sandy wanted was the daily walk—he knew nothing of the island but he saw clearly the scrub forests, the heather-covered badlands, the bird sanctuary—the walk along the beach with Madeleine, the occasional pressure of fingers on palm. Anything, as long as he could get a daily fix of this breeze, this wisteria breath that made him believe, with the pure exultation of his barefoot youth, in the soul.

Sandy was deep in the fog of these ruminations, when a new sound came to him, the sound of bells, a lighthouse warning him away from the rocks. At the second table, David Gordon was leading a tinkling of forks against glasses.

"Rabbi." Old Mrs. Starbuck raised herself up with a difficulty more profound than disease. "It has been an honor, indeed, to entertain you tonight." Enthusiastic applause came from the four corners of the ballroom, as much for the old lady's capitulation as for the magnificence of the dinner. "I know it is not polite to ask a guest to sing for his supper"—there was gaggle of titters over by the French windows—"but I was pleased to see that you admired my violin."

Sandy became aware, first of the fragrance, and then of the movement off his port shoulder. One of the waiters was standing, a bow in one hand, a violin in the other.

"It's been fifteen, more, twenty years," Sandy pleaded, knowing it would do no good.

"It has been twice as long, Rabbi," Mrs. Starbuck smiled, "since my violin has been played. We are understanding people, we Starbucks, *n'est-ce pas*?"

"Hear, hear!" one of the voices by the French windows shouted out, and people who had wandered off to the bathroom or out into the garden for a smoke rushed back in to the murmur that the rabbi was going to play old Mrs. Starbuck's scrimshaw violin.

"Please, Sandy." He hadn't seen her come about. Madeleine, herself, was urging him to his feet, her hand gripping his arm as if it were the neck of the violin. There was the mermaid, the whale, even more enticing out of the water of its glass case. He hadn't even held an instrument in the second half of his life. But the weight, the curves, the smell—he knew he couldn't resist, and he knew equally well that he had been hoping for this from the moment he had seen the instrument. He took the fiddle.

The room had gone silent, the candles alone flickered among the last crumbs of dessert. They were all watching him. What should he play? "Summertime" was his first thought, a little bit of dusky Gershwin, a cross-generational tune by a nice Jewish composer that he felt he could negotiate with dignity. But "Summertime" was too light for the occasion and there was always the danger that the audience might insist that he follow it with another piece.

Bach—that's what the violin was saying to him—play some Bach on my vacant strings, play some Bach into my lonely belly. So Bach it was—the Vivace from Bach's "G-minor Sonata," a perpetual motion of a piece, cascading six-teenth-notes from beginning to end, a real Jewish God of Vengeance, Moby Dick of a piece, quick and short enough for a Nantucket summer crowd. The Vivace in G minor, Sandy decided, with its triplet whitecaps, its perpetual unease—but easy enough that he'd had it memorized before he was old enough to daven. Sandy tucked the chinrest between his beard and shoulder, tuned the strings, and, with a bow to the Starbuck women, began.

The violin was brilliant—that was his first reaction. Who'd have suspected that an instrument exposed to the salt and fog of Nantucket could retain such vibrancy, such a confident voice as he passed easily through the personalities of the four strings. Still, there was something odd about the violin. It must be a top-heaviness due to the scrimshaw, Sandy thought, or the cloying smell of a violin that is polished more than it is played.

But gradually he heard, or rather, not heard, but felt a queasi-ness about the brilliance, felt it, not in his mind, but in the tips of his fingers as they pressed on the strings and met the scrimshaw of the fingerboard. He shook it off as a kind of craziness, thinking, now I have my first finger on the whale, now my third on the breast of the mermaid, no wonder I feel odd.

That wasn't it. There was another feeling, another sensitivity he had developed, even through the plastic gloves of forensics. It wasn't the design, but the fingerboard itself that was speaking to him every time his fingers pressed down on her surface. Had this violin belonged to some sad, young widow, who had memorialized the death of her whaling husband on this instrument of melancholy? Was the ghost—and being on Nantucket, Sandy permitted himself ghosts—of the widow, or maybe the ghosts of widow and husband together, watching over this violin, keeping it tuned, imbuing it with a despair that lived on long after their bodies had returned to the sea?

This fantasy—starring Madeleine as the bereaved young thing and Sandy himself as the waterlogged tar—inspired him through the first half of the Vivace. It added beauty to his playing, he thought. Surely, this was it, the connection with Madeleine, the presence that had gripped his hand the moment he stepped onto the portico of the Starbuck mansion.

With this confidence, he moved into the second half and allowed his eyes to lift from the violin to his audience. That's when it struck him. There were the men, sitting with their blazers and their scotches, their hair long and loosened by the Starbuck feast and summer. But next to them, where once there had been women, sat lattice upon lattice of bones and sinew. Over by the French windows, the giggly young things had been reduced to cheekbones and marrow. Across the table—no longer an aged French lady with a yellow eye, but a rotting liver and badly stitched flesh.

Sandy blinked once, twice. There were the men, there was David, looking more than faintly bored and dreaming about who knew what. But blink as he might, he could no longer see the women, no longer see old Mrs. Starbuck and the bridge ladies, the matrons and the debutantes, Jewish and otherwise. Worst of all, Madeleine had disappeared. The chair which moments before had supported the lanky bottom of his soulful Eve now held yards of intestines, kilometers of blood vessels, miles of hair, which wound through the room, around the legs of the tables, through the arms of the chandelier, delicate as lace, up to the inky strands that fell from the head of the mermaid on the scrimshaw fingerboard.

Sandy's music, the music of the violin, had scraped all sympathy, all humanity to the bone. He was back in the time before Eve, on the dissecting table of the sixth day, and blinking did no good. So he closed his eyes and kept playing, hoping that the dreams of Adam, the dreams that had grown a soul onto the anatomy of Eve, that had blinded him to the clinical details, would clear the salt mist from his vision.

But he couldn't close his fingers. As he played on, the truth grabbed the calluses at the tips and rode the nerves up arm and neck to his slightly balding brain. It was the fingerboard. The fingerboard was not scrimshaw at all.

Madeleine had been mistaken. It wasn't whalebone that old Mrs. Starbuck had brought with her from Europe after the War, this was no Nantucket ghost story—that was the message his fingers tapped out, had been tapping out from the first note. The fingerboard of this violin had once been a woman. This fingerboard had been meticulously carved from the humerus, the upper arm-bone, of a human woman, who, if not an Eve, had been, at least, a mature woman, a young mother, five-foot-three, his practiced fingers told him, a mother who had known terrible agony at the end. And as the message filtered through to his ears and turned the Bach into a nigun, into a Polish melody, a kaddish, a song for the dead, he realized who this woman was. It wasn't Madeleine—it hadn't been her breath, as he had thought all evening—and it certainly wasn't old Mrs. Starbuck. He didn't know the name of this woman, but he knew where she had died, what the music was that he had refused to hear for years. He heard the cry of this woman, of the nameless soul that had drained all the humanity from the women in the Starbuck ballroom, not in the voice of Selwyn's mother, but in a pitch and a timbre that sang directly and only to Sandy's ears, a song of history that all the forensics of the world could never explain.

And of course, because the fence he had built around his soul could only fall post by post, Sandy finished the Vivace. But the people who listened, and even those who were inclined to continue their conversations in whispers, remember a foggy chill as Rabbi Lincoln finished playing and, without a smile, or even a nod to his hostess, walked across the ballroom and through the French doors down to the harbor to give the scrimshaw violin a proper burial. Many of them said afterwards that it was months, even years, before they could listen to Bach again. As for Rabbi Doctor Alexander Abba Lincoln, there were no more trips to Nantucket, no more Friday nights.

The Hall of the Meteorites

Mary Morris

BEFORE I LIKED MEN, I liked rocks. I liked to wander the bluffs and ravines where I grew up and collect smooth, weathered stones. I put them on my shelves where other girls kept dolls and stuffed animals, and with my books on geology I identified and labeled them. Slate, mica, quartz, limestone, granite. What I found in the outside world, I brought into the house. Baby birds who'd fallen from nests, spiders that spun endless webs inside jars with punctured lids, the luna moth I captured as a caterpillar and released one spring day when it emerged from the cocoon it had woven in my room.

My mother taught me what I know of dinosaurs. She'd studied biology and wanted to be a teacher of life sciences. Instead, she had three children. But she kept a great love for the giant reptiles that had roamed the earth, for the minerals and elements, for outer space. In the cold wintery Saturdays of my youth, she would take me in the car downtown and we'd visit the Field Museum.

We always began in the Hall of the Dinosaurs, where she'd try to explain how these animals had lived before any of us were born. Often she'd joke and say even before *she* was born, but it was beyond me that anything had lived before, or would live after, me. I was fascinated by the bones of these long-dead creatures, and there was a place where children could reach up and rub a dinosaur's knee, smooth and hard as stones.

The one that amazed me the most was the giant marine lizard. There was a picture of it swimming in an incredibly rough sea and a sign that told how its remains had been found in a chalk bed in Kansas. I'd been to Kansas to visit an aunt, and there was no sea in Kansas. When I asked my mother about this, she just said that things change.

We would end our day at the planetarium sky show, where the lights dimmed and the heavens were illuminated overhead. A great disembodied voice would tell us, as we twisted our necks back and craned upward to see, that the universe was infinite, and if you traveled across it in a straight line, you'd end up right back where you started.

Much of this was lost on me, and I would grow tired, trying to understand, but my mother always wanted to stay for hours. Sometimes she'd try to stall before going home. She'd ask me if I wanted to look at the Hall of the Mammals again, if I wanted to buy some new stones for my collection. But usually I just wanted to go home. She'd look sad as we passed the glass cases filled with minerals and gems, the bones of great reptiles, on our way home.

Once as we walked to the car, the harsh wind blowing off Lake Michigan, my mother told me there was a whole side of life I hadn't seen yet and that none of it would make sense to me until I was as old as she, as old as a time that seemed as distant to me as the age of reptiles, as far away as the visions of the planetarium sky.

In eighth grade I discovered boys. I discovered them the same way I'd discovered rocks and butterflies and dinosaur bones. My mother explained them to me. She handed me a pink book one day and said, "Study this the way you study anything else. Then you'll know." And she added, "Well, you'll almost know."

I had known before that boys existed. I'd seen them putting on their baseball uniforms for Little League and I'd had snowball fights with them after school. But I'm not sure I understood what they were doing there. I'd always viewed them not as another sex, but as another species, as if I attended classes and went roller-skating with giraffes. But then one day my mother told me all, and I simply assumed I could apply my cataloguing spirit to them as well.

I thought I could collect and label whatever came my way, but I found myself at parties in darkened rooms with unknown entities, unidentifiable objects. Dancing in the dark, I touched bones, the muscles, the veins that coursed through their arms. I detected their scent, which at the time was mostly a cologne called Canoe, mingled with the pungent smell of athletic sweat.

I also began discovering things about my family. My father, for instance, developed a passion for woodworking. He devoted every spare moment to making chairs, tables, hatracks. He paneled the basement and turned it into a recreation room. He paneled bathrooms and put wooden frames around the bathtubs. All night and all day on weekends, after work, we heard him sawing, hammering, sanding.

During dinner, his fingers thumped on the tablecloth, eager to begin his hammering again. My mother said to him that we had enough chairs, enough tables. But he couldn't stop. He said he was doing it for us. Making the house beautiful for us. He constructed a new fence around the yard to protect us. His hammering became a clock, ticking away in my life, and when he'd built everything he could think to build, he was gone.

I went east to college and fell in love there for the first time. I fell in love with my lab partner, Benjamin Eiseman. I was pre-med, and we shared a lab bench, where we spent the weeks of Indian summer dissecting dogfish, frogs, cats. We opened a cat together, delicately prying it apart, and named every muscle, every vein. Benjamin was huge and clumsy, and at times our hands grazed as we worked inside animals. Before I knew what was happening, I fell in love with him.

One night he called to ask if I wanted to see a film. He said that *Superfluid* was playing at the physics department. We sat watching a film about the properties of a special liquid and all the time I was aware of the way his arm felt as it rested against mine. After the film, we drank Cokes in a café, then walked out onto the library roof. It was 1965, and as we stood on the roof, the lights of the entire city were suddenly obliterated. The night was as dark as a country road and we stood there for hours, holding hands. Then, when the lights began to come on, he turned me to him and kissed me. We stayed on the roof of that library, kissing until all the lights of the northeast came back on again.

We began an experiment. We carved windows into the shells of fertilized chicken eggs and covered the windows with isinglass. Under the light of the incubator in the lab we watched chickens grow—the formation of wings, of tiny beaks. And I saw the single path upon which my life was heading. I would marry Benjamin after college and we would have children. He would go to medical school and I would become a teacher of life sciences.

Then one night, after we'd been seeing one another for six weeks, he picked me up at my dorm and told me about Sarah. It was winter and he walked me over to the track, then began walking around the track, circling and circling, little clouds of breath rising from his lips. "I've got to tell you something," he said, "I should have told you a long time ago." We continued walking. "I never should have let it get this far." What he meant by that was that one night he had told me he loved me and we'd made love, my first time, in his dorm room while his roommate was out of town.

I can find no label for what I felt that night. Though it was almost twenty years ago and at an early stage in my history, the image is perfectly clear. We walked in that circle around the track, we walked for miles I think, and he told that he was in love with a girl he'd known since he was fourteen. That she sent him brownies that were still hot, that she knitted him the sweater he was wearing so that he'd be warm. That he planned to marry her as soon as college was done.

The earth, my mother had taught me, seeks equilibrium. Volcanoes erupt, hurricanes blow, forests ignite, all so that the earth can re-establish its balance. Nature, she'd told me, has its secret plan. I tried to devise my own and failed. I became obsessed with Benjamin.

He asked if I would keep seeing him and give him some time to make up his mind. I gave him four years. I could not get him out of my mind for a moment. I was like the robin who hears the worm in the ground. My head was cocked. I sensed his presence. I heard his footsteps when he walked into the lab. I knew when Sarah would be coming down, and once, when I saw them together, I followed them at a distance. I followed them for a long time as they walked around campus and I studied them. I noticed how their feet were not in sync, how her body met his well below the shoulder so that he looked as if he were straining when he walked with his arm around her.

I waited him out. I played hard to get, then gave him ultimatums. I would refuse to see him; then I would give in. For four years he begged me to be patient with him. He would see me during the week and then see Sarah on the weekend. He told me each week that he was going to make a decision soon. One week he did. He married Sarah right after graduation. He wrote once to say they were happy and were about to have a child. When the child was born, they sent me an announcement. It had a little bird on it, sitting in a nest. I never wrote him back.

It took me years to get back on the track. I moved to another city. I dated other men, but none struck me the way Benjamin had. It was around this time that my parents separated. I'd known it was coming, but that didn't make it any easier. She called me shortly after I got the baby announcement from Benjamin and sobbed that her life was over, that she didn't know what to do. I flew to the midwest and helped her settle into an apartment. Then I got on with my own life.

I relinquished my interest in natural history and became an identifier and cataloguer of primitive art. At times I traveled to faraway places and examined important discoveries to determine their worth, to situate them in time. I was very good at cooking utensils, weapons, and sacred idols. It was on such an expedition that I accidentally met the man who was to become my husband.

I was on a flight to Brazil, and a man sat next to me. He was a large, middle-aged man, and his feet had trouble fitting into the seat. He kept crossing and uncrossing his knees and finally said to me, "I travel so much, you'd think I'd remember to get an aisle." His name was Martin Garnet. He was a doctor who traveled to isolated places to set up medical clinics. He wore Old Spice, and I was quick to pick up the scent.

He called me when we both got back to the States and we began seeing each other. He was just getting over a bad marriage. I was still getting over Benjamin, though I'd begun to be interested in men again. We both traveled a lot, and when we could, we saw one another. He brought me gifts from duty-free shops all over the world, which I placed on a special shelf. Carved fish, shark's-teeth necklaces, miniature paintings on wood. He came back with fabulous stories about childbirth made painless by acupuncture, surgery done by hand, chronic illness cured by visits to the local oracle. I listened for hours to his tales of India, the jungles of Peru, and slowly, though I hadn't intended to, I began to care for him.

Martin defied classification. When I told him I'd never met anyone like him before, he replied, "There is no one like me." And he was correct. In the early stage of our courtship I should have had a sense of what life with Martin would be like. Once he was on a trip to the West Coast and had a day stopover before flying to Europe. He called to say he didn't think he could see me between trips because he needed to go to Brooklyn to get a pair of dress pants. "Pants?" I said over the phone. "Don't they have pants in Portland?" But he said he was on a tight schedule and didn't think he had time to buy pants. I told him to get his pants and keep walking in them.

But he didn't. He stayed. Then he went. He traveled to Pakistan, then came back for two days before leaving for L. A. Whenever he came back, he told me wonderful stories about what he'd seen and done. Then he'd leave again. I found myself traveling less, wanting to be with him more, and I found Martin, once he felt secure with me, traveling all the time. While he was in Brazil, I wrote him a letter. I said I was a fighting fish on a strong line and I was trying to get away. I didn't mail the letter. Instead, I tucked it into my appointment calendar.

One night Martin and I quarreled, because as soon as he got back from Brazil he had to leave for Nigeria. I left his place in a huff, got into a cab, and forgot my appointment calendar in the taxi. When I got home, I turned off my phone and took a long, hot bath. When I emerged, the light to my answering machine blinked. I knew it was Martin, calling to patch things up, saying he wasn't going to Nigeria after all.

Instead, the message said, "Hello, Monica Alberts. For a successful curator, you should put your name in your appointment calendar. I now know that your mother's name is Rochelle, that your parents have separated and your mother lives in Madison, that you are supposed to go to Peru in June, and that you had drinks with Betsy this afternoon. I'm afraid I woke Betsy up when I called, so you should apologize for me. Forgive me, but I also read your letter to Martin in an attempt to track you down. It's obvious that guy is driving you crazy, and my advice is don't marry him. I don't mean to pry, but that's my opinion. My name is Arnold Schnackler and I work in a lunar-receiving laboratory." He gave me the name of his university and phone numbers where he could be reached.

Arnold Schnackler's office wall was decorated with a map of the universe. His bedroom ceiling was filled with Day-Glo stars, and he'd teach me the names of the various constellations before we fell asleep. His work was studying objects coming from the moon that struck the earth, and he was devoted to finding life in outer space. He was also devoted to finding life on earth, and for a few weeks we had a good time.

Then Martin called from Nigeria one night when I wasn't home and left a grief-stricken message. He cut his trip short and came home. Arnold told me I was making the mistake of my life, but I said, "What can you do when love hits you over the head." When Martin came home, he said he wasn't going to travel much anymore. He wanted to be with me. And one night he proved it by handing me, over dinner, a large diamond. "Here," he said. "Add this to your collection of rocks."

Martin's heart was in the right place. But it wasn't with me. I thought, from what he'd promised, that love would make him want to travel less. Instead, it seemed to make him want to travel more. He traveled all over the world, dropping off his laundry between flights, and delivered papers on how to set up rural hospitals. He received super bonuses from all the airlines' advantage travel programs, and when he got these bonuses, he took me along if I could go.

When I told him I wanted a child, he agreed and traveled more. I thought of my father, building endless chairs and tables we didn't need, and how my mother was more alone with him than without him, how she begged him to stop. I understood now that some men couldn't stop.

Sometimes when Martin was away, I'd stand on the balcony of our building in Brooklyn and look at the stars. I wondered which ones were shining over him and what presents he'd bring me when he returned. But then I would feel lonely; once I tried to call Arnold Schnackler, the man from the lunar-receiving laboratory, to ask him if he'd discovered life in outer space and to tell him I could still name the constellations.

I found something happening to me. I found myself becoming a little cold inside, a little hard. It was as if a lump were in the middle of my chest, some solid thing I couldn't name. I called my mother once when I felt this way. I said to her, "I don't know myself anymore." And there was nothing she could say.

When Martin was back from one of his trips but about to leave again, I planned a romantic evening. I served dinner by candlelight and we drank champagne. Then I said, "How about if we go upstairs and get in bed?" and Martin said that was fine, but he was expecting two international calls, and if I didn't mind, he'd like to take them when they come in.

I stood up to clear the table and began rinsing and stacking the dishes. Martin said, "Darling, you shopped and cooked. I'll do the dishes."

I raised my fist high above the sink and brought it down flat on the dishes, smashing them to bits. "Then do them," I said, and I walked away.

We went to a marriage counselor to get back on a good track. The counselor suggested, since it was difficult for us to find time together, that we plan nice things to do that would be special, and that way we would have things to look forward to. She said that I needed to be more relaxed about time and Martin needed to be more attentive. It seemed` simple enough. So when we stopped seeing the marriage counselor, Martin said, "Your birthday is coming up in three months. Let's plan something nice." I suggested a picnic in the country, a climb on Bear Mountain. A quiet evening at home.

Six weeks before my birthday Martin told me he was excited because he'd been invited to the Soviet Union for a four-day conference on international health. I was very excited for him. Then he told me the dates and I reminded him that he was going to the Soviet Union over my birthday. He promised he'd be back in time to celebrate.

A few days before my birthday and his departure for the Soviet Union we went to dinner in a Chinese restaurant and I said, "Let's plan my birthday now." And he said he'd be back at seven in the morning and would come right home for a champagne toast. Then he said he just had two little things he had to do that day. He had to have breakfast with a health counselor from Martinique at eight-thirty and then lunch with some people from Saudi Arabia. "But the rest of the day I'm yours."

I spent my birthday alone, climbing Bear Mountain, and when I got off the mountain, I decided to give him one more chance. When I met him in the evening, I said, "I've never been bored with you, but I've never been so alone." Martin understood. He wanted to make it up to me. We planned our anniversary. We decided we'd spend a weekend in Vermont. It was September when Martin told me he had been invited to Afghanistan and I reminded him that he was going to Afghanistan over our anniversary. He said, "Maybe they can get somebody else."

And I said, "Maybe I can."

When I decided to move out, I called my mother to ask if she'd help me, and my father answered the phone. I said, "What're you doing there, Dad?" and he hesitated, then cleared his throat. He said he was living with my mother again. I said, "That's not possible."

And he replied, "Anything can happen in this world."

My mother came to help me move, the way I had helped her. She organized my closets and helped me pick out sheets and towels. She seemed to me vague and distant, and when I asked about my father, she told me, "It was easier this way." When she kissed me good-bye, she imparted her final wisdom. "There are some things," she said, "you have to find out for yourself."

I dug my way into a deep hole, from which I did not emerge for months. I went into a cave in which I found myself regressing in time, growing wild, primitive. I subscribed to *Natural History* and learned things I'd never known. Trees grow only if there is space between them, but if there are no other trees around, they'll burn out in the sun. Baby monkeys will choose a mother that cuddles over one that feeds. And sharks are missing the enzyme that produces anxiety. They go through the deep without depression or fear. I wanted to become a shark.

In the spring I emerged and released myself back into the world. I was learning the fine art of being alone, and I had almost mastered it when, while walking through the park one day, I heard someone calling my name. I turned to see a stranger, jumping up and down, shouting "Monica, is that you?" I saw a middle-aged man, rather stout and gray, his hairline receding. Yet he knew me, so I approached tentatively. "Benjamin," he said. "Benjamin Eiseman. You remember, the blackout, 1965."

I was shocked to think I had not recognized him. We hugged, and his arms felt flaccid; I was aware of his belly against mine.

Over coffee he told me that Sarah kicked him out about two years ago. "She hooked up with some guy who sells software in a computer store." Benjamin shook his head in disbelief. He told me that he'd never finished medical school because their baby died of heart failure, and that he taught biology in a high school in the town where he grew up. "Not what we expected, is it?"

I told him about the demise of my marriage and agreed with him. "Nobody told us it would be like this." I found I had little to say to him. As we paid the bill, he said, "So, do you still think about me?"

To my surprise, I realized that I hadn't thought of him in years. I hadn't thought of him at all since I'd been with Martin. "I've become obsessed with other things," I said.

I headed home, stunned by my encounter with Benjamin, thrown off course again, and wondering if I should move ahead with my divorce or try to work things out with Martin, as he wanted. I knew the answer would never again be a simple yes or no. Rather, it would be a slow unwinding, like a battery running down, decision by attrition.

I passed the Museum of Natural History. I didn't want to go back to my apartment right away, so I wandered in. I moved aimlessly through the museum, like a person trying to find something she's lost but can't quite remember what it is. I went into the Hall of the Dinosaurs, but they didn't seem so big anymore and I felt uneasy with their bones. I wandered downstairs. Through the Hall of Mammals, Primitive Man, Arctic Animals. I visited the ancestors' exhibit, but it didn't move me, either.

Then I saw the sign for the Hall of the Meteorites, and I went in. I watched a brief film that told how meteorites are the Rosetta stones of outer space, how they enable us to grasp the wonder of the world. I saw pictures of the wilderness of Siberia, where in Tunguska a giant fireball struck the earth and caused brushfires to burn for two decades. I walked around the small meteorites that lined the room, and they all had names: Gibeon, Guffy, Knowles, Diable.

And then in the middle of the room I paused in front of the greatest meteorite of them all, Ahnighito, which struck Greenland ten thousand years earlier and which the Eskimos believed had been hurled to the earth by the gods. Weighing thirty-one tons, Ahnighito is solid iron and parts have been polished where you can touch it.

Above the meteorites is a mirror, and I saw where coins had been tossed for good luck. Ahnighito means the Tent, and there are two other meteorites that were once part of Ahnighito. They are the Woman and the Dog. The tent, the woman, the dog—the simple needs of domesticity, all that is required for the happy life.

I reached up to rub the shiny part of the meteorites and thought of my hand, when I was a child, rubbing the knees of dinosaurs. I thought of my mother, giving my father another chance in the midwest; I tossed a penny on top of the Tent and saw in the mirror where it landed. Suddenly I realized that I was the same age as my mother when she first had brought me to the museum and taught me what she could of the world.

When I left, the sky had turned gray. I looked up and knew I'd never look at it in the same way again. That now I knew anything can strike us at any time. I contemplated the simple things and felt as I walked how easy it is for a heart to turn to stone.

Stone

Cynthia Ozick

JULES MCCORMICK was divorced from Madeline Washburn McCormick at the end of January, and in February he moved into the Marjorie Hotel. It was a relief to be there, even though he saw no one but retired schoolteachers in the elevators, and in the coffee shop at breakfast had to listen to their high, finicky, brooding comments on the cleanliness of the water tumblers. "That glass has a fingerprint on it," the old crones would complain, twitching their dry, ringless fingers. "There's lipstick on the rim," they would scold, and their own lips were flaking and unroseate. The Marjorie was mostly a women's hotel, an old maids' gathering ground, full of the gloom of failure and parsimony. The corridors were lit by forty-watt bulbs set yards apart, and the carpeting that Jules absently examined as he walked between the two rows of green doors toward his own was so worn that the plaiting underneath showed through.

Still, it was parsimony he was interested in, for the Marjorie provided an enormous, high-ceilinged, three-room suite at a rental considered reasonable for Manhattan, and Jules liked space. He had a collection of small sculptures, sporadically gleaned from auction barns and bargain cellars and junk shops. For a time it had looked as though he would have to commit the bulk of his assortment of "brick-knacks" (Madeline's sneering description of his pieces) to storage, which disturbed him, for he was forty-four and liked to have familiar objects about him. Then he had found the suite at the Marjorie, and everything was saved—the black boy in the red waistcoat holding out a ring, the cracked sun dial from some ruined estate-garden, a whole bower of inexpensive Roman goddesses, gesturing flirtatiously with hands of which the third and fourth fingers were always joined, a cherub with crumbling stone wings mounted on a mahogany pedestal—all the debris of other people's parks and drawing rooms, discarded by a generation that had outgrown a certain taste or style and had adopted the newer trends, microcephalic statues with holes in their chests and "textured" pieces built of driftwood and tobacco ash. But Jules liked his things just *because* they were out-of-date and embarrassing and unwanted. He even bought those giant lamp-bottoms with classical nymphs mourning for Eurydice as she descends into hell; he had one of these, and another depicting Paris awarding the Golden Apple to Athena. Whenever he passed a window displaying some forgotten object, however grotesque, rococo, or unendurable by ordinary standards it was, something would compel him to grieve over it. He would stop and meditate on it on his way to his office, and, returning, he would stop again. The more brown grime it had accumulated, the more beleaguered it was by surrounding objects, the more scandalous its

facade, the more nicked, battered, or scratched its protuber-
ances, the more he pitied it. He always tried to curb himself, to
please Madeline, but after a few days of staring at the thing,
whatever it was—baroque bird-bath, or four-feet-high imita-
tion Ionic column once used for a gate post, or only another
goddess without eye-pupils—he always went in and purchased
it. By then the proprietor knew his face, which he had seen lurk-
ing at the window more than once, and the price rose three
hundred per cent. Besides, Jules was no good at bargaining; and
no one was more aware of this primal collector's defect than
Madeline. "Twelve dollars! Don't tell me you paid *twelve dollars*
for that junk?" she would moan, handling the object with dis-
gust. And no matter what it was he came home with, she always
terminated his explanations or pleas or rages with the same
infuriating remark: "I'll give you fifty cents for it."

No wonder, people said when they heard about the divorce:
who would expect anything else?

Sometimes, walking in the deceitfully spring-like February
mornings to his office near the Empire State Building, Jules
would think of Madeline in Florida, where she had gone for the
winter—the residence requirement down there was a neat
ninety days, exactly the length of an ideal vacation—and he
imagined her sitting under a big orange beach umbrella, wearing sunglasses and holding one of those fashion magazines, not
reading it, but scanning the edge of the water where Barby
would be playing. Jules himself had never been to Florida, and
his notion of the life of an incipient divorcée waiting out her
time in a cabaña was perforce influenced by the travel posters.
Besides, Madeline was precisely the sort of girl who inhabited
the posters. She was only thirty-three, and her upper arms had
a dryad-haunted roundness, like young tree trunks. He had
never seen her deeply tanned, but he was sure that a copper
tinge would become her. Barby, poor thing, was practically an

albino, her hair and skin were so white. He hoped Madeline would smear her with that stuff they used to prevent burning; he didn't want his baby cooked. And imagine! he thought— she's going to stay down there, for keeps, to live—and he had a long sad vision of Barby slowly broiling on southern sands. Grounds of cruelty, sure, he said to himself, quoting the decree. He violently scooped up a dab of zinc-oxide-and-eugenol on his instrument and plugged it into the cavity; some of it fell on his patient's lip, burning it, and the man winced mildly. There she is cooking Barby, and I'm paying the alimony for cruelty, Jules thought angrily.

He walked back to the Marjorie in the cold late-February evenings; the walk made him feel better, the days were getting longer, and anyway he was beginning to appreciate the sounds of men's voices—men loading a truck and shouting together, men resting in doorways in a rumble of male gossip, a group of natty Madison Square lawyers standing on the courthouse steps hoarsely blending opinions. When he came into the lobby of the Marjorie, there were all the feminine voices again, pecking at his ears like bird-beaks. "The dentist," he heard hissed at his heels as he turned into the elevator. And then he was in his own rooms again, and there they were—the stone flowers, the rock-hearted maidens, the marmoreal children, and a note from the chambermaid, complaining about the dusting. He resolved to increase her tip, and looked around with satisfaction—the clay urn, half his size, that he'd bought in Connecticut the week before Barby was born; the bust of Zeus, shaggy-haired and with a scar on the forehead presumably in the place where Minerva had sprung full-grown, a most unusual representation that had once rested in a mansion in Oyster Bay: he was surprisingly content. Divorce had a finality, even in the toll of the syllables—a double chime of ending. He lifted a souvenir replica of the Liberty Bell (one of his oldest things, Madeline's really—she had bought it in a Friends' shop, passing through Philadelphia on their honeymoon), holding it up to his face and listening to the cry of its little hammer, all the while smiling at the corny symbolism of it. At least he had his things, his poor adopted vulgar orphans, dressed in their out-of-fashion hand-me-down flounces, and nobody whining in his ear about brick-knacks, common as bricks, cheap as bricks, ugly as bricks. He had the silent smiling company of goddesses saved from the garbage-dump, and if they had the smooth white eyeless gaze of blind coquettes, at least there was no finality about *them,* and they would go on eternally tempting his pity for their shattered anklebones and chipped elbows and gouged bloodless nostrils. There was a comfort in owning stone: it carried the conviction of permanence, and one knew it would outlast almost everything, especially oneself.

One morning Jules left the Marjorie rather earlier than usual As he approached the courthouse he saw a policeman beckoning a cluster of gaping people around a large van that had pulled up on the sidewalk. The crowd was moving reluctantly, and all the heads were lifted to the sky, the women clutching their hats with one hand. Jules looked up, and saw two men on the courthouse balustrade, high above the street, fitting a block and tackle to an enormous statue. It came slowly down, floating perilously over the crowd,, and swinging with remarkable precision into the open back of the truck. Meanwhile another pair of workers was preparing the next statue for a similar descent, and soon the long row of figures on the balustrade was standing in the mammoth truck, elbowing one another like a circle of gossipers. After the loading, the watchers began to scatter quickly, but, while the men were gathering up the coils of rope, Jules lingered to examine the figures. He had scarcely been aware of them in his daily walks; they had seemed so much a part of the courthouse that he had never given any thought to them. Still, he was surprised to notice how decayed they were, the veins in the arms eroded to a startling smoothness and the features distorted or broken. They made a pitiful congregation, Jules thought, pressing up close to get a better view. Their pedestals, which might have had inscriptions, had been left behind on the roof, and there was no way he could learn what they represented. He walked back to the open platform in the rear of the truck and began counting the marbles. There were ten statues in all, most of them -wearing robes or draperies that either dragged about their feet or exposed their gray knees, each one carrying objects which were obviously symbolic but which only confused Jules. There were no clues in the stern, battered faces peering out of their curious headdresses and forbidding beards; the ten sad ancients stood listlessly, like ten superannuated clerks in dressing-gowns wait-ing to be carted off to a home for the aged. Jules felt a tide of sor-row rise in his throat. Poor things! he thought, and looked up pityingly into the face of the figure nearest him. This one. had been loaded into the truck last of all, and loomed at the edge of the platform as though it were undecided about the journey and might at any moment leap off and escape into the street. Like the others, it was about eight feet tall, but it seemed larger, less pas-sive, more impatient of delay. The nine other figures were more neatly trapped, it was true, planted there in the *middle* of the truck, and had huddled together, shoulder to shoulder, in a league of companionship and defense. Only the tenth nameless giant stood at the rim of their alliance, its back rebelliously set against them, as though it had chosen its own way and needed no one. Jules studied it compassionately. The wrists and fingers were powerful, thick and heavily veined: the left hand supported an open book, but the right hand, overshadowing the other, held a great scimitar, with the thumb hard against the blade. Its head, half-turned, bewildered Jules; under the ring of a grand turban the brows jutted, the mouth withdrew, and Jules could not determine whether the face was warlike, like the scimitar, or visionary, like the book.

A band of workers, a dozen or so, had meanwhile climbed aboard the van, laughing and whistling, and had already shut the tailgate, securing it with a length of chain tied from post to post. The motor started and Jules scampered out of the way of a blast of exhaust. The men apparently had never squired so extraordinary a load, and they were enjoying it, hoisting themselves onto the shoulders of the figures, sitting on a head or two, squeezing through a pair of legs, like barbarians (Jules thought) cavorting atop the ruins of Rome. The truck moved off, agonizing under the weight of its stone crew; and Jules almost believed he heard a moan go up, faint and electrical, like a snap of faraway lightning, from the nine cowed prisoners in the middle of the truck, their crowns and hands helpless and ridiculous among the capering kidnappers. Only the tenth one, whose thumb was on his blade, bore no rider, and looked out over the locked gate toward Jules with an unyielding and puzzling gaze, until it was only a curious glint in the distant traffic.

The week following this incident, the weather grew imperceptibly warmer, and even the dusk felt spring-like. Jules was rather busy now—he always picked up a number of new patients in April and May, mostly executive secretaries who were preparing to go on a man-hunting cruise, having saved all year, and wished to improve their smiles, the better to gleam in Caribbean moonlight. Jules joshed mildly with them—he had with difficulty achieved a dentist's typical sense of humor, picking and probing like a steel explorer—but his mind kept slipping away from porcelain jackets and acrylic-faced gold inlays. ("Will it show gold? Will it?" the secretaries always wanted to know, clutching the stem of the mouth-mirror and grimacing.) This was his busiest time, and Madeline knew it; yet just a few days ago she had written him that she was bringing Barby north for her court-ordered bi-annual week with her father. This meant, of course, that Jules would have to close his office. It was an absurdly inconvenient time: June or July, the slow months, was what he had planned for. He wrote back and told Madeline that he couldn't shut things up right now, he was far too busy. Too bad, Madeleine snapped back via air mail special delivery, it was just too damn hot down in Florida; she was going up to Springfield to stay with her sister for a week or so, and then she was taking Barby to Maine for the summer. If Jules wanted Barby, he could keep her the week Madeline was in Springfield—otherwise he couldn't see her until October. Of course, if he wasn't interested enough in Barby to close his office for one measly week, if he was just too *busy* for the daughter over whom he had always pretended to fuss—well, it wouldn't surprise his ex-wife in the least. It was what she expected of him. Let him go grubbing money and squandering it on his pile of bricks.

Jules cancelled all his appointments for the last days of April, bought some saucepans and dishes for his as-yet unused kitchen, and sent a check for two tickets to the circus.

The work that belonged to the crucial lost week had at any rate to be done. At seven o'clock in the morning he was already perched on the high stool in his laboratory, setting teeth or casting an inlay or rescuing developed X-ray film, forgotten there by his busy assistant, from the hypo, hanging it neatly on brackets. At ten o'clock at night he plugged his last amalgam in the day's last molar, shut off the lights and went home exhausted.

It was, as he knew, Madeline's retribution. She meant him to suffer, for she was aware he could not easily endure the pressures of a crowded schedule. He often enough declared to her that he was not by nature equipped for his profession. It was a humorous profession, he complained; his office was always full of laughter, but he was not a natural clown, committed, as born buffoons, are, to the actual. As is the case with many dentists, his earlier intention had been to go to medical school, but for one reason or another he had not been admitted. It was not merely the greater prestige of medicine that had attracted Jules, although at twenty he was, to be sure, not uninfluenced by status. The truth was that misfortune excited him, distress lured his curiosity and his indulgence. As certain kinds of people have lusts, and are perpetually over-powered by them, so Jules claimed the burden of pity. But the chair over which he painfully stooped day after day was occupied by healthy, well-off patients, whose single and common curse was only a defective smile. As a young dentist, Jules had hoped to idealize his calling: bridgework, he had declaimed to his bride, was a species of sculpture; the human jaw a temple architecturally dependent on the buttress of the teeth; the reclamation of a mouth from decay a sort of archaeological reconstruction of a dead and classical city. But it was not long before he discovered the monotony of a sculpture that can only be uniform, the repugnance of a temple that has no shrine, and the hopelessness of any final resurrection. For the decay went on and on, reappearing incessantly, widening and deepening. The decay engulfed him at last. He concluded that dentistry was nothing more than eternal repair. When he had finished mending one row of teeth, new wastelands confronted him. There was no art because there was no end.

Nevertheless he continued all week long to remove impacted third molars, to stretch rubber dams, and to curette the gums of young ladies, but the process was futile and mechanical and, to his larger imagination, vengeful. He was preoccupied alternately by Madeline's vindictive sorcery (the ache in his spine) and by the prospect of his daughter's arrival, for it worried him that he might not succeed in renewing Barby's affection. So he did not, as it turned out, notice that the courthouse statues had been returned to their pedestals until they had been on the balustrade for several days.

Even from the ground he could see how dazzling the figures were: heroic marbles, strong-armed, gleaming. They stood proudly and stonily on the courthouse roof, displaying their various amulets and staring, relieved and restored, out beyond the heads of all the passersby who would never again be aware of them until time should once more have reduced them to idols craven and broken. Craning admiringly, Jules brooded faintly on a philosophy of repair which could end in majesty. He was alone in his position. No one else looked up. Yet what if he were the only one who cared? The marbles were, after all, in his line of interest, as he liked briskly to put it. But to himself he yearned sentimentally after their identities. The Muses, perhaps? But the Muses were, of course, women.

Startled, Jules counted again. Seven, eight, and . . . there were only nine figures on the balustrade. Which one was missing? The early sun was in his eyes. He put his hand up against it and tried to make out the characteristics of each. The empty pedestal, on the eastern end of the roof, looked dilapidated; it was the only one that had not been repaired, as though it were expected that it would remain unoccupied. Whose feet had been torn from it? With a little shiver, Jules took in the moment. The absent statue was the brave old man with the book and the scimitar, with whom he had made a covenant of pity.

In the days following, the unreclaimed pedestal stood vacant—until finally a trio of workmen with axes and a wheelbarrow hewed it into a mound of rubble, and carted it across the roof to a scaffold. Then the web of ropes and platforms vanished, the men who walked up the walls like steady hornets went away, and the serene community on the balustrade was left to brood undisturbed. It was plain that the tenth member would not return. Jules chalked it up to the inscrutable governmental mind and renewed his peregrinations in the slough of decay.

The circus tickets came at length, brought to his apartment one morning, along with the *Times,* by the Marjorie's septuagenarian bellboy. When he had grasped that the seats were precisely as he had ordered them, with a view of all three rings, Jules began to worry again. The circus took care of only one afternoon. What about the rest of the holiday? How would he entertain Barby? He had been too occupied to make plans, yet he wanted to give her a week she would remember with pleasure all summer, and talk about to Madeline. He intended to devise something extraordinary for each day. He meant to fill her conversation with his name and his gifts. He thought first of little expeditions—to the Bronx Zoo, the Brooklyn Children's Museum, even the Statue of Liberty. He determined that her visit should be a festival to boast about, later on, to the summer colony kids in Maine and perhaps less vividly to her Florida classmates in the fall. But the city trips would fade. He wanted her to experience something that she would really remember, that would impress her as connected with *him*—some sort of adventure that she could re-live long afterward.

The notion obsessed him, for it was Madeline he was after. Punishment for punishment. He would make her ears clamorous with his spite and his achievement. "When I was staying with Daddy," "One day Daddy and l," and so on. But even this was not enough; even this would not last. He wanted to capture his daughter forever, to deliver up to her some permanent radiance which would signify himself, which would burn out the eyes of her mother for envy's sake.

He was practicing frying eggs—he didn't propose to drag the poor child out to a restaurant every day for breakfast, all dressed up, before she had her lids open. Meanwhile he reflected on his ambition. Exactly what the adventure was to be he could not decide, but a moment later, opening the *Times* to read with his egg (more fat in the pan next time, and it won't taste so rubbery, he promised himself) he seized it unerringly. For there, right at the bottom center of the front page, was a photograph of the missing statue. He began reading excitedly:

ISLAMIC FOUNDER SAYS FAREWELL
TO 50-YR. MADISON SQUARE ROOST
Statue of Prophet Removed
From Row of Law-Givers

The State Department today acknowledged it had advised removal of a statue of Mohammed that has graced the roof of the Twenty-fifth Street Courthouse, for over half a century. The step was taken after three Islamic governments had submitted requests explaining that the Moslem faith frowns on graven images of human figures. A statue of the religious leader is particularly offensive to Moslems.

The Ambassadors of the complaining nations first learned of the existence of the idolatrous effigy when notice appeared in newspapers that the row of ten historical law-givers would be taken down for much-needed repairs. The State Department, acting on the Islamic plea that the statue be destroyed rather than renovated, then asked the Commissioner of Public Works to get rid of the statue, which was carved in Mexico and cost $20,000.

Returned to their pedestals are the nine other law-makers—Manu, Moses, Zoroaster, Lycurgus, Louis IX, Confucius, Solon, Justinian, and Alfred. Authorities are still undecided about the disposal of the half-ton Mohammed, who lies wrapped in excelsior in a New Jersey warehouse . . .

Wrapped in excelsior! Jules thought. The rebel with the scimitar lying captive on his back. And *excelsior!* "Ever upward." What a tragic pun, he remarked, remembering that the word was a motto, too, and he felt a renewal of his old sense of sorrow for the statue, which had not been meant for an idol at all, but only for a reminder of the triumph of iconoclasm. He read the figure again, and whistled at the waste: $ 20,000! But it was aesthetic waste also, imprisoning an impressive marble like that, invaliding it, keeping it from public view.

Just then Jules had his idea. He would buy the statue for Barby.

Barby had always been thrilled by his collection; indeed, she had taken his part against Madeline whenever a new acquisition had set off a fresh argument between them—a thing that occurred rarely enough in the child's presence, for they were, up to a point, careful parents—although not careful enough, it was remarked, to preserve their marriage for Barby's sake. But the sculptures, scattered throughout their old house on Long Island, had transformed each surprise-filled alcove into a paradise of discovery for the little girl; Jules had loved watching Barby's fingers delicately following the curve of a favorite garden-vase, or exploring the mysterious ear of a young comic god, or sadly stroking the cracked nose of an ancient nymph. She examined everything minutely, affectionately, and even with a kind of despair, as though she were wondering why there was no life in arms and necks that were hardly different, except for their smooth, cold texture, from her own.

"Run out in the yard, dear," Madeline would chide her, "the whole outdoors is full of children, and here you are poking about in corners."

"All right, Mama," Barby would answer obediently, but when Jules came home the incident would be savagely described to him.

"There's something the matter with that child! She spent all afternoon with those bathing beauties of yours. I'm sure they're encouraging an abnormal interest in nakedness," Madeline would complain.

"Nonsense," Jules said, "she dresses her dolls, doesn't she, and you don't see anything abnormal in *that.*"

"And how about that silly owl, or dove, or whatever it is," Madeline said, choosing a different tack, "she sat in her little rocker, looking up at it for half an hour, actually making *conversation* with the thing! "

"What did she say?" Jules asked with interest.

Madeline stared. "Say? I don't know what she said. I'm telling you that she *talked* to a lump of rock, and all you care about is what she said."

So the argument would really begin, and Jules would insist: that Barby was a normally fanciful child, and Madeline would accuse Jules of perverting Barby's imagination, and Jules would answer that if Madeline wanted to stunt her own daughter's obvious enjoyment of art that was *her* business, but as far as *he* was concerned he had every intention of encouraging it, and Madeline would echo him sneeringly, and observe that what he was *encouraging* was their child's withdrawal from reality, and that was a lovely thing to encourage in the name of art, if you could call that brick-pile *art,* because in *her* judgment she would give him fifty cents for the whole shebang.

Then Barby would come in hungry for dinner and smelling of sweaty corduroy pants, and Jules and Madeline would send her to wash up without another word between them. But Barby always knew, Jules thought, and in the unpleasant small-talk that followed the rage of the dispute she would search Jules's expression anxiously. "Daddy?" she would begin. "Daddy, I played a game with the bird today—the one that you said water's supposed to run out of its mouth—"

"Beak," Jules corrected.

"Beak, and I tried to make up a story about the bird when it used to live in the forest, but it wasn't a good story like you tell."

She was transparently flattering him, trying to make up to him for Madeline's anger, and already—a year before they had begun to talk about getting a divorce—she wore the bewildered, responsible look of children who are "not happy at home," who brokenly comfort or protect first one parent and then the other, and at last turn futilely into themselves.

When they parted, Jules told her she could choose one of his pieces to keep for herself.

Anything?

"Whichever one you like best." He smiled at her miserably. "Better make it portable."

He was not surprised when she selected a figurine he called King Midas' Daughter. That was an invention, of course; the statue was unidentified, having been separated from a group— a famous group, the dealer had assured him, which for all one knew was standing in the Metropolitan, but since this part of it, this young girl, so lost and exquisite, had been brutally severed from the rest, he could let Jules have her at an enormous bargain, considering the beauty of the work, the outstretched arms in perfect condition, the sad little mouth, about to speak, really Grecian in its execution, and all of it only eighteen inches high, a masterpiece for its size. It was Barby's favorite. She had insisted on setting it on her night-table, to admire before she fell asleep, and Jules was glad she had chosen it to take with her. Whenever she looked at it she would think of him; of all the stories he told her (Madeline disapproved of fairy tales) she liked King Midas best of all, and she had been delighted when he named the figurine after the poor turned-into-gold daughter. "Tell it again!" she always cried, and he would have to start all over again, patiently, explaining how there was once a king who loved his gold more than anything else in the world, and when he had finished she would smile at him teasingly and say, "And there was the little girl, all stiff, just as if you'd cast her, Daddy"—for once in his laboratory she had been impressed by the white hot whirling of his casting machine.

So King Midas' Daughter had traveled to Florida with Barby and Madeline, and a few weeks afterward there came a letter in Barby's hard-working fourth-grade scrawl, telling how the stone child had fallen from a table and had split down the middle. "Daddy Im Sory," the letter ended, and since then she had written nothing. But he knew from the queer little apology over her gawky signature that she was regretfully recalling everything—the mock christening they'd held for the figurine, the stories, the long afternoon she'd spent in his lab doggedly watching him play at being Midas.

It was, in a way, because of this—the destruction of his gift—that Jules decided to buy the statue of Mohammed. If he could contrive it, what a remarkable affair! An event of power and splendor! He quickly began to plan the outline of the story as he would tell it to Barby—the old, sad, brave hero abandoned; the tragic sojourn in the warehouse dungeon; the magnificent rescue; the restoration to the light: The accident—if it *was* an accident, Jules amended grimly—that had halved King Midas' Daughter under Madeline's probably rejoicing eye had produced in himself a desire to compensate—to retaliate—with some grand and celestial gesture, to delight Barby with some event not merely unforgettable, or impossible of being matched, but so overwhelming and magical that it would in some way mold or transform her.

He wrote to the Commissioner of Public Works. When an answer did not come at once, he telephoned; a series of bewildered secretaries assured him that as far as anyone knew, Mohammed was not for sale. He wrote again, protesting that the statue should not be left to crumble in darkness when there was a willing buyer. A letter came from the Public Works office, saying that disposal of the statue had not yet been resolved upon, but if at a future date a sale were contemplated, he would be among the first to hear of it.

Jules was now determined to own the statue. He could think of nothing else. The figure of Mohammed hovered urgently in his mind, pressing to be understood. He went to the library and examined a copy of the Koran, but he found it full of obscure poetry. Then he discovered an abridged edition of Gibbon and read in it about the complex wars of the Prophet's successors. But the most important fact he learned about Mohammed was also the most interesting: the Prophet's fierce unitarian bent, how he hated images, how he styled himself the most glorious idol-smasher of all.

No one, Jules suddenly realized, would have objected more to the statue of Mohammed than Mohammed himself.

He wrote another long, aggressive, detailed letter to the Commissioner of Public Works and waited tensely for the reply: only a dozen days lay between now and Barby's arrival. Meanwhile, in anticipation, he continued to rehearse the fables and romantic inventions she loved to hear—once there was a statue that existed by mistake, that had never *wished* to exist, and that was not *supposed* to exist : so was it real or not? And then he would sweep his palm upward to the form of the Prophet and grandly exclaim, Real!

The answer came on a Wednesday morning, three days before Madeline was to deliver Barby to his suite in the Marjorie.

> *Dear Dr. McCormick* (it read):
> *We are glad to inform you that we are now ready to negotiate for the sale of the Mohammed marble, with the condition attaching that it remain in a private collection.*

Since public exhibition has been denied to the statue, we are not able to dispose of it through any of the usual private or public channels. The remaining possibility would be the sale of the marble itself, as rubblework, to the terrazzo trade. In view of its value as a work of art, however, and in view of your expressed interest as a collector, we feel that your bid presents the only reasonable alternative to its neglect or destruction . . .

Jules bought the statue for three hundred dollars.

On Saturday morning, white-gloved and pleasantly brown-skinned, Madeline stepped out of the elevator, looking exactly as Jules had pictured her; nothing had altered but her complexion. Behind her came Barby, holding her mother's hand, lingering a little over the tapestried roses under her feet; she stood self-consciously aside during the businesslike reunion of her parents. Jules had stiffened excitedly, preparing for Barby's running kiss, straight into his arms; but she only reached up quietly for his check, with a little decorous lift of her chin that was new to her—out of consideration for Madeline, he thought, or perhaps it was merely that she was now too grown up to hurl herself at him. A momentary sense of alienation touched him as he led the two of them into his suite, listening to Madeline remind him about Barby's allergy to tomato-y foods: "She came out in purplish pimples *all* over her last time and they lasted for days—what in the name of mercy is *that?*" she broke off loudly.

A gigantic wooden crate stood in the center of the room.

He couldn't resist it. "A pile of bricks," he told her seriously. "I'm having a fireplace built in"

"But you *have* a fireplace," Barby said, starting to point; then suddenly she understood, or perhaps merely felt, his satire. She turned away and began to explore his rooms.

"Well, you've really gone all out this time," Madeline said, staring up at the unopened crate and shaping a brief sarcastic whistle. "What is it—a full-scale replica of Rockefeller Center?"

"Something of the sort," Jules agreed. He looked adoringly after his daughter; her hands were soaring prayerfully together, clutching a little plastic purse. "Barby, there's a container of milk on the kitchen table, and a glass, and some *special* cookies. No, turn right—there you are—"

They watched her white legs disappear behind a wall.

"I was afraid she'd get sunburned," Jules said.

"I know how to take care of my child," Madeline said. "I hope you do as well all week. *Please* remember about the tomatoes— not even catsup."

"All right."

"Well, I guess that's all. I'll be back for her Friday." She faced the door, hesitating. "Oh. I forgot. Jules, will you look at her teeth? I think she's got a cavity starting, in the back, on the right side—"

"Why do you let her eat so much candy?" he accused.

She met his look reluctantly. "Jules, she's a very nervous child. I think you should know that."

"She seems perfectly all right."

"No, you really want to be very careful of her."

"Has she been ill?" he asked quickly.

"Not really, except for the purple patches—Jules, I don't want you to excite her imagination. You know what I mean. Keep her outdoors and busy."

"Oh hell, Madeline! I'm perfectly capable of caring for the child—I have everything planned. I'm taking her to the circus."

"Oh, the circus, that's good, yes. Things like that. But nothing morbid, you know *exactly* what I mean, no stories. Those *things* of yours . . ." She waved at goddesses, urns, angels. "For her own good, I wish you'd see that she isn't affected by them."

"Affected?"

"Keep her away from them, Jules."

"I don't suppose," he attacked suddenly, "that figurine I gave her just fell off the table all by itself?"

"No," she admitted. She was curiously submissive. "I threw it."

"*Very* nice," he said, controlling himself. "It merely cost me twenty dollars."

"I know." She walked back into the room and looked up absently at the center ceiling-bulbs; they just missed the top of the crate. "Jules, I didn't intend to tell you this. You're responsible for it, of course, but that's no longer important. You'll be with Barby rarely enough. And I think you *should* have the privilege of seeing your daughter now and again, provided you take care." She circled the crate slowly; he was certain she was dying to know what it contained, but he was equally certain she would never deign to ask.

"Well?" he prodded, annoyed by her half-maternal, half-dramatic air.

"As I said, she's a terribly nervous child. She has—fantasies. That little statue you gave her—King Midas' Daughter—well, one afternoon I found her in hysterics over it, because it wouldn't come back to life. I told her it was only a doll made of stone, but she insisted it *had* to come back to life, because it happens that way in the story when King Midas repents."

"Oh come now, Madeline—"

"And—wait—I got so furious I tried to smash it, but it only broke in two. And then she said the charm *was* broken, the statue *had* come alive—she had seen its eyelids flicker just as I raised it to break it—but that I had killed it."

"Listen, if you want to know who's crazy, I'll tell you. It's *you*," Jules said bitterly. "I can just see it—she was angry at you because you'd interfered with her make-believe, as usual—and then when you broke the thing you only got her into a worse temper. It's perfectly simple."

"She was *convinced* I'd murdered it."

"Oh, quit psychoanalyzing the kid," Jules muttered, because he heard Barby coming down the hall. She had taken off her coat and hat and was already skipping a little; he marveled at how quickly she had grown used to his apartment. Or was it that she felt at home in the presence of his familiar clutter? It seemed to him, nevertheless, that the moment Madeline was gone, disappearing into the elevator like a departing spirit of malevolence, Barby came out of hiding. She danced around the crate like a little white witch; Jules could not help laughing for joy. He fetched her up— she was heavier than he remembered—and tickled her until she doubled up with glee. He greedily renewed his certainty of her beauty (that was Madeline's genetic contribution, surely not his) but she was lovelier than her mother, less wraithlike, except for the ghostly whiteness of her hair, which poured in long architectural flutes over her body as it wriggled in his arms. Her complexion was extraordinary, so marvelously layered that the blue strings of veins glowing translucently through her skin seemed like paths of pale jewels brocaded just beneath the surface. And he possessed her, and had the power to make her happy!

"It's a surprise for you, Barby! Now you wait, and I'll telephone downstairs for the bellboy to help me open this thing."

"What is it, Daddy?" she cried, hugging him excitedly.

"You'll see, be patient. It's for you," he said again. The man arrived with a hammer, a saw, and a crowbar. "Oh God," Jules exclaimed when he saw the armful of tools. "We don't need all those. Just the crowbar to pry it open. Easy now—watch it! Gently, this thing is fragile . . ."

The man disagreed indignantly. He had seen it being hoisted into the freight elevator, they had told him it weighed as much as two grand pianos . . . Little by little the wood gripping the nails splintered off, the nails bounced to the floor in showers, and the sides of the huge box fell away like suddenly opening petals.

The statue of Mohammed stood revealed.

"Get this packing stuff out of here," Jules directed, stepping over the boards to where Barby was waiting mutely. He was eager for the man to go, for he was trembling vaguely with anticipation and he wanted nothing to influence her response.

Barby's head came not far above the lowest half of the scimitar. She reached up and carefully encircled with her whole hand the giant index finger that was pointing on the open page of the book. Then she knelt and scrutinized the forward foot in its sandal.

"Do you like him?"

His question hung urgently.

"Oh *Daddy*," she italicized rapturously, "it's the biggest doll I ever owned!"

Jules laughed until he hurt. Madeline's bad-fairy admonitions were all at once swept away; he dismissed her as a small-time Lilith, and went on laughing at his adorable child. For Barby's dumbfounded digestion of what the crate actually *held* had swiftly turned into possessiveness.

"Is he *really* for me?"

"Of course."

"And I can take him to Maine with me?"

"Oh well, not really. It wouldn't be practical. But I'll keep him here for you, and whenever you come to visit, he'll be here for you to play with."

She pouted. "I wish I could take him with me."

"Mama wouldn't like it, would she? Besides, he isn't a traveling man." Then he remembered about the hegira. "Any more, I mean."

"Did he use to travel?"

"Oh yes, quite a bit, from city to city. In a caravan his uncle owned. Once he went to Mecca—that's his special city. You see, there's a story to him."

"Tell it !"

"All right." He took her up on his lap delightedly. "Once there was a good man named Mohammed. . . . That's who this statue is." She stared up at the great silent head and the brooding blind eyes as she listened. "Mohammed worshipped God, but all the other people in his neighborhood were bad and worshipped stone statues."

"Just like you, Daddy."

"What do you mean?" Jules said, startled.

"That's what Mama thinks. She says you worship stone."

He smiled. "Your mother meant something else," he said. "*That* worship means to like or admire very much. But these other people really *worshipped* the stone statues—they thought the statues were like God. But you can't see or touch God."

"Then what happened?" Barby said, impatient with metaphysics.

"Well, Mohammed went around telling people that they should break up their statues. Isn't it silly, he said, to carve something out of stone all by yourself and then to get down on your knees and call it God. Those statues aren't God—they're only idols."

He saw Barby carefully observing the statue in the room. "What's that big knife for?"

"The scimitar? Well, when some of the idol-worshippers refused to break up their statues, Mohammed pulled out his trusty scimitar and—pow! crash!—they knocked those idols to little bits."

"Oh," she breathed joyfully, "and did the people just have *fits?*"

"No, they were converted," Jules said. "When they looked down and saw those old statues scattered all over the place like pieces of a jigsaw puzzle, they knew their idols weren't powerful enough to be the one true God." He smiled to himself. He didn't mean to make a little Moslem out of her, although it wasn't too far-fetched, since one of her grandmothers was strongly

Unitarian. He only meant to armor her against Madeline's religion of anti-imagination, and, in a way, to convert her to himself.

So it was a success, his fantastic gift. She would remember it always; the event would dominate her until she was almost grown. The tremendous fact that he had proclaimed her the owner of so enormous an object was enough to influence her in his favor; it was comparable, on his own level, to his having inherited the Empire State Building—the donor would be remembered, if nothing else. But there *was* something else: his histories of the Prophet. They drew her to him with a wonderful intensity, and he gave himself tenderly and eagerly, expending all his resources, racking his brain for invention after invention, tale after tale, for she was insatiable. He supposed he would be exhausted, and in need of a vacation, when she was gone. Was there ever such a daughter? he wondered in amusement. And was there ever so ingenious a father?

On Sunday morning he took her to his office and checked her teeth and cleaned them with pumice and a rotary brush. Afterward, on their way to Madison Square Garden for the circus, they passed the courthouse and he showed her the nine other lawgivers and the empty place where Mohammed had been. She was so entranced by the thought that *her* statue had once stood right up *there*, on a rooftop, that only his rash promise of a hundred clowns got them to the circus on time. On Monday they went to the zoo. On Tuesday they sailed up the Hudson in a sightseeing boat. On Wednesday—

But on Wednesday a curious thing happened.

He had planned a walk through Central Park in search of the carousel, but just after breakfast a patient with a raging toothache telephoned. Jules was exasperated; he tried to put the woman off by suggesting a hot salt-water rinse, but when the telephone rang again half an hour afterward, he knew it was no use, and he would have to treat her in his office. He started to get Barby's headgear for her, then sensibly changed his mind. It was too hot for April. Why drag her crosstown and tire her before the day's outing had even begun? He would be back for her in forty-five minutes, and then they would set out on their pleasurable errand.

"If anything's the matter, Barby, you just pick up the telephone and call the desk downstairs. Is that clear? Now you wait for me, and rest, and I'll be back in less than an hour."

He caught a taxi going crosstown, and, crawling through traffic block by block in what had lived up to the promise of turning into a scorching spring heat, full of odious automobile effluvium, he was glad Barby had serenely agreed to remain behind. His mother-hennish dislike of leaving her alone in the hotel was alarmist and absurd: she was a sane child and would know how to proceed if there were a fire, or something equally improbable.

He took care of his patient, found another taxi for the even more tedious return trip, and by the time he opened the door of his suite he was thoroughly wilted. He felt foolishly relieved to see Barby sitting unharmed on the folding bed, which, at her request, he had set up at the feet of her new property.

"It's good you didn't come, Barby. Hot! I'm pooped." He bounced down beside her.

Then he noticed something odd in her expression. It was the look of decorum—that air of having secrets—which she had assumed when she had not wanted Madeline to see her running into her father's arms.

"Has anything happened? Mr. Greene—the bellboy—did he come here? Was the chambermaid here?"

"No," she answered tremulously.

"Then what's the matter?"

"Nothing." She hesitated. Sunlight was cascading through the window, lighting the strands of her hair like the thinnest of filaments. Nothing in this bright chamber could have frightened her; there was not a shred of gloom anywhere. Mohammed's white candescent breast hung unchanged by sun or shadow. The goddesses gleamed pleasantly in their stone arbors.

"What is it?" Jules repeated gently.

"Daddy—do we believe in Mohammed?"

"Now Barby. You know we're Presbyterians."

"But do we believe in him?" He saw that, from her point of view, he had not answered her question.

"No. Well, in a way. The Mohammedans believe some of the same things we do," he said unconvincingly.

"Oh." She looked thoroughly dissatisfied; she began again, groping. "Daddy, why did they take Mohammed off the roof?"

"I've told you, dear. Because the real Mohammed wanted all the statues destroyed. And *this* Mohammed is a statue."

"He's not the real Mohammed?" she wondered, leaning forward to examine the giant sandal with a baffled gesture.

"Of course not. They were going to break him up, but I bought him just in time. I saved him." He hoped she would not ask why the nine other figures, which he had not saved, had not been destroyed to please Mohammed. It was a logical rejoinder but luckily it did not occur to her. She was preoccupied with something else.

"I think he must be the real Mohammed," she observed decisively.

"What makes you think so?" Jules asked carefully, with a trace of fear. "Don't you understand what a statue is? You're getting mixed up," he went on when she did not answer. "The real Mohammed—the one who did all those things in the stories— has been dead for centuries. The real Mohammed could walk and talk. A statue can't."

"No," she agreed quietly, and he thought in relief and triumph that he had handled his explanation well. Madeline would have launched into jargon-edged hysterics about fantasies and withdrawal symptoms, instead of sensibly laying out definitions. For he was sure that it was only a certain fuzziness of definition that was disturbing Barby.

But her face was all at once bitterly distorted. "He didn't walk and he didn't talk. *I* talked to *him*."

"Darling," Jules began kindly. He understood now. In his absence she had hiddenly resumed her conversational game, and now, because Madeline had violently forbidden it, she was suffering from shame and guilt. That fanatic! he thought, angrily recalling Madeline's warning. She's trying to make Barby as literal-minded as herself; she'll end by making her ill. "Yes, darling," he said soothingly, caressing his daughter's smooth, solid little arms, "and wasn't it disappointing when old Mohammed didn't answer! That's the trouble with make-believe."

"But he did answer," she protested softly, looking at him with scared eyes. She's afraid I'll scream at her the way her mother does, Jules thought compassionately. She's afraid I'll punish her.

"You just *said* he didn't talk. Look, Barby," Jules said stoutly, "you *know* he's only a stone statue, don't you? You said yourself he's just a big doll. You do understand that, don't you?"

She nodded as if to reassure and console him.

"All right," he said, "then I'm satisfied he didn't manage to answer you if he can't talk. Where would his voice have come from?"

"It wasn't a voice."

He smiled at her ingenuity; she was improvising beautifully. And from her intonation, her thoughtful attitude, her little palms curved against her cheeks, he was almost persuaded to believe that she believed in her fable. "It wasn't a voice or a sound or anything. It was a sort of writing—a bunch of crooked letters that jumped out on that page, up there, like a rash of pimples."

"What color were the letters? Like your tomato rash?" Jules laughed.

"They weren't *a color*. They were sort of like"—she looked across the room to where the andirons were sun-dazzled gold points—"light."

"Well? What did they say?" But her earnestness troubled him.

"I don't know," she said simply. "I couldn't read them."

"Oh well," he said, dismissing it, "then we won't ever know." He tugged her away. "Come on, let's go find the carousel."

She lingered one moment more. "I thought if I looked at that writing long enough, I'd make it out. And I was just beginning to, only it disappeared when you came in."

He glanced up at the blank stone book, held by the sinewy marble hand; it looked all at once capable of brutality, queerly and suddenly warlike. "Nothing written up there now," he agreed, but he quietly resolved that he would not leave Barby alone again.

That evening he started to drag the folding cot into his own bedroom, so that she would not sleep near the statue. But when Barby tearfully protested, he left it where it was. The child was perfectly right. He didn't want to give her fears she didn't have.

The night passed peacefully. He stayed awake for most of it, listening for sounds from the next room. He heard nothing, and he went on tossing miserably, hating Madeline for the suspicions she had subtly put in his brain.

He must have fallen asleep near morning, for the sun was already turning the complex scene behind his closed eyelids into a vivid crimson when something, it felt like an earthquake, forced him to open them: in her flannel nightgown Barby was shaking him awake. "Daddy! The writing's come back!"

He was immediately and coldly alert. "All right, Barby. Show me." He leaped after her little pale heel-bottoms as they flickered rapidly ahead of him.

The statue of Mohammed rose up in the morning-lit room like some old Nereus white-foamed from the sea. His beard rippled wetly; the folds of his garments were luminous and almost without shadow, as if the light had poured liquidly and evenly into the crevices. The scimitar's edge glinted.

It's the sun, Barby. The reflection of the sun on the marble."

She was shaking her head, denying and denying; her head rained hair. "No. But they're gone now. They went away. The squiggly letters."

He knelt beside her. "Come, let's wash your face." He took her hand and she followed obediently. She let him squeeze the cold washcloth against her brow. But she was not feverish. Her skin was as cool as the water he was pressing against it. She stood passively waiting until he was finished with her.

"The letters were pretty dim," she said. "But when I started to watch them they got brighter. They got brighter right after I was wide awake."

"I'll tell you what," Jules said, "let's get dressed and go out for breakfast today. That'll be fun, for a change, what do you say?"

"I could read them," Barby said. "I could read them just as easy as anything. And they weren't even English."

Jules had heard about Joseph Smith finding the golden plates, Joan and the saintly voices—but he could not believe that this could have happened to his own child. Yet her sudden quiescence, her almost torpor, as if she were exhausted now by some terror or unendurable vision, did not altogether convince him that she had merely had a nightmare. She was no longer excited; she was instead calmly, frighteningly positive.

"I suppose they were Arabic letters," he said with mournful irony, and probed his memory in despair to see whether he had ever given her the basis for such imaginings. At the same time he was aware of the comic-strip humor of her noting—so literally!—what the language *wasn't*.

"I don't know if they were what you said, because I never saw letters like that before," she observed seriously.

"But you knew they were letters?"

"Oh yes, because I could read them, and anything you can read is *letters,* isn't it?"

He nodded, helplessly and pityingly. The child was hideously original. "I hope they said something really interesting," he went on lightly, "something worth getting me up for. Now let's get dressed for breakfast."

Jules walked down the long hall to the bathroom and plugged in his electric razor. The steady, loud buzz filled his ears, and in the soundlessness of not being able to hear other sounds, only the raucous monotonous dominating shaver, he abstractedly contemplated his face in the mirror. It looked ghastly with sleep-lessness and fright. He moved the razor across his left cheek, carving a pale path; just at that moment something, the touch or luster of his magically emerging bare skin, and a single bone that vaguely resembled Barby's, reminded him how deeply and sor-rowfully he loved her. It seemed to him suddenly that they ought to have stayed together, he and Madeline, in the house on Long Island, and given up greed for Barby's sake.

He thought he heard a noise. He clicked off the razor.

"Barby?"

"Uh-huh," she answered from the living room.

"Nothing. Okay," he called, and went back into the bath-room. He stretched his upper lip and slid the razor across it; a wave of grief struck him. Why had they not been kind to one another, and saved Barby? Oh, was she lost? What if it were true, Madeline's notion, what if she *were* what people charita-bly called a "nervous" child, no longer knowing the real from the unreal, what then? And if *he* had kneaded this distortion into her!

Thank God, Madeline was coming for her tomorrow, they would talk about it . . . But the strangeness of it! What did she think she had seen, poor angel, what crooked letters, what crazy intelligences, what—

He heard a terrifying sound.

The first thing he saw was the andiron, rolling across the floor and shining like a moon. It rocked twice more and stopped. Mohammed's hand, severed at the wrist, had fallen near a crumbled bit of robe, pointing nowhere. But the fingers of the right hand, still clutching a piece of scimitar, lay enmeshed in Barby's hair.

He fell to his knees to touch her blue-threaded flesh; it was smooth, cold, marvelously white. But her hair was staining rapidly, rivers of red through rivers of white. There was a vibration somewhere—not far. He remembered that his razor still dangled, singing, from its cord in the bathroom. He looked up at the face of the broken statue; the dead stone eyes said nothing. He looked down at the face of his daughter, shatterer of the shatterer of idols. And he saw only the agonizing whiteness of stone.

Everywhere Jules turned in the sunny room he saw stone.

An Unwelcome Guest

Jon Papernick

YOSSI BAR-YOSEF FELT his young wife Devorah stir in sleep.
He rolled over in bed, felt her warm breath against his face
and lay watching her until she was still again. Then she slept
quietly. A large round moon hung low over Jerusalem, its
white light spilling into their Muslim Quarter apartment. He
sat up in bed, reached for his kippah on the nightstand, and
placed it on his head. The night was silent in contrast to the
chaos of the day; Arab merchants hawking fruits and vegeta-
bles, pilgrims shouting prayers and curses, army patrols
strolling through the narrow stone streets. Now he could only
hear his wife's even breathing and the two soldiers joking quietly in Hebrew beneath their bedroom window. In a few hours
the muezzin would call the Ishmaelites to prayer for the first
time in the new day.

He got out of bed and made his way to the kitchen by moon-light, nearly skipping all the way in his bare feet. It was the month of Tishri and the stone floors were chilly even for early autumn. He filled a pot with water, lit the gas with a match, and stood by the stove for a moment thinking of his wife, his Devorah Bee: her soft olive skin, her curly brown hair, her green eyes, the way her body felt beneath his.

"You are welcome," the Arab man said, startling Yossi. "Welcome. Have a seat," he said gesturing to the empty chair at the kitchen table. "Welcome," the Arab man said again, smiling.

Yossi did not wonder how the old man had crept past the soldiers in the street, nor did he wonder how he had found his way through the locked door. He had waited every Passover for Elijah the Prophet to arrive and drink his cup of wine, and he prayed daily for the coming of the Messiah. Yossi knew that many people wandered the dreamy moonlit paths between sleep and prayer in this golden city of light and stone.

The Arab may have been sixty-five or seventy years old. His face was cracked like a wadi in the heat of summer, his nose round, bulbous, and pocked like a Judean hilltop, his thin salt and pepper mustache ratty, careless, a goatherd's mustache. He wore a black and white checked kaffiyeh on his head and a filthy striped caftan that reached almost to his slippered feet.

"Sit," said the Arab man in English. "We will share some tea and nana."

"What do you want here?"

The Arab man said nothing.

"My wife. She's sleeping."

"She sleeps like a baby."

The thought of someone invading his new wife's privacy,

someone even imagining Devorah asleep infuriated Yossi. He took a step forward and whispered through his teeth, "Get out! Why are you—"

"The water is ready," the Arab man said, cutting Yossi off.

Yossi turned his attention to the pot. The water bubbled over, hissing against the stove's flames.

"My name is Ziad."

"Who *are* you?" Yossi asked.

"I am Ziad Abu Youssif."

"You are in the wrong place. This is a private home," Yossi said, returning with the pot of water.

The old man only straightened his kaffiyeh on his head, smiled, and reached for a glass. He poured himself some water and said, "You are a rabbi?"

"No. No. I am studying. Near the Kotel."

The Arab man smiled a brown-toothed smile. "So you are a rabbi."

"I'm not a rabbi yet. I am studying," Yossi said, and then asked, "Why are you here?"

"This is my home, Rabbi," the Arab man answered in an even tone. "A tea bag, please."

"Your home?" Yossi said, surprised. "This is *my* home."

"How long have you stayed here?" the Arab man asked.

"Eight months."

"You are just married?" the Arab asked, taking a tea bag from a tin on the table. "Where are you from?"

"New York," Yossi answered.

"I was born in that room, where you sleep. My first son, Youssif, the dark one, was born in the same room. My father was born where you are sitting. This was not always a kitchen."

"If this is your house what color are the tiles on the floor of my bedroom?"

"The Jews are always changing things."

They sat in silence while their tea brewed in front of them. Then they drank. After a moment Yossi bit his lip at the corner, about to ask, "Why did you leave?" but before he had a chance, the old man said, "There were wars."

Yossi knew that many Arabs had fled Israel in 1948 and again during the Six-Day War. He had seen the squalid refugee camps and the anguished faces on his TV set, but he also knew the names Chmelnicki, Babi-Yar, and Auschwitz like a mantra. After a moment he said, "Abraham is your father as well as mine."

The old man did not seem to hear as he bent over to pick something up off the floor. It was a small wooden box. The Arab carefully placed it on the table between them. Yossi swallowed hard and thought about calling to the soldiers outside the window, but knew it would be useless. The bomb would go off before they could make it halfway up the stairs.

It had only been eight months since he and Devorah had stood under the huppa, only eight months since he had first kissed her after stomping the traditional glass representing the fragility of life, eight months since he had first touched his virgin wife. That was supposed to be the beginning; a family, a Jewish family in the heart of Jerusalem, and now, they were about to be blown to bits like that bus he had seen smoldering in the spring rain on Jaffa Street.

The Arab man undid a small latch and folded open a backgammon board.

"You play *shesh besh?*" he asked.

Yossi looked out the window and could see the moon higher over the city now, its light so bright, the face of the moon almost pulsing.

"It's the middle of the night."

The Arab began setting up the board, the white stones first, then the black stone disks in their places.

The old man took the last sip of his tea. "I will play you for the house. If you lose, I will live here again. If I lose, I will return to the Street of Chains begging for baksheesh."

Yossi was not interested in hearing about a broken man begging for shekels. He said, "No," and then said, "no," again.

"I am joking, of course," the Arab man said. "We will play for the right to speak."

Yossi would not get back to sleep now. He could feel his blood boiling through his body, his hands shaking, the small hairs at the back of his neck standing on end. "Okay. I'll play. Just let me check on my wife."

"But, it's your turn to roll." The Arab man had already rolled the first die: a four.

Yossi imagined his Devorah Bee curled up in bed, wetting her lips in sleep, kicking her leg against a bad dream. He thought of her slightly rounded belly and the child swimming within it. He stood halfway up from his chair, then picked up the die and rolled a three.

"My move first," the Arab man said. "Some more tea."

The old man rolled a six and a one. He moved the black stone to his side of the outer board, covering it with the one. Yossi rolled a two and a one. Already, one of his stones was unprotected. The Arab picked up the dice in his large hands and rolled. Then Yossi rolled. Only the sound of the dice clicking against the wooden board could be heard above the old man's labored breathing.

"Do you speak Hebrew?" the Arab asked.

"To read the Torah," Yossi answered, head down.

"Tell me, Rabbi, how did you get here?"

Yossi tried to move his two white stones from the inner board but could not. His pieces were almost entirely blocked in.

"Why here?" the Arab said.

"'If I should forget thee, O Jerusalem, may my right hand

forget its strength.' *Tehillim*. Psalm one thirty-seven," Yossi said.

"I do not forget," the Arab man said, holding out his right hand.

Yossi did not look up from the board and said matter-of-factly, "This land was given to Abraham by God. Abraham was the father of the Jews. We are here because we are Jewish. Because the land was promised to us by God."

The Arab rolled again, saying, "But we are both sons of Abraham."

Yossi rolled quickly and made his move. His mind was not on the game now. The Arab rolled the dice again.

"Abraham was the best of men," Yossi continued flatly, "but he contained some bad elements as we all do and those elements came out in his son Ishmael. He was the son of a slave girl. A wild man."

The old man's stones were all strongly in place on his side of the inner board. Yossi rolled but still could not move his two white stones trapped deep among the Arab's black stones. The Arab rolled and began removing his pieces from the board. "Beit 'Itab," he whispered. "Beit Mahsir," he said on his next roll. "Deir el Hawa," he said, removing two more pieces. "Jarash." "Lifta." "El Maliha." "Suba," he said, winning the game. Yossi cleared the board and began to set up another game.

"Deir Yassin!" the Arab said loudly. "Do you know Deir Yassin, Rabbi?"

Yossi motioned for the man to be quiet, he did not want to wake up his wife. The Arab lowered his voice.

"Do you know of Deir Yassin? No. It was a beautiful little village of orange and lemon trees, almond trees, and date palms on the outside of Jerusalem. Like the others, it is also erased from the face of the earth. Now it is called Givat Shaul. I'm sure you know Givat Shaul."

He did know Givat Shaul; his wife's aunt and uncle lived in an apartment not far from the mental institution. He had visited once or twice, but never saw a sign of Deir Yassin.

"You came to Deir Yassin one morning—"

Yossi interrupted, "I've never been—"

"It's my time to speak. I won the game. Now you must listen."

Yossi shifted uncomfortably in his chair.

"You came to Deir Yassin, a small quiet village at dawn. You were three hundred men with guns and mortars. You broke into homes, shot whole families, women and children, threw bombs into houses, machine-gunned us, butchered us, raped us. You took prisoners into the streets blindfolded and shot us dead. You left our bodies on the ground. You bound our hands, stripped us naked, put us in trucks, and drove us through the streets of Jerusalem. We were afraid and some of us ran."

Nonsense! Yossi thought. He had not even received his military training yet. He rolled the wooden die.

"You tried to scare the Arabs out of Jerusalem," the old man said and straightened his kaffiyeh. Then he rolled a three. It was Yossi's turn to roll first. The moon had moved behind some clouds, leaving them in almost complete darkness.

"Do you have a candle?" the old man asked.

Yossi stood up in silence, walked to the pantry, and returned with two Shabbat candles. He lit them.

"We'll play until the winner of three," the Arab said.

This time Yossi was determined not to get caught in the back of the board. He would rush his two white stones out from the very start and race the rest of his stones around to his side before the Arab could do the same. Yossi rolled, and then the old man, and then Yossi. They moved quickly, sliding their stones around the board, hypnotized by the rhythm of the rolling dice. He was so busy concentrating on the board that he did not notice the old man had been speaking in Arabic. Smelling tobacco smoke,

Yossi looked up from the table to find three more Arab men sitting on the kitchen floor beside the old man. He grabbed the table, nearly knocking the board to the floor as he tried to stand up. But he was unable, paralyzed in his seat. Two men slightly younger than Ziad wore kaffiyehs and took turns smoking from a tall gold-plated water pipe, a third ancient man with a battered fez planted on his head awkwardly fingered a set of worry beads. Yossi could still hear the soldiers' radio crackling faintly outside his kitchen window.

"Do not worry," Ziad said. "We are old men. There is nothing to fear. They are only my brothers and our blind father. Do not worry. Please. Please play."

The four men continued to talk in Arabic. Yossi, not understanding Arabic, did not know what to do. He took a deep breath but still could not fill his lungs.

Ziad asked Yossi, "Do you smoke the nargilah?"

"No. No," Yossi said, coughing. Then he remembered his pregnant wife as smoke filled the kitchen. Yossi excused himself.

From the bedroom doorway he saw Devorah asleep as before, her long hair splashed out onto the pillow. Yossi sat on the bed for a moment looking at her. Moonlight shined through the window and lit up her face. He kissed his index finger and touched it to the end of her nose.

"Sleep tight, my Bumblebee," he whispered and opened her night table drawer, removed his wife's mini 9 mm pistol, and placed it in his side pocket. Then he closed the bedroom door tight and hurried back to the kitchen half afraid of the encroaching Arabs, half determined to prove that he could win the game.

"She is sleeping?" Ziad asked.

Yossi nodded his head and sat down at the table.

"I shared that room with my brothers as a child," the old man said.

Yossi rolled the dice, ignoring him.

"There was a pomegranate tree at the window. My son Youssif liked to climb in it."

"It isn't there anymore," Yossi said, rolling a three and a one. He moved his first lone stone four spaces and said, "The tree is gone. There is no tree."

"I am just remembering," the old man said.

Yossi's white stone was open at the edge of the outer board one space short of safety. The old man paused a long time before rolling the dice again. With the moon high above the apartment the three Arabs sat cross-legged on the floor; two of them passing the water pipe back and forth between them, the older man continuing to fumble with his worry beads. It was only now with the moon out of the clouds that Yossi noticed the blind father's empty eye sockets.

"How would you feel if someone took that glass of tea from you?" Ziad asked.

"This glass?" Yossi said.

"Yes. That glass," the Arab said, rolling the dice.

"I would get another glass."

The old man rolled and promptly hit Yossi's single stone, removing it to the center bar. Yossi rolled, and entered in the fourth slot, moving his other lone piece from the first to third slot. His two stones were now open at the back end of the board. The Arab rolled again and Yossi found his stone back on the bar with the fourth and sixth slots occupied. He rolled a two and a three. His stone came off the center bar, but Yossi's stones were still hemmed in.

The Arab asked, "How old is your wife, Rabbi?"

"Nineteen," Yossi answered.

"And what is her name?" the Arab asked, rolling and knocking Yossi's stone to the bar again.

Yossi did not answer.

The game continued, and Yossi's stones were alternately knocked onto the center bar as the old man removed his pieces from the table two by two, whispering in Arabic. The Arab men on the floor clapped their hands on each other's shoulders—the blind old man mumbled something in Arabic that could have been a prayer.

"I've had enough of this. I'm going to sleep," Yossi said. He had not removed any of his stones from the table.

"But you can't. Nobody has won three games. Sit. Sit. I won the second game."

One of the Arab men got to his feet, a silver sheath shining among the folds of his caftan. Yossi fingered his wife's pistol in his pocket and said, "Okay. We'll play another game."

The old man picked up the stones in his hands and began chanting quietly the names he had just whispered: " 'Allar; 'Artuf; Beit Naqquba; Deir Aban; Ishwa'; El Jura; Kasla!" Do you know of the village of—"

"All right. It's time to play," Yossi said.

Yossi began setting up the board.

They played on, the dice rattling against the old wooden board. The men on the floor were anxious, groaning in discomfort with every move, shifting from one knee to the other. Yossi blocked the men from his mind, focusing only on the board. When he had established a lead he looked and flashed a confident wink at Ziad. The old man sat calmly, pondering his next move. Then he called out a question in Arabic and was answered by a woman's voice.

Four Arab women dressed in black stood over the kneeling men. One wore a hijab over her face, the other three sternly looked on. One of the women spoke loudly in guttural Arabic. The old man listened and turned to Yossi, who was beginning to remove his stones from the board.

"My wife, Zahira," Ziad said.

Yossi continued to play, ignoring her. His only interest now was to beat the old man, throw the Arabs from his home, and return to bed with his wife.

"These are my brothers' wives. And," he said, pointing to the tiny woman in the hijab, "this is our mother."

"It's your move," Yossi said.

The old man rolled. He had twelve stones left on the board. Yossi had six and rolled low but still removed two stones. The woman who had spoken to Ziad pushed her way forward and placed her hands on the table. Yossi saw the black under her fingernails, her eyes cold as the chipped stones on the board. Her face had the worn look of an old leather saddle. He rolled double four and won the game. The woman grabbed up the pieces and began to quickly reset the board. Yossi tried to place his hand on top of hers. She pulled away.

"Hevron!" he said, making eye contact with all the Arabs except the blind father. "We were neighbors in Hevron and you came to our homes," Yossi said, borrowing the tone of the old man, Ziad. "And you raped us, burned us, chopped off our hands."

"That is not true," the woman said.

"It is true," Yossi said.

"Liar!" the woman said louder.

"You were not born then," Ziad said.

"You came to our homes in the City of the Patriarchs—" Yossi said.

"Isra-ay-lee pig!" the woman yelled. "Liar!"

"—and tore us apart like fresh bread," he added.

"Arrogant Jew. Liar. Zionist," the woman shouted, and the men joined in shouting, knocking against the table. The woman stood face to face with Yossi and said, "You have no place here. Pig!" Then she spat in his face.

Yossi reached into his side pocket, pulled out his wife's pistol, and jammed it hard beneath the woman's ribs, doubling her over momentarily. He felt her soft stomach rebound against his hand.

"Quiet!"

The men moved back, but Zahira, the wife of the old man Ziad, stood her ground. "Put your toy away, yeled."

"It was a long time ago," the old man said.

"It was only sixty years ago," Yossi said.

"You were not born. You were not there," the old man said.

"Memory is in the blood," Yossi said. "I was there as I was at Sinai to receive the commandments. I was exiled from Spain. I wandered. And I remember pogroms beyond the Pale and the killing. I remember. And the camps, I remember that, too. Jews have been in Hevron since the time of Abraham. You have only lived there since the thirteenth century."

He waved the pistol at the Arabs and tasted blood in his mouth, sour and metallic. He wanted to lay the Arabs face down on the floor with their hands behind their backs, and fire a bullet into the brain of each. He would clean the floor with the old man's kaffiyeh and return to bed with his wife.

Zahira stepped closer, her weathered face inches from his. "Okay, boy," she said. "Shoot me." She pulled his pistol closer to her stomach. Yossi's hand was compliant. "I am all used up," she said. "Make me a martyr of the great battle." The men looked on impassively, the women stood stone-faced. Ziad, too, stared expressionless. "I am the mother of generations. But now I am finished. I am the husk of a pomegranate, my seeds have been scattered and grown. Shoot me. I am only a husk." Yossi pushed his pistol into her stomach and then pulled it back.

"Sit. We're going to play again," Yossi said.

The men sat, and the women did too.

Zahira reached forward and touched Yossi's cheek and said, "You are weak and sad."

"We will play?" Ziad said.

"Do not fear us," Zahira said. "We are old and not to be feared. But fear our children. Fear my son Youssif. He will burn your crops, tear down your home, and eat the flesh of your children."

Yossi rolled the dice.

"He will eat the flesh of your children," she repeated.

They began to play again, the Arab leading two games to one. The sky was turning from deep black to dark bruised blue. The moon was gone. Yossi slipped the pistol back into his pocket.

"The tea. It is cold," the old man said. Yossi stood up to boil another pot of water, then returned to his seat and rolled the dice. He opened with a solid four and two, occupying the four slot on the inner table. "My sweet wife was beautiful as a flower," Ziad said. "We married when she was fifteen. Her lovely name means flowers."

The old man rolled and Yossi turned to the woman. "I brought her to the place to take her gift, and my father and uncles waited outside the room with stones and knives—if she was not a virgin. But there was blood. . . . "

Yossi remembered his wife's red blood on the white bedsheet and the feeling that she was truly his.

"It hurt her and she cried and cried for days, did not stop."

Yossi rolled again.

"And we prayed that, *Inshallah,* we would have a strong boy who would not cry," Zahira, the old man's wife, said.

"And when he was born he cried," the old man said. "He cried for Palestine, and the bloodstained hilltops, and the weeping seashores. And I slapped his face and shook him and said, 'Do not be weak! You are an Arab!' And Youssif grew to be an angry barefoot boy."

The old man rolled and Yossi watched him slide the stones around the board with his rough fingers. The smell of hashish mixed with the smell of tobacco filled the room. Yossi was afraid to look up, feeling the weight of claustrophobia on him. He just stared at the board and at the old man's chipped black stones.

"It's your turn," the old man said.

The room was jammed with Arabs. The children had arrived. Eight young men with thick hair and mustaches crowded around the table with the others. Yossi could feel one of the newcomers breathing at his neck. Some drank beer from brown bottles, others smoked. They were all slim and strong and Yossi was afraid. The kitchen was so crowded that the Arabs pressed right up against the table and chairs.

"I need room," Yossi said and the woman called out, "Lebensraum?" and laughed. "I need room," Yossi said again, but the Arabs either could not or would not move. Then he thought of his wife alone in the bedroom and wanted to run to her.

"It's your turn," the old man said. Yossi stared blank-faced. "My sons," the old man said. "And my brothers' sons."

"I don't want to play."

"But you must. We are the majority," the Arab said.

Yossi wanted to call the soldiers down below, but couldn't raise his voice to speak. His wife's pistol in his pocket comforted him, but he knew he would never use it. He rolled again. Then the old man rolled. The young Arabs pressing in toward the table kept a running commentary of the game in Arabic. One imitated the sound of the clicking dice with his tongue. Yossi rolled again and he was leading. He removed his first stone from the board. The old man held up his empty cup and said, "Your pot is burning." Black smoke rose from the stove.

"Your house is on fire," the woman said.

Yossi pushed his chair back into one of the Arabs, stood up and forced his way to the stove. The Arabs laughed, and as he waded through them and tried to pull his kippah from his head, one reached into his pocket. Someone had thrown a dish towel into the flame. Yossi dropped it into the sink with the blackened pot and turned on the water.

"Some more tea," the old man said in a cracking voice.

When Yossi returned to the table his white stone was on the bar and six or seven of the Arab's stones had been spirited away without even a single roll of the dice.

"Where is the tea?" the old man asked.

"There is no tea," Yossi said. "Put the stones back or I won't play."

"All right. I will put them back and you will play."

"Where is your toy?" the woman asked.

Yossi felt his side pocket. His wife's pistol was gone and had been replaced with a slab of olive wood. Yossi's head felt light and then heavy.

"You will play now," the old man said.

Yossi's stomach churned and his mouth tasted bitter, acidy. With the pieces back in place, he rolled again, more determined than ever to beat the Arabs. "When I win you'll give me back my gun," Yossi said.

"You still don't understand. We make the rules," the old man said.

Yossi bit his lip and rolled again—double four. A lucky roll. Five stones left. The room still smelled of hashish now mixed with body odor and Yossi's head felt too heavy for his neck. The Arabs rolled. Then Yossi—two more stones off the board.

"Which one is Youssif?" Yossi asked.

The young Arabs laughed and one called out, "Youssif no home."

"Youssif is not here yet," the old man said.

Yossi put his hand to his forehead and rolled again—two more stones.

"You have won," the old man said, picking the last stone off the board with his battered fingers. "Now tell me of the six million, or some other lies, Rabbi."

"Tell me, Jew," the woman said. "Tell me some more fairy stories."

Yossi remembered the burned-out carcass of the bus on Jaffa Street, the shattered glass, the body parts scattered in the street. The bomb blast had woken him and Devorah in their apartment within the walls of the Old City. He had rushed from their bedroom to see, arriving while the acrid smell of burning flesh was still thick in the air.

"Bus number eighteen. I was there when the second bus blew up."

"Good. We have a bomb-maker here," the woman said, pronouncing the second "b" as she pointed to the young Arabs.

"He's a terrorist and should be killed," Yossi said, remembering the *Hesed shel Emet* workers cleaning flesh from the statue of the winged lion that sat perched atop the Generali Building.

"That is not very humane. Does your Torah allow that, Rabbi?" the old man said, setting up the board.

"The Torah of Israel is not about being humane," Yossi said. "This is the land of Isaac and Jacob. This is the land of my fathers and the land of my children and it will be the land of their children. This is our land. The land of Israel. The land of the Jewish people. I don't give a damn about your orange trees and date palms and pomegranate trees. You do not belong here. You are Amalek. I should have poisoned your tea."

"You should have," the old man said. "But your right hand forgot its strength."

"What?" Yossi said, stunned.

"I have read your books, Rabbi. Does it not say, if someone is going to kill you, it is your duty to rise early and kill him first? Yes, I am Amalek and you are not welcome here. You have scattered my children, chopped down my trees, thrown me from my home," the Arab said. "I am a son of Ishmael and you are a son of Isaac. But for that, we are not enemies. We are enemies because you came to make a family in Al-Quds. The land of Palestine is an Islamic holy possession, given to future Muslims until Judgment Day. You are a cancer and you must be cut out." The Arab paused for a moment. "Now it is your turn to roll again."

Before Yossi had a chance to reply, he heard what sounded like a window smashing in his wife's room, the glass shattering onto the stone floor. Yossi's stomach turned. He tried to stand up but was forced down by his shoulders.

"Help!" he called, before the old man pulled off his checked kaffiyeh and stuffed it into Yossi's mouth with the help of his laughing nephews.

"If I forget thee, let my tongue cleave to the roof of my mouth," the old man said, shaking his head.

"Psalm one thirty-seven," Yossi thought, sickened.

Yossi could hear someone stepping through the broken glass. His wife, in a panic, would rise in search of her gun, pull open her night table drawer, and find it empty. The taste of the dirty kaffiyeh in his mouth made Yossi want to throw up.

"*Hakol b'seder?*" a soldier called from beneath the kitchen window.

"*B'seder,*" one of the Arabs answered.

"*Lo b'seder,*" Yossi thought in Hebrew. "It's not okay. There are Arabs in my kitchen!"

"*Tov,*" the soldier said. Then there was silence.

The old man placed the dice in Yossi's hand. He dropped them onto the board.

"A good roll," the old man said, moving Yossi's pieces around the table. "Do you have *mazel* tonight?" the Arab man said mockingly.

The sky outside the window was turning quickly from a deep blue to a glowing purple. The bald old man reached into his caftan, removed Devorah Bee's mini 9 mm pistol and placed it on the table. Yossi struggled but could not move. He was held in place by three of the young Arabs. "My children studied at the revolutionary school. They drank anger and ate fury and threw stones. But they are not just bomb-makers and pickpockets. They will be the leaders of this land." The old man prodded the pistol with his index finger and spun it on the board. There was an inscription on the handle.

"What's this?" the old man said, " 'DARLING DEVORAH: FOR A SAFE LIFE IN JERUSALEM. LOVE DADDY.' A thoughtful gift, and practical, may it protect her from all harm. And a very pretty name. What does Devorah mean?"

Yossi blinked his eyes hard and fast as if he were trying to say, "Fuck you. Fuck your mother you filthy Arab." The woman picked up the gun and held it against Yossi's temple. Then she pulled his kippah from his head and dropped it to the floor. "It is almost time to pray," she said.

Yossi prayed to his God, wishing Moses had never led his people out of the wilderness, wishing that he had never come to this violent desert land, wishing that he and Devorah were safe in bed back in New York.

The old man looked on, his big eyes pitying, his pink peeling head almost glowing as the sun continued to rise.

Yossi looked at the woman, her face as hard as fire-forged steel. And then the muezzin cried, calling the Arabs to prayer. "*Ull-aaaaaaw-hoo-Ak-bar! Ull-aaaaaaw—hoo-Ak-bar!*" And the unwelcome guests, as surprisingly as they had arrived, began disappearing into the blue morning light. The blind father, the wives, the mother, the woman, the sons, and the nephews dropped to their knees, foreheads on the floor. And were gone. The old man, too, climbed from his chair and vanished. Yossi pulled the dirty kaffiyeh from his mouth and ran to the hallway, his heart breaking in his throat. The bedroom door opened and out stepped Youssif, a tall handsome Arab in a sweater and slacks. He held a broken bottle in his hand.

Youssif stepped past him, dropping the bloodied bottle to the floor.

"She is not dead," Youssif said. "She is only crying for the ghosts of her children and their children, too."

The sun continued to rise, the muezzin wailing in Arabic, "There is no God but Allah and Muhammad is the messenger of Allah."

"Paskudnyak"

Sonia Pilcer

Paskudnyak: From Polish/Ukranian, a man or woman who is nasty, mean, odious, contemptible, rotten, vulgar, insensitive, and dirty.

WE LIVE IN BROOKLYN, America. 24 Park Place. *Crowned Heights.* That's what I was supposed to tell a person if I got lost. My mother worried about losing me like a loose button on her baby blue cardigan sweater.

Our building was a dark tenement with a bomb shelter and the sign: NO LOITERING, NO SPITTING, NO PLAYING BALL. From early morning until it got dark, the big children played Chinese handball against the wall while we chased each other in and out of alleyways. Everyone talked about the Dodgers. The Franklin Avenue shuttle thundered above us.

My father worked in a knitting mill in another state, New

Jersey. His fellow workers on the machines, beer-drinking Americans, spoke neither Polish, Yiddish, German, nor even Russian, all of which he knew, so he had to learn English. In his freshly-laundered T-shirt, all could see the blue numbers B48356 swell on the inside of his forearm as Heniek forced a loose bolt into the scalding maw.

All day, Genia's silver needle imposed order, repaired broken seams, worn elbows and knees, created lively imitations of what she saw in shop windows. *"Hello, young lover, whoever you are..."* She mangled Hit Parade tunes as she sewed. *"Shrink boats are a-coming..."*

A neighbor, Mrs. Pellini, often dropped in for a cup of instant coffee. "Can you please to let out a little at the waist—God save me. I eat too much!—raise the hem, move over the buttons." My mother called it her pin money and hid the dollars in her private drawer, where she kept her cultured pearls and her father's cigarette case. She had found it hidden under a floorboard in her parents' apartment in Lodz after the war. Whenever Heniek objected to something she bought, Genia raised the specter of her pin money. He responded that she couldn't ride the subway with what she earned.

In the spring, she sewed matching cotton dresses for us. *Truskawkis*, strawberries printed on a white background, the sleeves and waist finished with red velvet piping. As we modeled before the full-length mirror on the closet door, she cried in delight, "Look, Zosha, we're exactly the same." On a Sunday afternoon when the sun lit even our street in the subway's shadow, we wore our identical dresses to the Brooklyn Botanical Gardens. My father took pictures with his Leica from Germany as mother and daughter posed like movie stars, under a blossoming cherry tree.

In lieu of living family, my parents belonged to a large network of Polish Jews. All were survivors. Their names were music notes, the ladies of the arbeit-lager: Lola, Stella, Minka, Ruzha, Fela, Blanca, Lusia, Manusha.

Every second Wednesday, they played canasta in our living room. As they tossed bright plastic chips and picked up cards, blue numbers flashing on the insides of their arms, the stories multiplied.

"Pish posh. I knew Mushka in the camp when she wasn't such a fancy lady. She cleaned toilets with the rest of us."

"If Bolek hadn't given me his piece of bread, I wouldn't be here. Lucky me, I was dealt two red threes!"

I understood Polish so none of it escaped me as I played with my mother's box of buttons under the mahogany coffee table. It had books about the Warsaw Ghetto Uprising and Auschwitz with photographs of concentration camp survivors in torn shifts, shaven heads—amidst bowls of celery stalks, cream cheese with scallions and radishes, Ritz crackers.

"I wouldn't give Uzek a broken cent. Now he's an important man in B'nai B'rith. During the war, he had a big mouth."

The delivery was off-hand. Lineups, beatings, starvation discussed as casually as yesterday's weather. Their voices rose with excitement as they regaled one another with tales of daredevil escapes, morsels of wartime gossip, teasing each other's memories as at a college reunion. After all, most of them had been in their teens when the war broke out.

"You remember Yola? She was the not bad-looking one with crooked teeth, who went with the German. He gave her crabs."

When I was in fifth grade, we left behind the concrete shadow of the Franklin Avenue shuttle and moved uptown to the Heights. Washington Heights, that is, above Harlem and below Dyckman. We could see New Jersey across the Hudson River, the neon roller coaster at Palisades Amusement Park, and, looming larger than God, the George Washington Bridge.

"The Riviera" was carved in stone over the entrance to our apartment building. Curse words sprayed in black paint decorated the marble columns. When I wasn't out, leaning on parked cars, passing a single Salem among giggly teenage girls, I sat on the third floor fire escape of my parents' pink bedroom. I watched 161st Street for hours: boys pitched broomstick baseball, slithering on their stomachs to plunk wax-melted bottle-caps into skully boxes. Nearby, completely ignoring them, girls hopped between chalked potsy boxes, bounced pink balls through all the letters of the alphabet, jumped double Dutch without getting tangled in the two ropes, flying from side to side. Children whizzed past on tricycles as bent-over old ladies crawled up the block, pushing shopping carts of groceries. In the afternoon's fading sunlight, mothers wheeled black-hooded baby carriages.

As I sat on the fire escape, pigeons pecked at my lunch, an egg salad sandwich, which I had refused to eat the day before. The white bread was moist and pulpy. "I'm not throwing away food that could save someone's life," Genia insisted, placing it next to me on the windowsill. "If I have to, I'll give it to you every day of your life. You can't have anything until you eat your sandwich."

I crumbled pieces of the crust and tossed them to a fat, gray pigeon, who snatched them in his beak. We were both content. What my mother didn't know was that I had discovered Chico's miraculous French fries across the street from school. When you stuck your hand in the brown paper bag, the grease and ketchup flavored your fingers, which you could lick, and the taste lasted all day. It cost fifteen cents for regular, and a quarter for large. I rarely had enough money to buy, but I took dibs on my friends' fries.

The Heights made Brooklyn—mostly Italian, Irish, and Jewish—seem tame. Especially the streets east of Broadway. We rode the uptown AA past 116th Street, 125th, to 161st, our station, a dark, piss-scented grotto littered with broken bottles of

Thunderbird. When you got to the street, St. Nicholas, you had to walk fast without seeming scared. Men lurked in parked cars, in doorways, hanging out of windows with their pants open. They exposed themselves, jerked off in front of you, followed you for blocks breathing heavily, whispering things in a voice that got inside of you, creeping into your sleep: *mi puta, te amo* . . . I never told my parents. They had to know, I figured, or they didn't want to know.

My mother was called to my new school, P.S. 28. I stood like a hostage in the principal's office.

"Your daughter was caught cheating on a math test," said Mrs. Washington, my teacher.

"No, I wasn't."

She raised the sleeve of my blouse to reveal numbers, drawn with blue ink on my forearm. "Look."

My mother's eyes met mine. I could see her shock.

"Thank you for telling me," Genia said stiffly. "I'll take care of it."

When we were outside, she screamed, "You're not normal!"

Spitting on her handkerchief, she tried to rub out the numbers. The blue ink resisted. She continued, spitting and rubbing, wiping the tears that flowed from her eyes on her sleeve. Slowly, the numbers began to unwrite themselves.

"How could you do such a disgusting thing?" she cried.

"I wanted to be like you!" I answered.

Just as I marched in her high heels, donned her black pillbox hat with the veil, imitated how she opened her mouth when she applied her red lipstick.

"What are you talking about?" she demanded.

"Will I have a tattoo when I get older?" I asked.

At that moment, my mother unbuttoned the sleeve of her shirtwaist dress. "Look, idiot! Your father has numbers, not me."

The High Holidays descended upon us. It began with Rosh Hashanah. My father poured red wine into the engraved silver goblets from his family's home. He had dug them up after the war. Now he stood at the head of the table, mumbling in Hebrew as he held the goblet his father had once held.

"Heniek," Genia said, sitting down at the table. "Enough already. We're hungry and you're still *davening*."

"Quiet!" he said sharply. "No wonder Zosha doesn't know nothing. There's no respect."

Then came Yom Kippur, the Day of Repentance. The only time of the year I didn't have to eat. I wasn't even supposed to brush my teeth.

They lit *yortzeit* candles. "Here," my father said, passing me the prayer book opened to *Zikhronot*. Remembrance.

He pointed to a passage. "Read this in English." *May we never abandon our memories. May our memories inspire deeds which lead us to life and love, to blessings and peace.*

I looked at my parents. Their memories did not lead them to peace, only tearful re-telling of loss. In fact, they did nothing but remember. My mother pacing from room to room in the apartment, weeping inconsolably. When I wanted to go outside, she turned on me. "*Paskudnyak!* It's the day I lost my whole family."

After months of gaga adoration, I finally succeeded in becoming one of the Cleopatras. They were a tough, cigarette-smoking clique of girls who rushed home after school to worship at the shrine of American Bandstand, then slithered through the streets in teased-out hairdos with satin bows clipped above the bangs, Liz Taylor makeup and the cheapest, tackiest gear this side of Frederick's of Hollywood. Felicidad flashed black see-through tops, her major bosom popping out of a black lace push-up bra. Cookie was a color freak; this week's special, purple: purple sweater, skirt, tights, shoes, and headband. Lola's glittering turquoise eyeliner started at her lobes and stopped at the bridge of her nose. I wore a tight black skirt, off-black runny stockings, white lipstick, but my claim to fame was my hair. When fully teased and sprayed, it measured four and a half inches high.

Wherever the Cleopatras went, acne-ridden boys with greasy pompadours followed, buzzing around us. Their transistors wailed, "When a man loves a woman . . ." as they flicked Duncan yoyos at each other, cut loud farts, made gross remarks, and ran after us, attacking with water balloons and pea shooters.

Usually Felicidad and Cookie made out with Hector and Jesus, but sometimes they switched. I had a secret crush on Carlos, Jesus's brother, who was a dead ringer for George Chakiris in West Side Story. We exchanged furtive, burning glances, consummated at Cookie's party where we had French-kissed during Seven Minutes of Heaven.

At sunset, the Cleopatras met on 158th Street, across the street from Mt. Sinai shul. We smoked Salems, teased our hair higher and sprayed it, as the Jews prayed at the evening Sabbath service.

My father looked up from his New York Times. We rarely encountered each other. During the week, he left for work while I was at school and returned after midnight. Most Saturdays he worked, but not today. "Where are you going?" he demanded.

"Out," I said.

"You look like a tramp," he said, inspecting me.

Transistor radio plugged to my ear, I lip-synched "My boyfriend's back and you're gonna be in trouble," having gotten myself semi-dolled up in Pink Passion lipstick, a chartreuse satin blouse, tight black skirt with slit on the side, off-black stockings, and roach-killer boots.

"Everyone dresses like this," I told him. Then figuring I'd be clever, I added, "Dad, this is the style in America."

"Who cares about style? Genia!" he called. "You let her leave the house like this?"

My mother rushed out of the kitchen, wiping her hands on the dishtowel tied around her waist. "What do you want me to do?" she demanded. "Lock her up?"

"You should do something before she gets locked up by the police. A Jewish girl walking on the street like that," he grumbled, picking up the newspaper, which had fanned at his feet.

I put my hand out, saying softly, "Mom, I need my allowance."

"Talk to your father," she said, returning to the kitchen.

"Dad." I approached slowly. "Can I have two dollars and fifty cents, please. Cookie and Lola and me are going to the movies."

Without looking up, he said, "Tramps. Streetwalkers. Not companions for you. Why don't you wash that crap off your face."

The downstairs buzzer would sound in five minutes.

He sat there in his dictator pose.

"Please," I insisted. "You owe me my allowance."

"Give me peace!" he cried. "You won't get a penny until you wash your face. Look at you."

"What's wrong with the way I look?"

For a moment, our eyes met. Then he turned back to his paper. "I don't trust you," he said.

The downstairs bell buzzed three times. I buzzed back, knowing that my friends would wait five minutes, then leave.

"Please, Dad."

"Leave me alone!" he cried out. Then suddenly, he was screaming. "I survived for this? To see my own daughter turn into filth. I should have died in the camps."

"It's my allowance, Dad," I screamed back. "You owe me it!"

His newspaper did not stir as they gathered at the wall on Riverside Drive without me, feet swinging as they slapped each other five, strutting their stuff to 181st Street where they headed for the balcony smoking section of the R.K.O. Coliseum. My father was immovable.

Finally, overcome by tears, I gave up. As I walked to my room, I heard a cheerless laugh. "Zosha, come here," he called me.

I turned to face my father. Two dollars dangled from his fingers. "Here, *paskudnyak*," he said.

As I tried to grab the bills, his hand withdrew. He repeated this trick. It amused him, his daughter leaping up and down like a seal.

"What do you have to cry about?" he mocked. "I never had nothing, not even before the war." He handed me two dollars. "Go to the stinking movies."

Running up the stairs, toes numb from my roach-killer boots, I found Cookie and Lola in the back row of the R.K.O. balcony. They weren't alone. This guy with a toppling pompadour had his arm around Lola. Both smoked cigarettes. On the screen, Natalie Wood and Steve McQueen were making out in *Love with a Proper Stranger*. So were Cookie and Jesus. And sitting next to Jesus—I couldn't believe it—his gorgeous brother, Carlos.

I, of course, sat down at the other end of the row. It was the only cool thing to do. Cookie beckoned me. "Hey yo!" But I shook my head and watched what happened when Natalie Wood went all the way.

I felt the heat of his presence before I turned. Carlos had slipped in next to me, his arm tactfully draping my seat. "Hi," he whispered in my ear. "How you doin'?"

"Fine."

Those were the only words exchanged. As we watched Natalie Wood discover she was in trouble, Carlos's arm moved stealthily from the seat, grazing my shoulder, to firmly surround me. Soon, his lips were teasing mine. I couldn't resist. I wanted his lips against mine, and then, his tongue. I kissed him as hard as I could, thinking of how much I hated my father.

We kept kissing, but he moved closer, holding me tighter, rubbing his knee softly against my thighs. I felt breathless. Meanwhile, Steve McQueen took Natalie Wood to get the "operation."

"How you doin'?" he whispered.

"Fine," I answered, my voice quaking. "You?"

We just kept kissing, my lips bruising, I didn't care, as he hugged me harder, rubbing his knee between my legs. I clutched his arms, pushing against him. I felt hot, my cheeks flushed, out of breath. Suddenly, I was panting like I might hyperventilate. Was this an orgasm? It was so different from when I did it alone.

We were slipping out of our seats. I threw myself against his hipbone, his leg. More. "Oh, Carlos," I sighed, trying to muffle my breathing. But he was panting too, pressing against me, grinding against my hip.

"*Mi caracita.*"

Suddenly, the flash of a light beamed on our faces. "What are you doing?" an outraged voice demanded.

We pulled ourselves up to a sitting position, trying to hastily straighten out our clothes. "Nothing," said Carlos, tucking in his shirt.

"We won't have this," declared the middle-aged black woman in a navy bellhop suit. Her flashlight formed a yellow triangle around us. "You must leave."

"We paid our money," Carlos said.

"You leave right now or I'll call the guard," she threatened.

"Fuck you and your family," Jesus called out.

"Punks," the usher muttered, walking back up the aisle.

"Yo, Carlos!" Jesus called from across the row. "What's happen?"

"It's cool, man."

"Hey, Spic and Span," an angry voice shouted, "Shut the fuck up!"

"Your mother!" another voice called.

As Natalie Wood wept desperate tears because she was in love with Steve McQueen but he would never respect her since she'd gotten pregnant when she went all the way with him, we felt the clamp of strong fingers on our shoulders. Carlos and I were ushered out of the theater by a short guy with incredibly muscular arms. "I'm calling your parents, you hoodlums."

"I don't know what you do, who you're with," Genia said as we rode the bus to Yeshiva Rabbi Soleveichik on 185th Street, where my father insisted she enroll me. "It's better here. You'll be with Jewish children, not the goyim on the street."

But I despised Judaism. Lighting candles to remember the dead. Holidays and high holidays, which introduced yet more taboos. Why did they talk about *shvartzes* like subhumans? As if Jews were a different race and we mustn't consort with anyone else.

My mother's inconsistent rites of observation! Bacon and ham were okay, but no pork chops. Spare ribs from the Chinese restaurant were okay too. The two-faced double standards for inside and outside the home. Every Saturday, my mother turned on the radio to listen to the "Make-Believe Ballroom," watched the "Million Dollar Movie," and so did I. But if I was going outside, I had to observe Shabbos and not wear pants.

"You must look decent. They tried to destroy us," she told me. "Now we must show how well we dress."

For my interview with the rabbi, my teased hairdo was forcibly reduced by fifty percent. My mother made me wear my blue pleated skirt with a white ruffled blouse—Israel's colors, she reminded me. But I sported my black leather roach-killer boots. I was a slum goddess, after all.

Inside the red brick building, all the boys wore yarmulkes. As they raced through the halls, their arms filled with books, the strings of their tzitzit streamed behind them like leashes. The girls walked quietly. Upon noticing me, they began to whisper among themselves. One boy grunted loudly, "Ugh." As I seemed to scratch my head, I gave them all a subtle third finger.

In the elevator, my mother raised her slip. She then pulled down the hem of her blue wool dress. "All right?" she asked, turning around. "I copied this pattern from *Vogue*."

We entered a musty-smelling office, papers strewn over the old, scratched-up desk and on the chair, leather bound volumes from ceiling to floor. As the rabbi looked up from the text on his desk, I could see his long, white beard, white *peyes* and sharp blue eyes.

He opened a book with large Hebrew letters. "Will you read these?" he said, pointing with his finger.

"I don't know how," I said, staring down blankly, of course, recognizing the *aleph, bet, daled, gimel, hay* . . .

"Haven't your parents sent you to Hebrew school?" the rabbi inquired.

I nodded. Our text, *The History of the Jewish People,* started with Abraham and Moses, through Disraeli, to Ben Gurion, Leonard Bernstein, and Bernie Schwartz, known to his fans as Tony Curtis. The teacher was a balding, dogmatic man who despised questions, especially from girls. A crocheted yarmulke with a black circle in its center was bobby-pinned to his short hair. When he turned around to write on the blackboard, I imagined shooting a rubber band and paper clip. Bull's-eye!

"Young lady," the rabbi demanded, "Don't make me angry. What's the first letter of the Hebrew alphabet?"

"Aleph." I nearly spat the word.

His blue eyes observed me from their pink pockets. "You don't want to go to Yeshiva? Why? Don't you want an education?"

Yeshiva meant four hours of religion in addition to regular

school. I crossed my arms. "I'm an atheist," I said, having come across the word in *The Fountainhead* by Ayn Rand.

"Don't be rude," my mother misunderstood. "She doesn't mean that," she apologized, cuffing me on the back of my neck.

The rabbi studied me, shaking his head. "You speak because you don't know. Is that what you want? To be stupid like the rest of the world?"

"I don't want to go to yeshiva," I declared, wondering why Jews always thought they were so smart.

"Do you think you'd be happier going to public school?" he asked.

I nodded.

"You know there won't be many white children," he said.

"I don't care," I said.

"You like the colored?" my mother asked. "When they beat you up, you weren't so happy."

A group of older girls had followed me after school. "Balloonhead!" they called. "Shake it, don't break it, took your momma nine months to make it." Their taunts grew louder. "She thinks she's hot." I walked fast, knowing Broadway wasn't far. They followed on my heels. "Hey girl," someone called, "when I talk to you, you listen." I started to run. Suddenly, a girl grabbed my arms from behind and threw me down. I landed on my knees, the concrete ripping my stockings. My knees bled as I made my way home. My mother had found my bloody stockings in the garbage.

"Have you no shame?" the rabbi demanded suddenly.

I stared at the ground, not to meet his stinging eyes.

"After what your parents went through," he said.

I crossed my arms, not answering him.

"Say something!" my mother urged. "What's wrong with you?"

I shifted my weight to the other foot.

"We can't force you to learn." The rabbi shrugged. "She doesn't belong here, Mrs. Palovsky."

My mother nodded. "I didn't think so. It was my husband's idea. In Poland, his family was very religious."

The rabbi was through with us, but Genia continued. "My family was assimilated. Still they took us away and murdered everyone."

"We must honor the memory of those who perished," the rabbi said, standing up slowly. His dark jacket was stained. "May everything work out for the best, God willing."

"Are you happy now?" she asked as we walked out of the building. "Now you can rot on the street with your juvenile delinquent friends."

"They're not juvenile delinquents," I insisted. "They just like to dress tough."

"But, Zosha, you belong with these people? Their families drink and the husbands beat up the wives. *Paskudnyak!* Why can't you be normal—like Daddy and me?"

First Date

Jonathan Rosen

IT WAS STRANGE for Lev to be back in Roosevelt Hospital. When his father was there he had always hurried in and out of the lobby but now he was stuck in the vast, vaulted, impersonal space, waiting for Deborah, who was already twenty minutes late.

He was beginning to regret his invitation. What had he been thinking? A rabbi!

Lev had liked watching her drink from the fountain, the way she stooped into the gleaming white hollow and then pulled away with her face and hair all spangled with water; the way she stood laughing at herself. But the professional air of concern put him off. The hand on the shoulder—had she put a hand on his shoulder? There was something a little preachy about her. As if she was always up on the dais. Of course that might have been the platform shoes. But she seemed to be looking down from some remote moral perch. *I can't, it's a fast day.*

He would be justified in leaving because she was now half an hour late.

He was considering doing just that when the security guard manning the front desk, who had been eyeing him for the last ten minutes, beckoned.

"You waiting for the lady rabbi?" He asked.

Lev said he was and the man gave him a folded piece of paper. He opened the note quickly and read:

> *Dear Lev,*
> *I am SO sorry. Somebody died and I didn't have your number! I have to do the funeral—I'm pinch-hitting for another rabbi. I'll understand if you just go to the game, but if you want to find me, I'll be at Riverside Chapel on 76th and Amsterdam. The funeral starts at noon. With apologies—Deborah*

Well, there it was. He had a feeling that death was never far from this woman, even though she herself had such a lively air.

Lev did not feel like going to Yankee Stadium alone but he was pretty sure he did not want to attend a stranger's funeral. Still, he found himself heading uptown to Riverside Chapel. He was wearing jeans and sneakers and a black polo shirt, hardly funeral-wear, but he figured he could slip in and find Deborah before things began, say a quick hello and a quick goodbye. It would be only polite to let her know that he had gotten her note.

He had been to Riverside Chapel before. He had grown up near it on the Upper West Side and had often walked through clustered mourners out on the sidewalk. The upper windows were all blotted out with a milky white film. He had been fascinated since childhood by the side entrance with its wide, riveted steel doors, cryptically lacking handles, like the doors of a bank vault—through which, one imagined, corpses came and went in the dead of night. He sometimes stopped to stare through the ground floor window at the ominous display of tombstones provided by "Sprung Monuments." There was always the creepy, unarticulated expectation that one of the tombstones would bear his own name.

A dark suited "greeter," stationed in the lobby, nodded impersonally at Lev as he entered the funeral parlor.

"Corngold?" The man asked.

Lev did not know what funeral he was going to but he said yes.

"Second floor."

Lev took the stairs. He was claustrophobic at the best of times and there was something about a funeral home that made him more eager than ever to avoid the enclosed space of the waiting elevator. The second floor was filled with mourners milling around like guests at a lugubrious cocktail party. The atmosphere was muted but there were odd, merry outbursts—"Cindy, you made it!"—a reunion atmosphere of hugs and kisses amid the murmured comments, "It's better this way, she won't suffer," and the unrelated chitchat. "The stock was doing gangbusters a week ago," a man said ruefully behind him.

Lev felt awkward crashing a funeral but he was, after all, a journalist, and intruding into other peoples' calamities was not altogether alien to him. Besides, there was an ethnic familiarity in the air, a sort of genetic overlap. Everyone's face seemed once-removed from faces he knew. These might have been his relatives. There was a Jewish undertow pulling everyone at some occult level toward a shared past—or was it a common future? Someone flashed him a big familial smile and then, looking closer, took it back.

Lev spotted Deborah in a far corner of the room. She was dressed in a lavender business suit and her hair was pulled back tight and twisted into a bun. She was talking to a little man in a dark suit whom Lev presumed was a funeral director. The funeral director nodded discretely, like a hit man receiving instructions, and then disappeared into a side room.

Deborah straightened up and surveyed the crowd. She saw Lev and broke into a big smile, moving toward him immediately. She seemed uncowed by the crowd or the occasion.

"You must hate me," she said, a little breathlessly. "Rabbi Zwieback has a stomach bug. He was supposed to do this one. If you want to just take off I'll totally understand."

"Would you mind if I stayed?" Lev hadn't expected to but he was suddenly curious. The idea of watching her perform appealed in an odd, almost perverse way.

"Sure," she said. She seemed pleased, a little flattered. "It should take about half an hour. You can skip the burial—but if you want, I've got my car and we can drive straight to the stadium from the cemetery."

She laughed a little nervously, at the absurdity of it all.

"Or you can see how you feel after the service. This must be kind of weird."

"Kind of," said Lev.

Deborah smiled at him but her eyes were already darting around the room nervously. She was looking for the funeral director.

Lev noticed that in her left her ear, along with a simple pearl earring, there were several tiny, unused holes, not merely in the lobe but perforating the delicate outer rim of her ear.

"Who died?" Lev asked.

"Irma Corngold."

Ah, Jewish names, thought Lev. Depriving even the dead of dignity.

"She was ninety," said Deborah. "I have to interview her family to get a little info for the eulogy. I've never met her."

The little man in the dark suit had come back. He was holding several black ribbons attached to safety pins in his hand. Deborah took them and counted them out.

"We're short," she said reproachfully, as if to a dishonest merchant.

"There are six," the man said.

"There should be seven," Deborah said. "Four children, three sisters."

"I was told six," the man said defensively.

"Well we need one more."

Deborah seemed exasperated all of a sudden.

"Bring them to the Rabbi's Room" she said as the man went off.

"This guy is such a nitwit," she muttered to Lev under her breath. A change had come over her. But then she smiled, a little sheepishly. Lev had a slightly detached, scrutinizing way of staring that made her self-conscious.

"Does it matter that I'm not dressed right?" he asked.

"Oh don't worry about that," said Deborah. "You look great. But you might want a kippa." She patted her own head demonstratively. Several stray strands of hair had come loose from her bun and hung curling over her ears like the peyes of Hasidic Jews. It exaggerated the exotic aura of her face, the high, wide cheekbones and Asiatic shape of her eyes.

"Will you be okay if I go do some things?" she asked. Lev assured her that he would be fine and Deborah went off to the "Rabbi's Room" where the sisters, children and grandchildren were waiting in seclusion from the others. Lev helped himself to a black nylon kippa from a wicker basket and, head covered, felt calmer, camouflaged. He considered signing the guest book but thought better of it, and, to avoid the crowd, opened a side door and entered the room where the funeral itself would take place.

Except for an elderly couple sitting in the back row, the room was empty. It was a religiously neutral chapel with a rounded ceiling painted blue with gold stars. Lev took a seat a few rows from the front. There was a podium and flowers and, on one wall, stained glass windows of indecipherable images in blue and purple—purposely blurred, Lev decided, for ecumenical use. It was only after he had sat in the cool silence for a few moments that he realized there was also a coffin in the room.

The coffin stood at the front, resting on a stand with wheels. How had he overlooked it? It was of pale polished wood and there was a Jewish star in a circle carved neatly on top. The fact that there was a body in the box, that someone who had been alive was now dead, struck Lev with unexpected force. He felt the narrow sides of the coffin confining his own breath, shrinking the boundaries of his body. He inhaled deeply.

But it wasn't him. Irma Corngold, or what had been Irma Corngold, was in there. He tried to figure out where the head was and where the feet were. Probably the Jewish star was over the head.

"Where are you now?" he thought. As soon as he thought this he imagined the whispering presence of Irma Corngold's soul still hovering. He shivered away this superstitious inkling—he was prone to them—and was grateful when the doors were propped open and people began to drift into the chapel.

When the chapel was full and everyone had sat in murmuring, uncomfortable silence for what seemed a long time, the little funeral director came in and asked everyone to rise, like the bailiff at a trial when the judge is about to enter. Lev stood with the others as the immediate family, wearing their little black ribbons on their lapels, filed somberly in and took their seats in the front row of the chapel. Deborah was in the lead and, instead of sitting down, she went immediately up the few stairs and stood behind the lectern, looking out calmly over the crowd.

Behind him somebody said, in a harsh whisper, "A woman rabbi!"

"Why not?" said her companion. "We have one in Florida."

"She's a doll," said somebody else. Lev felt an unexpected flush of pride that he was . . . what? Her date? He stared at her—everyone was staring at her—and she made fleeting eye contact with him. Unless he was mistaken, Deborah had winked speedily in his direction.

The gesture was charming and disconcerting. It suggested that the whole funeral was a performance; that the wood coffin and the flowers and the mourners were all just props and extras in a play. He tried to renew eye contact but Deborah stared implacably out over the seats, her gaze everywhere and nowhere, the way a lifeguard scans the ocean. She had tucked the few curling strands back into her bun and was now wearing a black rabbinical robe over her lavender suit. She kept gazing out over the assembled mourners, even after the few stragglers who came in through a rear door had found their seats and a deep hush had fallen on the room.

Then, out of the deepening silence, she began to speak:

A voice says: Cry out! And I say: What shall I cry?

All flesh is grass, and all its beauty is like the flower of the field. The grass withers, the flower fades, when a wind of the Lord blows upon it. Surely the people are grass. The grass withers, the flower fades; but the word of our God shall endure forever.

She had begun barely above a whisper, so that the old people shifted and strained forward and the hush in the room became even deeper, a layered silence. But as she spoke Deborah's voice grew clearer and louder so that by the time she finished reading the paragraph of Isaiah aloud, people had again settled back in their seats. Now she was chanting the Twenty-third Psalm in Hebrew.

Her voice rose and fell in gentle waves. Her eyes had a faraway look. Lev was close enough to see that she was on the brink of tears, but her voice did not falter. She invited members of the family to come up and speak. Little by little, an image of Irma took shape in Lev's mind. Her mother had died in the influenza epidemic of 1918. She had been only nine but she had helped raise her siblings, all of whom, except sister Sophie, sick with arrhythmia in Florida, were gratefully present. She had married Max, who sold pharmaceutical supplies. He had died twenty-four years ago of a brain tumor. It had not been easy. It had been a hard life and a good life and a prosperous life and a sad life. And now she was in a box with a star on it.

But now Deborah, back at the lectern, was reading, in her sonorous voice, a passage out of her rabbi's manual. Her broad face, above the black robe, was luminous.

Fear not death; we are destined to die. We share it with all who ever lived, with all who ever will be. Bewail the dead, hide not your grief, do not restrain your mourning. But remember that continuing sorrow is worse than death. When the dead are at rest, let their memory rest, and be consoled when the soul departs.

Death is better than a life of pain, and eternal rest than constant sickness.

People nodded at this but others shifted uncomfortably. How many here, Lev wondered, believed in "eternal rest"? What did the word *eternal* mean? It was a child's question but one he realized he wanted to know the answer to. He would like to have raised his hand and asked.

But then, as if in answer to his thought, Deborah declaimed:

"... *seek not to understand what is too difficult for you, search not for what is hidden from you. Be not over-occupied with what is beyond you, for you have been shown more than you can understand* ..."

Lev drifted off with this. He found the formulation oddly

comforting, though it was no answer at all. When he tuned back in Deborah was thanking the family members and friends for their beautiful words. She added a few observations she had gleaned in her interview. But Lev was only half-listening. He was looking at Deborah's bright eyes, her full lips forming words he could scarcely focus on. He was thinking, suddenly, "She's beautiful."

He wondered vaguely what she looked like under her robe and if she would sleep with him. Unlikely on a first date. And of course, he'd have to go to the cemetery first.

Deborah was chanting, in a soft, rich voice, *El Maleh Rachamim*, the prayer for the dead. This time she did cry—her high cheekbones were shining and it was as if she were somehow linked to each body in the chapel; Lev felt her little sob release an echoing sob in the throats around him. And he understood that in some perverse way, everybody in the chapel had fallen in love with her.

And then it was over and people were again standing as the box with Irma's body was wheeled slowly down the aisle. People were weeping. The realization that this was final, that this was death, filled the room. The immediate family followed behind the coffin and people were reaching out to them.

Deborah brought up the rear. People hugged the mourners and several pulled at Deborah's sleeve as well.

"Beautiful," someone murmured.

"Thank you, Rabbi," someone else said.

She looked suddenly small. The towering apparition chanting *El Maleh Rachamim* was gone. In her black robe, Deborah looked like a college student at a graduation. She caught Lev's eye and flashed him a half smile. Like the wink, Lev found it a little disconcerting and also oddly thrilling.

When the mourners had passed and his turn came he left his pew and moved out the door. Separating himself quickly from the crowd he took the stairs and went outside where the limousines were already idling their engines. Lev felt a sense of release in the bright sunshine. The coffin would be taken down in its own elevator and loaded unobtrusively into a hearse. But Lev was free, and he had an impulse to just keep going, down the bright sidewalk.

But he stayed put and soon Deborah was standing beside him. She was no longer wearing the black robe and she looked transformed yet again. She was a real person in a lavender suit that buttoned over breasts, with a skirt that seemed slightly crooked and white stockings that had a run in one leg, moving like a zipper toward the inner thigh.

"Hi."

"That was great," Lev said, with genuine enthusiasm.

Deborah shook her head. "I called one daughter Ellen but her name's Elena. I forgot to give the address for shiva."

She seemed uncomfortable. Lev said nothing. He stood squinting in the bright light, trying to regain his bearings.

"Listen, I don't want to pressure you," Deborah said suddenly, "but I've got to get into the procession."

They walked in silence to the corner.

"Somebody took my car when I got here. Let's see if I can get it back—last time they lost it."

She again had the unexpected, imperious tone that seemed to say, "I'm surrounded by idiots," though she laughed disarmingly at herself right after. Her car was fetched without difficulty and when she opened the door of the little red Honda, Lev found himself climbing in beside her.

"Follow that car," he said, pointing to the hearse that was just now emerging from the parking garage underneath the funeral home. He glanced at Deborah to see if she was offended but she was busy nosing into traffic, taking her place behind the hearse and two black limousines.

Lev could not help noticing that Deborah had on only a bra under the lavender blazer. He thought the V of naked flesh a little daring for a funeral, though she'd worn a robe for the service. There was a chain around her neck suspending a small gold star of David. Judaic icons seemed kitschy to Lev, as a rule, but this small sharp star had a delicate beauty—a tiny echo of the star on Irma Corngold's coffin, nestling above Deborah's breasts.

"Not a bad turnout for an old lady," Deborah said.

Lev was looking around the car trying to learn what he could about its owner. There were a number of cassettes on the dashboard: Shlomo Carlebach, Ray Charles, Sinead O'Connor, Melissa Ethridge, K.D. Lang (was she a lesbian? he wondered suddenly), Lauren Hill and—most surprising—Marion Anderson singing gospel.

"Do you do a lot of funerals?" he asked.

"Too many. It's weird when you don't know the person who died. *Shit!*"

A cab had darted between her and the procession. Deborah swerved around it and cut off another car pulling out of a parking spot. The driver gave her the finger.

"It's a funeral, asshole!" she shouted back. Lev was glad the windows were closed and the air conditioning was on.

"Sorry," Deborah said, scrunching up her face amusingly. "I don't like city driving. I'll be fine when we get on the highway."

Lev checked to make sure his seat belt was on.

"Anyway, funerals can be strange."

"I thought you did a beautiful job."

"Well, thank you. I'm mostly an emcee. That's my main job. To facilitate, to create a ritual framework for other people's grief, for their stories."

"It's quite a job. You're really at the heart of things."

"I suppose so. Funerals aren't so different from the rest of life," she said. She was talking without turning her head, keeping her eye on the car in front of her, which had pulled over to the side to let other members of the cortège catch up.

Deborah pulled over as well and took the opportunity to reach back and grab a plastic bag from the back seat.

"It's time you learn the most important lesson about funerals," she said.

"What's that?" Lev asked, genuinely curious.

"Food!" Deborah said. "Always bring your own."

Lev laughed in surprise.

"Seriously," said Deborah. "The funeral *started* at noon. Then you go to the cemetery—which is always out in Long Island or New Jersey or a part of Queens you've never heard of. It'll be three or, more likely, four before anyone makes it back to shiva, which is in the Village at her daughter's place. Then you have to attack the lox like a starved hyena, which is really humiliating for everyone. You expect Jews to know better than that."

Deborah had opened the bag on her lap and was rummaging through it. She removed a box of raisins, a bag of baby carrots, and two sandwich-shaped squares of tinfoil.

"I have tuna and egg salad."

"Tuna," said Lev.

He took the sandwich she handed him gratefully. He was, he realized, starving.

What Must I Say to You?

Norma Rosen

WHEN I OPEN THE DOOR for Mrs. Cooper at two in the afternoon, three days a week, that is the one time her voice fails us
both. She smiles over my left shoulder and hurries out the words
"Just fine," to get past me. She is looking for the baby, either in the
bassinet in the living room or in the crib in the baby's room.
When she finds her, she can talk more easily to me through the
baby. But at the doorway again, in the early evening, taking leave,
Mrs. Cooper speaks up in her rightful voice, strong and slow: "I
am saying good night." It seems to me that the "I am saying" form,
once removed from herself, frees her of her shyness. As if she had
already left and were standing in the hall, away from strangers,
and were sending back the message "I am saying good night."

Maybe. I know little about Mrs. Cooper, and so read much
into her ways. Despite the differences between us, each of us

seems to read the other the same—tender creature, prone to suffer. Mrs. Cooper says to me, many times a day, "That is all right, that is all right," in a soothing tone. I say to her, "That's such a help, thank you, such a help." What can I guess, except what reflects myself, about someone so different from me?

Mrs. Cooper is from Jamaica. She is round-faced and round-figured. She is my age, thirty, and about my height, five-five. But because she is twice my girth (not fat; if there is any unfavorable comparison to be drawn, it may as well be that I am, by her standard, meager) and because she has four children to my one, she seems older. She is very black; I am—as I remember the campus doctor at the women's college I attended saying—" surprisingly fair." Though, of course, not Anglo-Saxon. If you are not Anglo-Saxon, being fair counts only up to a point. I learned that at the women's college. I remember a conversation with a girl at college who had an ambiguous name—Green or Black or Brown. She said in the long run life was simpler if your name was Finkelstein. And I said it was better to be dark and done with it.

Mrs. Cooper has been coming to us, with her serious black bulk and her beautiful voice, for some months now, so that I can get on with my work, which is freelance editorial. The name is lighthearted enough, but the lance is heavy and keeps me pinned to my desk. Mrs. Cooper's work, in her hands, seems delightful Though she comes to relieve me of that same work, it is a little like watching Tom Sawyer paint a fence—so attractive one would gladly pay an apple to be allowed to lend a hand. Even the slippery bath, the howls as my daughter's sparse hairs are shampooed, become amusing mites on the giant surface of Mrs. Cooper's calm. They raise Mrs. Cooper's laugh. "Ooh, my! You can certainly sing!"

I sneak from my desk several times an afternoon to watch the work and to hear Mrs. Cooper speak. Her speech, with its trotty

Jamaican rhythm, brings every syllable to life and pays exquisite attention to the final sounds of words. When she telephones home to instruct the oldest of her children in the care of the youngest, it is true that her syntax relaxes. I hear "Give she supper and put she to bed." Or "When I'm coming home I am going to wash the children them hair." But the tone of her voice is the same as when she speaks to me. It is warm, melodious. Always the diction is glorious—ready, with only a bit of memorizing, for Shakespeare. Or, if one could connect a woman's voice with the Old Testament, for that.

"God is not a God of confusion." Mrs. Cooper says that to me one day while the baby naps and she washes baby clothes in the double tub in the kitchen. I have come in to get an apple from the refrigerator. She refuses any fruit, and I stand and eat and watch the best work in the world: rhythmic rubbing-a-dubbing in a sudsy tub. With sturdy arms.

She says it again. "God is not a God of confusion, that is what my husband cousin say." A pause. "And that is what I see."

She washes; I suspend my apple.

"It is very noisy in these churches you have here." She has been in this country for three years—her husband came before, and later sent for her and the children, mildly surprising her mother, who had other daughters and daughters' kids similarly left but not reclaimed—and still she is bothered by noisy churches. Her family in Jamaica is Baptist. But when she goes to the Baptist church in Harlem, she is offended by the stamping and handclapping, by the shouted confessions and the tearful salvations. "They say wherever you go you are at home in your church. But we would never do that way at home."

She lifts her arms from the tub and pushes the suds down over her wrists and hands. "But I will find a church." The purity of her diction gives the words great strength. The tone and timbre would be fitting if she had said, "I will build a church."

Again she plunges her arms in suds. "Do you ever go," she asks me, "to that church? To that Baptist church?"

Now is the time for me to tell her that my husband and I are Jewish—and so, it occurs to me suddenly and absurdly, is our three-month-old daughter, Susan.

It is coming to Christmas. I have already mentioned to my husband that Mrs. Cooper, who has said how her children look forward to the tree, will wonder at our not having one for our child. "I don't feel like making any announcements," I tell my husband, "but I suppose I should. She'll wonder."

"You don't owe her an explanation." My husband doesn't know how close, on winter afternoons, a woman is drawn to another woman who works in her house. It would surprise him to hear that I have already mentioned to Mrs. Cooper certain intimate details of my life, and that she has revealed to me a heartache about her husband.

"But I think I'll tell her," I say. "Not even a spray of balsam. I'd rather have her think us Godless than heartless."

My husband suggests, "Tell her about Chanukah"—which with us is humor, because he knows I wouldn't know what to tell.

Mrs. Cooper stands before my tub in the lighted kitchen. I lean in the doorway, watching her. The kitchen window is black. Outside, it is a freezing four o'clock. Inside, time is suspended, as always when the baby sleeps. I smell the hot, soaped flannel, wrung out and heaped on the drainboard, waiting to be rinsed in three pure waters. "We don't attend church," I say. "We go— at least, my husband goes—to a synagogue. My husband and I are Jewish, Mrs. Cooper."

Mrs. Cooper looks into the tub. After a moment, she says, "That is all right." She fishes below a cream of suds, pulls up a garment, and unrolls a mitten sleeve. She wrings it and rubs it and plunges it down to soak. Loving work, as she performs it—mother's work. As I watch, my body seems to pass into her body.

I am glad that my reluctance to speak of synagogues at all has led me to speak while Mrs. Cooper is working. That is the right way. We never, I realize while she scrubs, still seeming to be listening, talk face to face. She is always looking somewhere else—at the washing or the baby's toy she is going to pick up. Being a shy person, I have drilled myself to stare people in the eyes when I speak. But Mrs. Cooper convinces me this is wrong. The face-to-face stare is for selling something, or for saying, "Look here, I don't like you and I never have liked you," or for answering, "Oh, no, Madam, we never accept for refund after eight days."

The time Mrs. Cooper told me her husband had stopped going to church altogether, she was holding Susan, and she uttered those exquisite and grieved tones—"He will not go with me, or alone, or at all any more"—straight into the baby's face, not mine.

Mrs. Cooper now pulls the stopper from the tub and the suds choke down. While she is waiting, she casts a sidelong look at me, which I sense rather than see, as I am examining my apple core. She likes to see the expression on my face after I have spoken, though not while I speak. She looks back at the sucking tub.

When Mrs. Cooper comes again on Friday, she tells me, as she measures formula into bottles, "My husband says we do not believe Christmas is Christ's birthday."

I, of course, do not look at her, except to snatch a glance out of the corner of my eye, while I fold diapers unnecessarily. Her expression is calm and bland, high round cheekbones shining, slightly slanted eyes narrowed to the measuring. "He was born, we believe, sometime in April." After a bit, she adds, "We believe there is one God for everyone."

Though my husband has told me over and over again that this is what Jews say, Mrs. Cooper's words move me as though I have never heard them before. I murmur something about my work, and escape to my desk and my lance again.

Mrs. Cooper has quoted her husband to me several times. I am curious about him, as I am sure she is about my husband. She and my husband have at least met once or twice in the doorway, but I have only seen a snapshot of her husband: a stocky man with a mustache, who is as black as she, with no smiles for photographers. Mrs. Cooper has added, in the winter afternoons, certain details important to my picture.

Her husband plays cricket on Staten Island on Sundays and goes on vacations in the summer without her or the children, sometimes with the cricketers. But to balance that, he brings her shrimps and rice when he returns at 1:00 A.M. from cricket-club meetings on Friday nights. His opinion of the -bus strike in the city was that wages should go up but it was unfair to make bus riders suffer. About Elizabeth Taylor he thought it was all just nonsense; she was not even what he called pretty—more like skinny and ugly.

In most other respects, it seems to me, he is taking on the coloration of a zestful America-adopter. There are two kinds of immigrants, I observe. One kind loves everything about America, is happy to throw off the ways of the old country, and thereafter looks back largely with contempt. The other kind dislikes, compares, regrets, awakens to *Welt* and *Ichschmerz* and feels the new life mainly as a loss of the old. Often, the two marry each other.

Mr. Cooper, though he still plays cricket, now enjoys baseball, the fights on television, his factory job and union card, and the bustle and opportunity of New York. I mention this last with no irony. Mr. Cooper's job opportunities here are infinitely better than in Jamaica, where there aren't employers even to turn him down. He goes to school two nights a week for technical training. He became a citizen three years ago, destroying his wife's hopes of returning to Jamaica in their young years. But she dreams of going back when they are old. She would have servants there, she told me. "Because there aren't enough jobs, servants are cheap." Her husband, in her dream, would have a job, and so they would also have a car. And a quiet, gossipy life. She likes to move slowly, and this, as she herself points out, is very nice for my baby.

Christmas week comes, and we give Mrs. Cooper presents for her children. And since Christmas day falls on the last of her regular three days a week, we pay her for her holiday at the end of the second day. "Merry Christmas, Mrs. Cooper," I say. "Have a happy holiday."

Mrs. Cooper looks with interest at the baby in my arms, whom she had a moment before handed over to me. Suddenly she laughs and ducks her knees. Her fingers fly with unaccustomed haste to her cheek and she asks, "What must I say to you?"

"You can wish me the same," I say. "We have a holiday. My husband gets the day off, too."

I am glad that Mrs. Cooper has not grown reticent, since her embarrassment at Christmas, in speaking to me of holidays. Soon she is telling me how her children are looking forward to Easter. The oldest girl is preparing already for her part in a church play.

I fuss with the can of Enfamil, helping Mrs. Cooper this way when what I want is to help her another way. "Will your husband come to the play?" I ask casually.

"I am not sure," she says. After a while, "We haven't told him yet." Another little while. "Because it seems also he is against these plays." Then, with just enough of a pause to send those tones to my heart, she says, "I think he will not come."

Because the Judaeo-Christian tradition will have its little joke, Passover week sometimes coincides with Easter week, overlaying it like a reproach. It does the year Mrs. Cooper is with us. First, Good Friday, then in a few days is the first day of Passover.

"This year," my husband says, "because of Susie, to celebrate her first year with us, I want us to put a mezuzah outside our door before Passover."

"I'm not in favor." I manage to say it quietly.

"You don't understand enough about it," my husband says.

"I understand that much."

"Do you know what a mezuzah is? Do you know what's in it?" Taking my silence as an admission of ignorance, my, husband produces a Bible. "Deuteronomy," he says. He reads:

"Hear, 0 Israel: The Lord our God, the Lord is one Lord:
And thou shalt love the Lord thy God with all thine
     heart, and with all thy soul, and with all thy might.
And these words, which I command thee this day, shall
     be in thine heart:
And thou shalt teach them diligently unto thy children,
     and shalt talk of them when thou sittest in thine
     house, and when thou walkest by the way, and when
     thou liest down, and when thou risest up. . . ."

All this and more is written on a parchment that is rolled up tight and fitted into the metal or wooden mezuzah, which is no more than two inches high and less than half an inch across and is mounted on a base for fastening to the doorframe. My husband finishes his reading.

"And thou shalt write them upon the door-posts of
     thine house, and upon thy gates:
That your days may be multiplied, and the days of your

children, in the land which the Lord swore unto your fathers to give them, as the days of heaven upon the earth."

The words might move me if I allowed them to, but I will not allow them to.

My husband closes the Bible and asks, "What did your family observe? What was Passover like?"

"My grandfather sat on a pillow, and I was the youngest, so I found the matzos and he gave me money."

"No questions? No answers?"

"Just one. I would ask my grandfather, `Where is my prize?' And he would laugh and give me money."

"Is that all?" my husband asks.

"That was a very nice ceremony in itself," I say. "And I remember it with pleasure, and my grandfather with love!"

"But besides the food, besides the children's game. Didn't your grandparents observe anything?"

"I don't remember."

"You sat at their table for eighteen years!"

"Well, my grandmother lit Friday-night candles, and that was something I think she did all her life. But she did it by herself, in the breakfast room."

"Didn't they go to a synagogue?"

"My grandmother did. My grandfather did, too, but then I remember he stopped. He'd be home on holidays, not at the services."

"Your parents didn't tell you anything?"

"My parents were the next generation," I say. "And I'm the generation after that. We evolved," I say—and luckily that is also humor between my husband and me.

But my husband rubs his head. It's different now, and not so funny, because this year we have Susan.

My husband was born in Europe, of an Orthodox family. He is neither Orthodox nor Reform. He is his own council of rabbis, selecting as he goes. He has plenty to say about the influence of America on Jewishness, Orthodox or not. "The European Jew," my husband says, "didn't necessarily feel that if he rose in the social or economic scale he had to stop observing his Jewishness. There were even a number of wealthy and prominent German Jews who were strictly observant."

"I'm sure that helped them a lot!" This is as close as I come to speaking of the unspeakable. Somewhere in the monstrous testimony I have read about concentration camps and killings are buried the small, intense lives of my husband's family. But why is it I am more bitter than my husband about his own experiences? And why should my bitterness cut the wrong way? It is the word "German" that does it to me. 'My soul knots in hate. "German!" Even the softening, pathetic sound of "Jew" that follows it now doesn't help. All words fail. If I could grasp words, I would come on words that would jump so to life they would jump into my heart and kill me. All I can do is make a fantasy. Somewhere in New York I will meet a smiling German. In his pocket smile the best export accounts in the city—he is from the land of scissors and knives and ground glass. Because I am surprisingly fair, he will be oh, so surprised when I strike at him with all my might. "For the children! For the children!" My words come out shrieks. He protests it was his duty and, besides, he didn't know. I am all leaking, dissolving. How can a mist break stone? Once we exchange words it is hopeless; the words of the eyewitness consume everything, as in a fire:

> "The children were covered with sores.... They
> screamed and wept all night in the empty rooms
> where they had been put.... Then the police would

go up and the children, screaming with terror, would be carried kicking and struggling to the courtyard."

How is it my husband doesn't know that after this there can be no mezuzahs?

"It's too painful to quarrel," my husband says. He puts his hands on my shoulders, his forehead against mine. "This is something I want very much. And you feel for me. I know you feel for me in this."

"Yes, I do, of course I do." I use Mrs. Cooper's trick, and even at that close range twist my head elsewhere. "Only that particular symbol—"

"No, with you it's all the symbols." My husband drops his hands from my shoulders. "You don't know enough about them to discard them."

I don't have the right to judge them—that is what I feel he means. Since I was not even scorched by the flames of their futility. As he was, and came out cursing less than I.

"But besides everything else"—I take hasty shelter in practicalness—" a mezuzah is ugly. I remember that ugly tin thing nailed to the door of my grandmother's room. If I spend three weeks picking out a light fixture for my foyer, why should I have something so ugly on my door?"

Then, as my husband answers, I see that this shabby attack has fixed my defeat, because he is immediately reasonable. "Now, that's something else. I won't argue aesthetics with you. The outer covering is of no importance. I'll find something attractive."

The next night my husband brings home a mezuzah made in the East. It is a narrow green rectangle, twice the normal size, inlaid with mosaic and outlined in brass. It does not look Jewish to me at all. It looks foreign—a strange bit of green enamel and brass.

"I don't like it," I say. "I'm sorry."

"But it's only the idea you don't like?" My husband smiles teasingly. "In looks, you at least relent?"

"It doesn't look bad," I admit.

"Well, that is the first step." I am happy to see the mezuzah disappear in his dresser drawer before we go in to our dinner.

When Mrs. Cooper comes next day, she asks, "What have you on your door?"

I step out to look, and at first have the impression that a praying mantis has somehow hatched out of season high on our doorway. Then I recognize it. "Oh, that's . . ." I say. "That's . . ." I find I cannot explain a mezuzah to someone who has never heard of one.

While Mrs. Cooper changes her clothes, I touch the mezuzah to see if it will fall off. But my husband has glued it firmly to the metal doorframe.

My husband's office works a three-quarter day on Good Friday. I ask Mrs. Cooper if she would like time off, but she says no, her husband will be home ahead of her to look after things. I have the impression she would rather be here.

My husband comes home early, bestowing strangeness on the rhythm of the house in lieu of celebration. I kiss him and put away his hat. "Well, that was a nasty thing to do." I say it lazily and with a smirk. The lazy tone is to show that I am not really involved, and the smirk that I intend to swallow it down like bad medicine. He will have his way, but I will have my say—that's all I mean. My say will be humorous, with just a little cut to it, as is proper between husband and wife. He will cut back a little, with a grin, and after Mrs. Cooper goes we will have our peaceful dinner. The conversation will meander, never actually pricking sore points, but winding words about them, making pads and cushions, so that should they ever bleed, there, already softly wrapped around them, will be the bandages our words wove. Weave enough of these bandages and nothing will ever smash, I say. I always prepare in advance a last line, too, so that I will know where to stop. "When mezuzahs last in the doorway bloomed," I will say tonight. And then I expect us both to laugh.

But where has he been all day? The same office, the same thirty-minute subway ride to and from each way, the same lunch with the same cronies. . . . But he has traveled somewhere else in his head. "Doesn't anything mean anything to you?" he says, and walks by me to the bedroom.

I follow with a bandage, but it slips from my hand. "I know a lot of women who would have taken that right down!" It is something of a shout, to my surprise.

He says nothing.

"I left it up. All I wanted was my say."

He says nothing.

"I live here, too. That's my door also."

He says nothing.

"And I don't like it!"

I hear a loud smashing of glass. It brings both our heads up. My husband is the first to understand. "Mrs. Cooper broke a bottle." He puts his arms around me and says, "Let's not quarrel about a doorway. Let's not quarrel at all, but especially not about the entrance to our home."

I lower my face into his tie. What's a mezuzah? Let's have ten, I think, so long as nothing will smash.

Later, I reproach myself. I am in the living room, straightening piles of magazines, avoiding both kitchen and bedroom. A woman, I think, is the one creature who builds satisfaction of the pleasure she gets from giving in. What might the world be if women would continue the dialogue? But no, they must give in and be satisfied. Nevertheless, I don't intend to take back what I've given in on and thereby give up what I've gained.

I am aware of Mrs. Cooper, boiling formula in the kitchen, and of my baby, registering in sleep her parents' first quarrel since her birth. "What must I say to you?" I think of saying to my daughter—Mrs. Cooper's words come naturally to my mind.

I go to the kitchen doorway and look at Mrs. Cooper. Her face indicates deaf and dumb. She is finishing the bottles.

When Mrs. Cooper is dressed and ready to leave, she looks into the living room. "I am saying good night."

"I hope you and your family will have a happy Easter," I say, smiling for her.

I know in advance that Mrs. Cooper will ask, "What must I say to you?"

This time she asks it soberly, and this time my husband, who has heard, comes in to tell Mrs. Cooper the story of Passover. As always in the traditional version, there is little mention of Moses, the Jews having set down from the beginning not the tragedy of one but their intuition for the tragedy of many.

When my husband leaves us, Mrs. Cooper takes four wrapped candies from the candy bowl on the desk, holds them up to be sure I see her taking them, and puts them in her purse. "I do hope everything will be all right," she says.

"Oh, yes," I say, looking at the magazines. "It was such a help today. I got so much work done. Thank you."

I hear that she is motionless.

"I will not be like this all the days of my life." It is a cry from the heart, stunningly articulated. I lift my head from the magazines, and this time I do stare. Not be like what? A Jamaican without a servant? A wife who never vacations? An exile? A baby nurse? A woman who gives in? What Mrs. Cooper might not want to be flashes up in a lightning jumble. "I am going to find a church," she says, and strains her face away from mine.

I think of all the descriptions of God I have ever heard—that He is jealous, loving, vengeful, waiting, teaching, forgetful, permissive, broken-hearted, dead, asleep.

Mrs. Cooper and I wish each other a pleasant weekend.

Solid Food

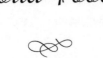

Lucy Rosenthal

SOME INCIDENTAL intelligence from the family archives:

In the early, carefree years of their marriage, Annette and Edward English were exotics, elegant and original, with equally original friends. Like the Russian émigré Mikail Ivanov, who with russet pencils sketched me, their baby, and rendered a glowing naked cherub, chin lifted, lying on her belly, with her feet raised, soles and all, to the air. Annette loved the drawing, loved the baby, loved Mikail, and she glued the sketch to the first page of the photograph album in which she kept the record of the baby's first year.

One day when Annette was introducing her baby to solid foods, and with no great margin of patience was mopping strained pear sauce from the baby's chin, her husband came in with a newspaper, and the mess the baby was making was upstaged by another one, more ramifying. The year was 1939. Dear, warm, ruddy Mikail, who loved his smokes, who sampled Edward's port, who loved his vodka, who loved the baby, who loved the Russian language and spoke broken English with a pure Moscow accent, was a Communist.

There was nothing wrong with that. Annette and Edward had their secret sympathies. It was an evil world, and from a safer distance but like their friend Mikail, Annette and Edward embraced the promise extended by the Union of Soviet Socialist Republics, the Hammer and Sickle.

Their devoted friend Mikail was an idealist, so much so that the signing of the Stalin-Hitler pact in August caused him to snap. For Stalin to shake hands and break bread with Hitler was too much for him.

As a gesture of protest, the newspaper said, Mikail Ivanov hired a private plane and a pilot who would fly him up over the city. High up over New York Harbor, Mikail Ivanov, whose real name was Walter Johnson, shot and killed the pilot, and the plane, after a brief moment's shudder, plunged straight into the water.

Both bodies were recovered later that night.

My mother wept: Mikail couldn't bear the bestial world. He killed a man, my father said. It was a sin to take another man with him.

But Mikail Ivanov had never existed. It developed that Walter Johnson didn't even speak Russian.

The true story emerged in the newspapers in the days that followed. Walter Johnson was nobody much. A petty thief, leaving under different names a trail of mostly misdemeanors, at first, which soon escalated into felonies. (My mother, at length, reported discovering some of her jewelry missing.) His brief career as a somebody had been in the false persona of Mikail Ivanov.

Shocked, grieved, on that first morning, even before all the facts were in, my mother left me in my high chair and stole into her bedroom. She unearthed the photograph album from the drawer where she kept it, and poking at dried glue, managed to remove the drawing from its place of honor in the album. It became, in her agitation, torn and crumpled.

Sitting in my high chair, with pear sauce caking on my chin and neck, I began to wail. My father lifted me and pressed me against his chest, indifferent to the stains that were being transferred to his shirt.

My mother returned and together they put me down, on their bed, while I cried on. Briefly, she left me to show my father what was left of the portrait. *Oh, no,* he said, why? It frightens me, she said, that he was so close to the baby. I won't allow any of this to touch her. It already has, said my father. Some time later, after a fashion, my mother restored the portrait with scotch tape.

It was thought that my father had persuaded her to do this. But it had nothing to do with my father at all. The fact is, my mother had been in love with Mikail Ivanov.

Some introduction to solid food, is all I can say.

Mrs. Saunders Writes to the World

Lynne Sharon Schwartz

MRS. SAUNDERS PLACED her white plastic bag of garbage in one of the cans behind the row of garden apartments and looked about for a familiar face, but finding nothing except two unknown toddlers with a babysitter in the playground a short distance off, she shrugged, gazed briefly into the wan early spring sun, and climbed the stairs back to her own door. She was looking for someone because she had a passion to hear her name spoken. But once inside, as she sponged her clean kitchen counter with concentrated elliptical strokes, she had to acknowledge that hearing "Mrs. Saunders" would not be good enough anymore. She needed—she had begun to long, in fact, with a longing she found frightening in its intensity—to hear her real name.

She squeezed the sponge agonizingly over the sink, producing a few meager drops. No one called her anything but Mrs.

Saunders now. Her name was Fran. Frances. She whispered it in the direction of the rubber plant on the windowsill. Fran, Franny, Frances.

Anyone seeing her, she thought, might suspect she was going crazy. Yet they said it was good to talk to your plants. She could always explain that she was whispering to them for their health and growth. Fran, Franny, Frances, she breathed again. Then she added a few wordless breaths, purely for the plants' sake, and felt somewhat less odd.

There was no one left to call her Fran. Her husband had called her Franny, but he was long dead. Her children, scattered across the country, called her Ma when they came at wide intervals to visit, or when she paid her yearly visit to each of the three. Except for Walter, she reminded herself, as she was fussy over accuracy, except for Walter, whom she saw only about once every year and a half, since he lived far away in Oregon and since his wife was what they called unstable and couldn't stand visitors too often or for too long a period.

Her old friends were gone or far off, and the new ones stuck to "Mrs. Saunders." The young people who moved in and out of these garden apartments thought of themselves as free and easy, she mused, but in fact they had their strange formalities, like always calling her Mrs. Saunders, even though they might run in two or three times a week to borrow groceries or ask her to babysit or see if she needed a lift to the supermarket. She pursed her lips in annoyance, regarded her impeccable living room, then pulled out the pack of cigarettes hidden in a drawer in the end table beside her chair. Mrs. Saunders didn't like these young girls who ran in and out to see her smoking; it wasn't seemly. She lit one and inhaled deeply, feeling a small measure of relief.

It wasn't that they were cold or unfriendly. Just that they didn't seem to realize she had a name like anyone else and might wish to hear it spoken aloud once in a while by someone other than herself in her darkened bedroom at night, or at full volume in the shower, mornings. And though she knew she could say to her new neighbors, "Call me Fran," as simply as that, somehow whenever the notion came to her the words got stuck in her throat. Then she lost the drift of the conversation and worried that the young people might think her strange, asking them to repeat things they had probably said perfectly clearly the first time. And if there was one thing she definitely did not want, she thought, stubbing the cigarette out firmly, it was to be regarded as senile. She had a long way to go before that.

Suddenly the air in the neat room seemed intolerably stuffy. Cigarette smoke hung in a cloud around her. Mrs. Saunders felt weak and terribly unhappy. She rose heavily and stepped out onto her small balcony for a breath of air. Jill was lounging on the next balcony with a friend.

"Oh, hi, Mrs. Saunders. How are you? Isn't it a gorgeous day?" Tall, blond, and narrow-shouldered, Jill drew in a lungful of smoke and pushed it out with pleasure.

"Hello, Jill dear. How's everything?"

"Struggling along." Jill stretched out her long jean-clad legs till her feet rested on the railing. "Mrs. Saunders, this is my friend, Wendy. Wendy, Mrs. Saunders. Mrs. Saunders has been so terrific to us," she said to Wendy. "And she never complains about the kids screeching on the other side of the wall."

"Hi," said Wendy.

"Nice to meet you, Wendy," said Mrs. Saunders. "I don't mind the children, Jill, really I don't. After all, I had children of my own. I know what it's like."

"That's right. Three, aren't there?"

"Yes," Mrs. Saunders said. "Walter, Louise, and Edith. Walter was named after his father."

"We named Jeff after his father, too," Wendy remarked.

"Mrs. Saunders sometimes babysits for Luke and Kevin," Jill explained to Wendy. "They adore her. Sometimes they even tell us to go out so she can come and stay with them. I don't know what it is you do with them, Mrs. Saunders."

She smiled, and would have liked to linger with the two young women, but suddenly she had to go in, because a furious sob rose in her throat, choking her. She threw herself down on the bed and wept uncontrollably into the plumped-up pillows. Everyone in the world had a name except her. And it would never change. Nobody here, at this stage in her life, was going to come along and start calling her Fran. Franny, surely never again. She remembered the days—they were never far from her mind—when her husband was sick and dying in the bedroom upstairs in the old house, and fifteen, maybe twenty times a day she would hear his rasping, evaporating voice calling, "Franny, Franny." She would drop everything each time to see what it was he wanted, and although she had loved him deeply, there were moments when she felt if she heard that rasping voice wailing out her name once more she would scream in exasperation; her fists would clench with the power and the passion to choke him. And yet now, wasn't life horribly cruel, she would give half her remaining days to hear her name wailed once more by him. Or by anyone else, for that matter. She gave in utterly to her despair and cried for a long time. She felt she might die gasping for breath if she didn't hear her own name.

At last she made an effort to pull herself together. She fixed the crumpled pillows so that they looked untouched, then went into the bathroom, washed her face and put on powder and lipstick, released her gray hair from its bun and brushed it out. It looked nice, she thought, long and still thick, thank God, falling down her back in a glossy, smooth sheet. Feeling young and girlish for a moment, she fancied herself going about with it loose and swinging, like Jill and Wendy and the other young girls.

Jauntily she tossed her head to right and left a few times and reveled in the swing of her hair. As a matter of fact it was better hair than Jill's, she thought, thicker, with more body. Except it was gray. She gave a secretive smile to the mirror and pinned her hair up in the bun again. She would go into town and browse around Woolworth's to cheer herself up.

Mrs. Saunders got a ride in with Jill, who drove past the shopping center every noon on her way to get Luke and Kevin at nursery school. In Woolworth's she bought a new bathmat, a bottle of shampoo and some cream rinse for her hair, a butane cigarette lighter, and last, surprising herself, two boxes of colored chalk. She couldn't have explained why she bought the chalk, but since it only amounted to fifty-six cents she decided it didn't need justification. The colors looked so pretty, peeking out from the open circle in the center of the box—lime, lavender, rose, yellow, beige, and powder blue. It was spring, and they seemed to go with the spring. It occurred to her as she took them from the display case that the pale yellow was exactly the color of her kitchen cabinets; she might use it to cover a patch of white that had appeared on one drawer after she scrubbed too hard with Ajax. Or she might give Luke and Kevin each a box, and buy them slates as well, to practice their letters and numbers. They were nice little boys, and she often gave them small presents or candy when she babysat.

Feeling nonetheless as though she had done a slightly eccentric thing, Mrs. Saunders meandered through the shopping center, wondering if there might be some sensible, inexpensive thing she needed. Then she remembered that the shoes she had on were nearly worn out. Certainly she was entitled to some lightweight, comfortable new shoes for spring. With the assistance of a civil young man, she quickly was able to find just the right pair. The salesman was filling out the slip. "Name, please?" he said. And then something astonishing happened. Hearing so unexpectedly the word that had been obsessing her gave Mrs. Saunders a great jolt, and, as she would look back on it later, seemed to loosen and shake out of its accustomed place a piece of her that rebelled against the suffocation she had been feeling for more years than she cared to remember.

She knew exactly the answer that was required, so that she could find reassurance afterwards in recalling that she had been neither mad nor senile. As the clerk waited with his pencil poised, the thing that was jolted loose darted swiftly through her body, producing vast exhilaration, and rose out from her throat to her lips.

"Frances."

She expected him to look at her strangely—it was strange, she granted that—and say, "Frances what?" And then, at long last she would hear it. It would be, she imagined, something like making love years ago with Walter, when in the dark all at once her body streamed and compressed to one place and exploded with relief and wonder. She felt a tinge of that same excitement now, as she waited. And it did not concern her that the manner of her gratification would be so pathetic and contrived, falling mechanically from the lips of a stranger. All that mattered was that the name be spoken.

"Last name, please." He did not even look up.

Mrs. Saunders gave it, and gave her address, and thought she would faint with disappointment. She slunk from the store and stood weakly against a brick wall outside. Was there to be no easing of this pain? Dazed, she stared hopelessly at her surroundings, which were sleek, buzzing with shoppers, and unappealing. She slumped and turned her face to the wall.

On the brick before her, in small letters, were scratched the words "Tony" and "Annette." An arrow went through them. Mrs. Saunders gazed for a long time, aware that she would be late meeting Jill, but not caring, for once. She broke the staple on the

Woolworth's bag, slipped her hand in, and drew out a piece of chalk. It turned out to be powder blue. Shielding her actions with her coat, she printed in two-inch-high letters on the brick wall outside the shoe store, FRANNY. Then she moved off briskly to the parking lot.

At home, after fixing herself a light lunch, which she ate excitedly and in haste, and washing the few dishes, she went back down to the garbage area behind the buildings. In lavender on the concrete wall just behind the row of cans, she wrote FRANNY. A few feet off she wrote again, FRANNY, and added WALTER, with an arrow through the names. But surveying her work, she took a tissue from her pocket and with some difficulty rubbed out WALTER and the arrow. Walter was dead. She was not senile yet. She was not yet one of those old people who live in a world of illusions.

Then she went to the children's playground, deserted at naptime, and wrote FRANNY in small letters on the wooden rail of the slide, on the wooden pillars of the newfangled jungle gym, and on the concrete border of the sandbox, in yellow, lavender, and blue, respectively. Choosing a quite private corner behind some benches, she crouched down and wrote the six letters of her name, using a different color for each letter. She regarded her work with a fierce, proud elation, and decided then and there that she would not, after all, give the chalk to Luke and Kevin. She was not sure, in fact, that she would ever give them anything else again.

The next week was a busy and productive one for Mrs. Saunders. She carried on her usual round of activities—shopping, cooking, cleaning her apartment daily, and writing to Walter, Louise, and Edith; evenings she babysat or watched television, and once attended a tenants' meeting on the subject of limited space for guest parking, though she possessed neither a car nor guests; she went to the bank to cash her social security check, as well as to a movie and to the dentist for some minor repair work on her bridge. But in addition to all this she went to the shopping center three times with Jill at noon, where, using caution, she managed to adorn several sidewalks and walls with her name.

She was not at all disturbed when Jill asked, "Anything special that you're coming in so often for, Mrs. Saunders? If it's anything I could do for you . . . "

"Oh, no, Jill dear." She laughed. "I'd be glad if you could do this for me, believe me. It's my bridge." She pointed to her teeth. "I've got to keep coming, he says, for a while longer, or else leave it with him for a few weeks, and then what would I do? I'd scare the children."

"Oh, no. Never that, Mrs. Saunders. Is it very painful?" Jill swerved around neatly into a parking space.

"Not at all. Just a nuisance. I hope you don't mind—"

"Don't be ridiculous, Mrs. Saunders. What are friends for?"

That day she was more busy than ever, for she had not only to add new FRANNYs but to check on the old. There had been a rainstorm over the weekend, which obliterated her name from the parking lot and the sidewalks. Also, a few small shopkeepers, specifically the butcher and the baker, evidently cleaned their outside walls weekly. She told Jill not to pick her up, for she might very likely be delayed, and as it turned out, she was. The constant problem of not being noticed was time-consuming, especially in the parking lot with its endless flow of cars in and out. Finished at last, she was amazed to find it was past two-thirty. Mrs. Saunders was filled with the happy exhaustion of one who has accomplished a decent and useful day's work. Looking about and wishing there were a comfortable place to rest for a while, she noticed that the window she was leaning against belonged to a paint store. Curious, she studied the cans and color charts. The colors were beautiful: vivid reds, blues, golds, and violets, infinitely more beautiful than her pastels. She had never cared much for pastels anyway. With a sly, physical excitement floating through her, Mrs. Saunders straightened up and entered.

She knew something about spray paint. Sukie, Walter's wife, had sprayed the kitchen chairs with royal blue down in the cellar last time Mrs. Saunders visited, nearly two years ago. She remembered it well, for Sukie, her hair, nose, and mouth covered with scarves, had called out somewhat harshly as Mrs. Saunders came down the steps, "For God's sake, stay away from it. It'll choke you. And would you mind opening some windows upstairs so when I'm done I can breathe?" Sukie was not a welcoming kind of girl. Mrs. Saunders sighed, then set her face into a smile for the paint salesman.

As she left the store contentedly with a shopping bag on her arm, she heard the insistent beep of a car horn. It was Jill. "Mrs. Saunders, hop in," she called. "I had a conference with Kevin's teacher," Jill explained, "and then the mothers' meeting to plan the party for the end of school, and after I dropped the kids at Wendy's I thought maybe I could still catch you."

Jill looked immensely pleased with her good deed, Mrs. Saunders thought, just as Louise and Edith used to look when they fixed dinner on her birthday, then sat beaming with achievement and waiting for praise, which she always gave in abundance.

"Isn't that sweet of you, Jill." But she was not as pleased as she tried to appear, for she had been looking forward to the calm bus ride and to privately planning when and where to use her new purchases. "You're awfully good to me."

"Oh, it's nothing, really. Buying paint?"

"Yes, I've decided to do the kitchen and bathroom."

"But they'll do that for you. Every two years. If you're due you just call the landlord and say so."

"But they don't use the colors I like and I thought it might be nice to try. . . ."

"It's true, they do make you pay a lot extra for colors," Jill said thoughtfully.

Mrs. Saunders studied the instructions on the cans carefully, and went over in her mind all the advice the salesman had given her. Late that evening after the family noises in the building had subsided, she took the can of red paint down to the laundry room in the basement. She also took four quarters and a small load of wash—the paint can was buried under the wash—in case she should meet anyone. She teased herself about this excessive precaution at midnight, but as it happened she did meet one of the young mothers, Nancy, pulling overalls and polo shirts out of the dryer.

"Oh, Mrs. Saunders! I was frightened for a minute. I didn't expect anyone down here so late. So you're another night owl, like me."

"Hello, Nancy. I meant to get around to this earlier, but it slipped my mind." She took the items out of her basket slowly, one by one, wishing Nancy would hurry.

"Since I took this part-time job I spend all my evenings doing housework. Sometimes I wonder if it's worth it." At last Nancy had the machine emptied. "Do you mind staying all alone? I could wait." She hesitated in the doorway, clutching her basket to her chest, pale and plainly exhausted.

"Oh no, Nancy dear. I don't mind at all, and anyhow, you look like you need some rest. Go on and get to sleep. I'll be fine."

She inserted her quarters and started the machine as Nancy disappeared. The clothes were mostly clean; she had grabbed any old thing to make a respectable-looking load. The extra washing wouldn't hurt them. With a tingling all over her skin and an irrepressible smile, she unsealed the can. Spraying was much easier than she had expected. The *F*, which she put on the wall behind the washer, took barely any time and effort. Paint dripped thickly from its upper left corner, though, indicating she had pressed too hard and too long. It was simple to adjust the pressure, and by the second *N* she felt quite confident, as if she had done this often before. She took a few steps back to look it over. It was beautiful—bold, thick, and bright against the cream-colored wall. So beautiful that she did another directly across the room. Then on the inside of the open door, rarely seen, she tried it vertically; aside from some long amateurish drips, she was delighted at the effect. She proceeded to the boiler room, where she sprayed FRANNY on the boiler and on the wall, then decided she had done enough for one night. Waiting for the laundry cycle to end, she was surrounded by the red, lustrous reverberations of her name, vibrating across the room at each other; she felt warmed and strengthened by the firm, familiar walls of her own self. While the room filled and teemed with visual echoes of FRANNY, Mrs. Saunders became supremely at peace.

She, climbed the stairs slowly, adrift in this happy glow. She would collect her things from the dryer late tomorrow morning. Lots of young mothers and children would have been in and out by then. Nancy was the only one who could suspect, but surely Nancy didn't come down with a load every day; besides, she was so tired and harassed she probably wouldn't remember clearly. Mrs. Saunders entered her apartment smiling securely with her secret.

Yet new difficulties arose over the next few days. The deserted laundry room at night was child's play compared to the more public, open, and populated areas of the development. Mrs. Saunders finally bought a large tote bag in Woolworth's so she could carry the paint with her and take advantage of random moments of solitude. There were frequent lulls when the children's playground was empty, but since it was in full view of the balconies and rear windows, only once, at four-thirty on a Wednesday morning, did she feel safe, working quickly and efficiently to complete her name five times. The parking lot needed to be done in the early hours too, as well as the front walk and the wall space near the mailboxes. It was astonishing, she came to realize, how little you could rely on being unobserved in a suburban garden apartment development, unless you stayed behind your own closed door.

Nevertheless, she did manage to get her name sprayed in half a dozen places, and she took to walking around the grounds on sunny afternoons to experience the fairly delirious sensation of her identity, secretly yet miraculously out in the open, sending humming rays toward her as she moved along. Wherever she went she encountered herself. Never in all her life had she had such a potent sense of occupying and making an imprint on the world around her. The reds and blues and golds seemed even to quiver and heighten in tone as she approached, as if in recognition and tribute, but this she knew was an optical illusion. Still, if only they could speak. Then her joy and fulfillment would be complete. After her walks she sat in her apartment and smoked and saw behind her closed eyes parades of brilliantly colored FRANNYs move along in the darkness, and felt entranced as with the warmth of a soothing physical embrace. Only once did she have a moment of unease, when she met Jill on her way back in early one morning.

"Mrs. Saunders, did anything happen? What's the red stuff on your fingers?"

"Just nail polish, dear. I spilled some."

Jill glanced at her unpolished nails and opened her mouth to speak, but apparently changed her mind.

"Fixing a run in a stocking," Mrs. Saunders added as she carried her shopping bag inside. She sensed potential danger in that meeting, yet also enjoyed a thrill of defiance and a deep, faint flicker of expectation.

Then one evening Harris, Jill's husband, knocked on Mrs. Saunders' door to tell her there would be a tenants' meeting tomorrow night in the community room.

"You must have noticed," he said, "the way this place has been deteriorating lately. I mean, when we first moved in four years ago it was brand-new and they took care of it. Now look! First of all there's this graffiti business. You must've seen it, haven't you? Every kid and his brother have got their names outside— it's as bad as the city. Of course that Franny character takes the cake, but the others are running her a close second. Then the garbage isn't removed as often as it used to be, the mailboxes are getting broken, there's been a light out for weeks in the hall. . . . I could go on and on."

She was afraid he would, too, standing there leaning on her doorframe, large and comfortably settled. Harris was an elementary-school teacher; Mrs. Saunders guessed he was in the habit of making long speeches. She smiled and wondered if she ought to ask him in, but she had left a cigarette burning in the ashtray. In fact she had not noticed the signs of negligence that Harris mentioned, but now that she heard, she was grateful for them. She felt a trifle weak in the knees; the news of the meeting was a shock. If he didn't stop talking soon she would ask him in just so she could sit down, cigarette or no cigarette.

"Anyhow," Harris continued, "I won't keep you, but I hope you'll come. The more participation, the better. There's power in numbers."

"Yes, I'll be there, Harris. You're absolutely right."

"Thanks, Mrs. Saunders. Good night." She was starting to close the door when he abruptly turned back. "And by the way, thanks for the recipe for angel food cake you gave Jill. It was great."

"Oh, I'm glad, Harris. You're quite welcome. Good night, now."

Of course she would go. Her absence would be noted, for she always attended the meetings, even those on less crucial topics. Beneath her surface nervousness the next day, Mrs. Saunders was aware of an abiding calm. Buoyed up by her name glowing almost everywhere she turned, she felt strong and impregnable as she took her seat in the community room.

"Who the hell is Franny anyway?" asked a man from the neighboring unit. "She started it all. Anyone here got a kid named Franny?" One woman had a Frances, but, she said, giggling, her Frances was only nine months old. Mrs. Saunders felt a throb of alarm in her chest. But she soon relaxed: the nameplates on her door and mailbox read "Saunders" only, and her meager mail, even the letters from Walter, Louise, and Edith, she had recently noticed, was all addressed to Mrs. F. Saunders or Mrs. Walter Saunders. And of course, since these neighbors had never troubled to ask. . . . She suppressed a grin. You make your own bed, she thought, watching them, and you lie in it.

The talk shifted to the broken mailboxes, the uncollected garbage, the inadequacy of guest parking, and the poor TV reception, yet every few moments it returned to the graffiti, obviously the most chafing symptom of decay. To Mrs. Saunders the progress of the meeting was haphazard, without direction or goal. As in the past, people seemed more eager to air their grievances than to seek a practical solution. But she conceded that her experience of community action was limited; perhaps this was the way things got done. In any case, their collective obtuseness appeared a more than adequate safeguard, and she remained silent. She always remained silent at tenants' meetings—no one would expect anything different of her. She longed for a cigarette, and inhaled deeply the smoke of others' drifting around her.

At last—she didn't know how it happened for she had ceased to pay attention—a committee was formed to draft a petition to the management listing the tenants' complaints and demanding repairs and greater surveillance of the grounds. The meeting was breaking up. They could relax, she thought wryly, as she milled about with her neighbors, moving to the door. She had done enough painting for now anyway. She smiled with cunning and some contempt at their innocence of the vandal in their midst. Certainly, if it upset them so much she would stop. They did have rights, it was quite true.

She walked up with Jill. Harris was still downstairs with the other members of the small committee which he was, predictably, chairing.

"Well, it was a good meeting," Jill said. " I only hope something comes out of it."

"Yes," said Mrs. Saunders vaguely, fumbling for her key in the huge, heavy tote bag.

"By the way, Mrs. Saunders . . ." Jill hesitated at her door and nervously began brushing the wispy hair from her face. "I've been meaning to ask, what's your first name again?"

In her embarrassment Jill was blinking childishly and didn't know where to look. Mrs. Saunders felt sorry for her. In the instant before she replied—and Mrs. Saunders didn't break the rhythm of question and answer by more than a second's delay—she grasped fully that she was sealing her own isolation as surely as if she had bricked up from inside the only window in a cell.

"Faith," she said.

The longing she still woke with in the dead of night, despite all her work, would never now be eased. But when, in that instant before responding, her longing warred with the rooted habits and needs of a respectable lifetime, she found the longing no match for the life. And that brief battle and its outcome, she accepted, were also, irrevocably, who Franny was.

The profound irony of this turn of events seemed to loosen some old, stiff knot in the joints of her body. Feeling the distance and wisdom of years rising in her like sap released, she looked at

Jill full in the face with a vast, unaccustomed compassion. The poor girl could not hide the relief that spread over her, like the passing of a beam of light.

"Isn't it funny, two years and I never knew," she stammered. "All that talk about names made me curious, I guess." Finally Jill turned the key in her lock and smiled over her shoulder. "Okay, good night, Mrs. Saunders. See you tomorrow night, right? The boys are looking forward to it."

The Reverse Bug

Lore Segal

"LET'S GET THE ANNOUNCEMENTS out of the way," said Ilka, the teacher, to her foreigners in Conversational English for Adults. "Tomorrow evening the institute is holding a symposium. Ahmed," she asked the Turkish student with the magnificently drooping mustache, who also wore the institute's janitorial keys hooked to his belt, "where are they holding the symposium?"

"In the New Theatre," said Ahmed.

"The theme," said the teacher, "is 'Should there be a statute of limitations on genocide?' with a wine-and-cheese reception—"

"In the lounge," said Ahmed.

"To which you are all invited. Now," Ilka said in the bright voice of a hostess trying to make a sluggish dinner party go, "what shall we talk about? Doesn't do me a bit of good, I know, to ask you all to come forward and sit in a nice cozy clump. Who would like to start us off? Tell us a story, somebody. We love stories. Tell the class how you came to America."

The teacher looked determinedly past the hand, the arm, with which Gerti Gruner stirred the air—death, taxes, and Thursdays, Gerti Gruner in the front row center. Ilka's eye passed over Paulino, who sat in the last row, with his back to the wall. Matsue, a pleasant, older Japanese from the university's engineering department, smiled at Ilka and shook his head, meaning "Please, not me!" Matsue was sitting in his usual place by the window, but Ilka had to orient herself as to the whereabouts of Izmira, the Cypriot doctor, who always left two empty rows between herself and Ahmed, the Turk. Today it was Juan, the Basque, who sat in the rightmost corner, and Eduardo, the Spaniard from Madrid, in the leftmost.

Ilka looked around for someone too shy to self-start who might enjoy talking if called upon, but Gerti's hand stabbed the air immediately underneath Ilka's chin, so she said, "Gerti wants to start. Go, Gerti. When did you come to the United States?"

"In last June," said Gerti.

Ilka corrected her, and said, "Tell the class where you came from, and, everybody, please speak in whole sentences."

Gerti said, "I have lived before in Uruguay."

"We would say, '*Before that I lived,*' " said Ilka, and Gerti said, "And *before that* in Vienna."

Gerti's story bore a family likeness to the teacher's own superannuated, indigestible history of being sent out of Hitler's Europe as a little girl.

Gerti said, "In the Vienna train station has my father told to me . . ."

"*Told me.*"

. "*Told me* that so soon as I am coming to Montevideo . . ."

Ilka said, "*As* soon as I *come,* or more colloquially, *get* to Montevideo..."

Gerti said, "*Get* to Montevideo, I should tell to all the people..."

Ilka corrected her. Gerti said, "*Tell* all the people to bring my father out from Vienna before come the Nazis and put him in concentration camp."

Ilka said, "In *the* or *a* concentration camp."

"Also my mother," said Gerti, "and my Opa, and my Oma, and my Onkel Peter, and the twins, Hedi and Albert. My father has told, 'Tell to the foster mother, 'Go, please, with me, to the American Consulate'"

"*My* father went to the American Consulate," said Paulino, and everybody turned and looked at him. Paulino's voice had not been heard in class since the first Thursday, when Ilka had got her students to go around the room and introduce themselves to one another. Paulino had said that his name was Paulino Patillo and that he was born in Bolivia. Ilka was charmed to realize it was Danny Kaye of whom Paulino reminded her—fair, curly, middle-aged, smiling. He came punctually every Thursday. Was he a very sweet or a very simple man?

Ilka said, "Paulino will tell us his story after Gerti has finished. How old were you when you left Europe?" Ilka asked, to reactivate Gerti, who said, "Eight years," but she and the rest of the class, and the teacher herself, were watching Paulino put his right hand inside the left breast pocket of his jacket, withdraw an envelope, turn it upside down, and shake out onto the desk before him a pile of news clippings. Some looked sharp and new, some frayed and yellow; some seemed to be single paragraphs, others the length of several columns.

"You got to Montevideo..." Ilka prompted Gerti.

"And my foster mother has fetched me from the ship. I said, 'Hello, and will you please bring out from Vienna my father before come the Nazis and put him in—*a* concentration camp!'" Gerti said triumphantly.

Paulino had brought the envelope close to his eyes and was looking inside. He inserted a forefinger, loosened something that was stuck, and shook out a last clipping. It broke at the fold when Paulino flattened it onto the desk top. Paulino brushed away the several paper crumbs before beginning to read: "La Paz, September 19."

"Paulino," said Ilka, "you must wait till Gerti is finished."

But Paulino read, "Señora Pilar Patillo has reported the disappearance of her husband, Claudio Patillo, after a visit to the American Consulate in La Paz on September 15."

"Gerti, go on," said Ilka.

"The foster mother has said, 'When comes home the Uncle from the office, we will ask.' I said, 'And bring out, please, also my mother, my Opa, my Oma, my Onkel Peter...'"

Paulino read, "A spokesman for the American Consulate contacted in La Paz states categorically that no record exists of a visit from Señor Patillo within the last two months...."

"Paulino, you really *have* to wait your turn," Ilka said.

Gerti said, "'Also the twins.' The foster mother has made such a desperate face with her lips."

Paulino read, "Nor does the consular calendar for September show any appointment made with Señor Patillo. Inquiries are said to be under way with the Consulate at Sucre." And Paulino folded his column of newsprint and returned it to the envelope.

"Okay, thank you, Paulino," Ilka said.

Gerti said, "When the foster father has come home, he said, 'We will see, tomorrow,' and I said, 'And will you go, please, with me, to the American Consulate?' and the foster father has made a face."

Paulino was flattening the second column of newsprint on his desk. He read, "New York, December 12 ..."

"*Paulino*," said Ilka, and caught Matsue's eye. He was looking expressly at her. He shook his head ever so slightly and with his right hand, palm down, he patted the air three times. In the intelligible language of charade with which humankind frustrated God at Babel, Matsue was saying, "Calm down, Ilka. Let Paulino finish. Nothing you can do will stop him." Ilka was grateful to Matsue.

"A spokesman for the Israeli Mission to the United Nations," read Paulino, "denies a report that Claudio Patillo, missing after a visit to the American Consulate in La Paz since September 15, is en route to Israel. . . ." Paulino finished reading this column also, folded it into the envelope, and unfolded the next column. "U.P.I., January 30. The car of Pilar Patillo, wife of Claudio Patillo, who was reported missing from La Paz last September, has been found at the bottom of a ravine in the eastern Andes. It is not known whether any bodies were found inside the wreck," Paulino read with the blind forward motion of a tank that receives no message from any sound or movement in the world outside. The students had stopped looking at Paulino; they were not looking at the teacher. They looked into their laps. Paulino read one column after the other, returning each to his envelope before he took the next, and when he had read and returned the last, and returned the envelope to his breast pocket, he leaned his back against the wall and turned to the teacher his sweet, habitual smile of expectant participation.

Gerti said, "In that same night have I woken up . . ."

"That night I *woke* up," the teacher helplessly said.

"*Woke* up," Gerti Gruner said, "and I have thought, What if it is even now, this exact minute, that one Nazi is knocking at the door, and I am here lying not telling to anybody anything, and I have stood up and gone into the bedroom where were sleeping the foster mother and father. Next morning has the foster mother gone with me to the refugee committee, and they found for me a different foster family."

"Your turn, Matsue," Ilka said. "How, when, and why did you come to the States? We're all here to help you!" Matsue's written English was flawless, but he spoke with an accent that was almost impenetrable. His contribution to class conversation always involved a communal interpretative act.

"Aisutudieddu attoza unibashite innu munhen," Matsue said.

A couple of stabs and Eduardo, the madrileño, got it: "You studied at the university in Munich!"

"You studied acoustics?" ventured Izmira, the Cypriot doctor.

"The war trapped you in Germany?" proposed Ahmed, the Turk.

"You have been working in the ovens," suggested Gerti, the Viennese.

"Acoustic ovens?" marveled Ilka. "Do you mean stoves? Ranges?"

No, what Matsue meant was that he had got his first job with a Munich firm employed in soundproofing the Dachau ovens so that what went on inside could not be heard on the outside. "I made the tapes," said Matsue. "Tapes?" they asked him. They figured out that Matsue had returned to Japan in 1946. He had collected Hiroshima "tapes." He had been brought to Washington as an acoustical consultant to the Kennedy Center, and had come to Connecticut to design the sound system of the New Theatre at Concordance University, where he subsequently accepted a research appointment in the department of engineering. He was now returning home; having finished his work— Ilka thought he said—on the reverse bug.

Ilka said, "I thought, ha ha, you said `the reverse bug'! "

"The reverse bug" was what everybody understood Matsue to say that he had said. With his right hand he performed a row of air loops, and, pointing at the wall behind the teacher's desk, asked for, and received, her okay to explain himself in writing on the blackboard.

Chalk in hand, he was eloquent on the subject of the regular bug, which can be introduced into a room to relay to those outside what those inside want them not to hear. A sophisticated modern bug, explained Matsue, was impossible to locate and deactivate. Buildings had had to be taken apart in order to rid them of alien listening-devices. The reverse bug, equally impossible to locate and deactivate, was a device whereby those outside were able to relay *into* a room what those inside would prefer not to have to hear.

"And how would such a device be used?" Ilka asked him.

Matsue was understood to say that it could be useful in certain situations to certain consulates, and Paulino said, "My father went to the American Consulate," and put his hand into his breast pocket. Here Ilka stood up, and, though there was still a good fifteen minutes of class time, said, "So! I will see you all next Thursday. Everybody—be thinking of subjects you would like to talk about. Don't forget the symposium tomorrow evening!" She walked quickly out the door.

Ilka entered the New Theatre late and was glad to see Matsue sitting on the aisle in the second row from the back with an empty seat beside him. The platform people were already settling into their places. On the right, an exquisite golden-skinned Latin man was talking, in a way people talk to people they have known a long time, with a heavy, rumpled man, whom Ilka pegged as Israeli. "Look at the thin man on the left," Ilka said to Matsue. "He has to be from Washington. Only a Washingtonian's hair gets to be that particular white color." Matsue laughed. Ilka asked him if he knew who the woman with the oversized glasses and the white hair straight to the shoulders might be, and Matsue said something that Ilka did not understand. The rest of the panelists were institute people, Ilka's colleagues—little Joe Bernstine from philosophy, Yvette Gordot, a mathematician, and Leslie Shakespere, an Englishman, the institute's new director, who sat in the moderator's chair.

Leslie Shakespere had the soft weight of a man who likes to eat and the fine head of a man who thinks. It had not as yet occurred to Ilka that she was in love with Leslie. She watched him fussing with the microphone. "Why do we need this?" she could read Leslie's lips saying. "Since when do we use microphones in the New Theatre?" Now he quieted the hall with a grateful welcome for this fine attendance at a discussion of one of our generation's unmanageable questions—the application of justice in an era of genocides.

Here Rabbi Shlomo Grossman rose from the floor and wished to take exception to the plural formulation: "All killings are not murders; all murders are not 'genocides.'"

Leslie said, "Shlomo, could you hold your remarks until question time?"

Rabbi Grossman said, "Remarks? Is that what I'm making? Remarks! The death of six million—is it in the realm of a question?"

Leslie said, "I give you my word that there will be room for the full expression of what you want to say when we open the discussion to the floor." Rabbi Grossman acceded to the evident desire of the friends sitting near him that he should sit down.

Director Leslie Shakespere gave the briefest of accounts of the combined federal and private funding that had enabled the Concordance Institute to invite these very distinguished panelists to take part in the institute's Genocide Project. "The institute, as you know, has a long-standing tradition of `debriefings,' in which the participants in a project that is winding down sum up their thinking for the members of the institute, the university, and the public. But this evening's panel has agreed, by way of an experiment, to talk in an informal way of our notions, of the history of the interest each of us brings to this question—problem—at the point of entry. I want us to interest ourselves in the *nature of inquiry:* Will we come out of this project with our original notions reinforced? Modified? Made over?

"I imagine that this inquiry will range somewhere between the legal concept of a statute of limitations that specifies the time within which human law must respond to a specific crime, and the Biblical concept of the visitation of punishment of the sins of the fathers upon the children. One famous version plays itself out in the 'Oresteia,' where a crime is punished by an act that is itself a crime and punishable, and so on, down the generations. Enough. Let me introduce our panel, whom it will be our very great pleasure to have among us in the coming months."

The white-haired man turned out to be the West German ex-mayor of Obernpest, Dieter Dobelmann. Ilka felt the prompt conviction that she had known all along—that one could tell from a mile—that that mouth, that jaw, had to be German. Leslie dwelled on Dobelmann's persuasive anti-Nazi credentials. The woman with the glasses was on loan to the institute from Georgetown University. ("The white hair! You see!" Ilka whispered to Matsue, who laughed.) She was Jerusalem-born Shulamit Gershon, professor of international law, and longtime adviser to Israel's ongoing project to identify Nazi war criminals and bring them to trial. The rumpled man was the English theologian William B. Thayer. The Latin really was a Latin—Sebastian Maderiaga, who was taking time off from his consulate in New York. Leslie squeezed his eyes to see past the stage lights into the well of the New Theatre. There was a rustle of people turning to locate the voice that had said, "My father went to the American Consulate," but it said nothing further and the audience settled back. Leslie introduced Yvette and Joe, the institute's own fellows assigned to Genocide.

Ilka and Matsue leaned forward, watching Paulino across the aisle. Paulino was withdrawing the envelope from his breast pocket. "Without a desk?" whispered Ilka anxiously. Paulino upturned the envelope onto the slope of his lap. The young student sitting beside him got on his knees to retrieve the sliding batch of newsprint and held onto it while Paulino arranged his coat across his thighs to create a surface.

"My own puzzle," said Leslie, "with which I would like to puzzle our panel, is this: Where do I, where do we all, get these feelings of moral malaise when wrong goes unpunished and right goes unrewarded?"

Paulino had brought his first newspaper column up to his eyes and read, "La Paz, September 19. Senora Pilar Patillo has reported the disappearance of her husband, Claudio Patillo..."

"Where," Leslie was saying, "does the human mind derive its expectation of a set of consequences for which it finds no evidence whatsoever in nature or in history, or in looking around its own autobiography?... Could *I please* ask for quiet from the floor until we open the discussion?" Leslie was once again peering out into the hall.

The audience turned and looked at Paulino reading, "Nor does the consular calendar for September show any appointment..." Shulamit Gershon leaned toward Leslie and spoke to him for several moments while Paulino read, "A spokesman for the Israeli Mission to the United Nations denies a report..."

It was after several attempts to persuade him to stop that Leslie said, "Ahmed? Is Ahmed in the hall? Ahmed, would you be good enough to remove the unquiet gentleman as gently as necessary force will allow. Take him to my office, please, and I will meet with him after the symposium."

Everybody watched Ahmed walk up the aisle with a large and sheepish-looking student. The two lifted the unresisting Paulino out of his seat by the armpits. They carried him reading, "The car of Pilar Patillo, wife of Claudio Patillo . . ."—backward, out the door.

The action had something about it of the classic comedy routine. There was a cackling, then the relief of general laughter. Leslie relaxed and sat back, understanding that it would require some moments to get the evening back on track, but the cackling did not stop. Leslie said, "Please." He waited. He cocked his head and listened: it was more like a hiccupping that straightened and elongated into a sound drawn on a single breath. Leslie looked at the panel. The panel looked. The audience looked all around. Leslie bent his ear down to the microphone. It did him no good to turn the button off and on, to put his hand over the mouthpiece, to bend down as if to look it in the eye. "Anybody know—is the sound here centrally controlled?" he asked. The noise was growing incrementally. Members of the audience drew their heads back and down into their shoulders. It came to them—it became impossible to not know—that it was not laughter to which they were listening but somebody yelling. Somewhere there was a person, and the person was screaming.

Ilka looked at Matsue, whose eyes were closed. He looked an old man.

The screaming stopped. The relief was spectacular, but lasted only for that same unnaturally long moment in which a howling child, having finally exhausted its strength, is fetching up new breath from some deepest source for a new onslaught. The howl resumed at a volume that was too great for the small theatre; the human ear could not accommodate it. People experienced a physical distress. They put their hands over their ears.

Leslie had risen. He said, "I'm going to suggest an alteration in the order of this evening's proceedings. Why don't we clear the hall—everybody, please, move into the lounge, have some wine, have some cheese while we locate the source of the trouble."

Quickly, while people were moving along their rows, Ilka popped out into the aisle and collected the trail of Paulino's news clippings. The young student who had sat next to Paulino found and handed her the envelope. Ilka walked down the hall in the direction of Leslie Shakespere's office, diagnosing in herself an inappropriate excitement at having it in her power to throw light.

Ilka looked into Leslie's office. Paulino sat on a hard chair with his back to the door, shaking his head violently from side to side. Leslie stood facing him. He and Ahmed and all the panelists, who had disposed themselves about Leslie's office, were screwing their eyes up as if wanting very badly to close every bodily opening through which unwanted information is able to enter. The intervening wall had somewhat modified the volume, but not the variety—length, pitch, and pattern—of the sounds that continually altered as in response to a new and continually changing cause.

Leslie said, "We know this stuff goes on whether we are hearing it or not, but this . . . " He saw Ilka at the door and said, "Mr. Patillo is your student, no? He refuses to tell us how to locate the screaming unless they release his father."

Ilka said, "*Paulino?* Does Paulino *say* he 'refuses'?"

Leslie said to Paulino, "Will you please tell us how to find the source of this noise so we can shut it off?"

Paulino shook his head and said, "It is my father screaming."

Ilka followed the direction of Leslie's eye. Maderiaga was perched with a helpless elegance on the corner of Leslie's desk, speaking Spanish into the telephone. Through the open door that led into a little outer office, Ilka saw Shulamit Gershon hang up the phone. She came back in and said, "Patillo is the name this young man's father adopted from his Bolivian wife. He's Klaus Herrmann, who headed the German Census Bureau.

After the Anschluss they sent him to Vienna to put together the registry of Jewish names and addresses. Then on to Budapest, and so on. After the war we traced him to La Paz. I think he got into trouble with some mines or weapons deals. We put him on the back burner when it turned out the Bolivians were after him as well."

Now Maderiaga hung up and said, "Hasn't he been the busy little man! My office is going to check if it's the Gonzales people who got him for expropriating somebody's tin mine, or the R.R.N. If they suspect Patillo of connection with the helicopter crash that killed President Barrientos, they'll have more or less killed him."

"It is my father screaming," said Paulino.

"It's got nothing to do with his father," said Ilka. While Matsue was explaining the reverse bug on the blackboard the previous evening, Ilka had grasped the principle. It disintegrated as she was explaining it to Leslie. She was distracted, moreover, by a retrospective image: Last night, hurrying down the corridor, Ilka had turned her head and must have seen, since she was now able to recollect, young Ahmed and Matsue moving away together down the hall. If Ilka had thought them a curious couple, the thought, having nothing to feed on, had died before her lively wish to maneuver Gerti and Paulino into one elevator just as the doors were closing, so she could come down in the other.

Now Ilka asked Ahmed, "Where did you and Matsue go after class last night?"

Ahmed said, "He wanted to come into the New Theatre."

Leslie said, "Ahmed, forgive me for ordering you around all evening, but will you go and find me Matsue and bring him here to my office?"

"He has gone," said Ahmed. "I saw him leave by the front door with a suitcase on wheels."

"He is going home," said Ilka. "Matsue has finished his job."

Paulino said, "It is my father screaming."

"No, it's not, Paulino," said Ilka. "Those screams are from Dachau and they are from Hiroshima."

"It is my father," said Paulino, "and my mother."

Leslie asked Ilka to come with him to the airport. They caught up with Matsue queuing, with only five passengers ahead of him, to enter the gangway to his plane.

Ilka said, "Matsue, you're not going away without telling us how to shut the thing off!"

Matsue said, "Itto dozunotto shattoffu."

Ilka and Leslie said, "Excuse me?"

With the hand that was not holding his boarding pass, Matsue performed a charade of turning a faucet and he shook his head. Ilka and Leslie understood him to be saying, "It does not shut off." Matsue stepped out of the line, kissed Ilka on the cheek, stepped back, and passed through the door.

When Concordance Institute takes hold of a situation, it deals humanely with it. Leslie found funds to pay a private sanitarium to evaluate Paulino. Back at the New Theatre, the police, a bomb squad, and a private acoustics company from Washington set themselves to locate the source of the screaming.

Leslie looked haggard. His colleagues worried when their director, a sensible man, continued to blame the microphone after the microphone had been removed and the screaming continued. The sound seemed not to be going to loop back to any familiar beginning, so that the hearers might have become familiar—might, in a manner of speaking, have made friends—with one particular roar or screech, but to be going on to perpetually new and fresh howls of pain.

Neither the Japanese Embassy in Washington nor the

American Embassy in Tokyo had got anywhere with the tracers sent out to locate Matsue. Leslie called in a technician. "Look into the wiring!" he said, and saw in the man's eyes that look experts wear when they have explained something and the layman says what he said in the beginning all over again. The expert had another go. He talked to Leslie about the nature of the sound wave; he talked about cross-Atlantic phone calls and about the electric guitar. Leslie said, "Could you look *inside* the wiring?"

Leslie fired the first team of acoustical experts, found another company, and asked them to check inside the wiring. The new man reported back to Leslie: He thought they might start by taking down the stage portion of the theatre. If the sound people worked closely with the demolition people, they might be able to avoid having to mess with the body of the hall.

The phone call that Maderiaga had made on the night of the symposium had, in the meantime, set in motion a series of official acts that were bringing to America—to Concordance—Paulino Patillo's father, Claudio/Klaus Patillo/Herrmann. The old man was eighty-nine, missing an eye by an act of man and a lung by an act of God. On the plane he suffered a collapse and was rushed from the airport straight to Concordance University's Medical Center.

Rabbi Grossman walked into Leslie's office and said, "Am I hearing things? You've approved a house, on this campus, for the accomplice of the genocide of Austrian and Hungarian Jewry?"

"And a private nurse!" said Leslie.

"Are you out of your mind?" asked Rabbi Grossman.

"Practically. Yes," said Leslie.

"You look terrible," said Shlomo Grossman, and sat down.

"What," Leslie said, "am I the hell to do with an old Nazi who is postoperative, whose son is in the sanitarium, who doesn't know a soul, doesn't have a dime, doesn't have a roof over his head?"

"Send him home to Germany," shouted Shlomo.

"I tried. Dobelmann says they won't recognize Claudio Patillo as one of their nationals."

"So send him to his comeuppance in Israel!"

"Shulamit says they're no longer interested, Shlomo! They have other things on hand!"

"Put him back on the plane and turn it around."

"For another round of screaming? Shlomo!" cried Leslie, and put his hands over his ears against the noise that, issuing out of the dismembered building materials piled in back of the institute, blanketed the countryside for miles around, made its way down every street of the small university town, into every back yard, and filtered in through Leslie's closed and shuttered windows. "Shlomo," Leslie said, "come over tonight. I promise Eliza will cook you something you can eat. I want you, and I want Ilka— and we'll see who all else—to help me think this thing through."

"We . . . I," said Leslie that night, "need to understand how the scream of Dachau is the same, and how it is a different scream from the scream of Hiroshima. And after that I need to learn how to listen to the selfsame sound that rises out of the Hell in which the torturer is getting what he's got coming. . . ."

His wife called, "Leslie, can you come and talk to Ahmed?"

Leslie went out and came back in carrying his coat. A couple of young punks with an agenda of their own had broken into Patillo/Herrmann's new American house. They had gagged the nurse and tied her and Klaus up in the new American bathroom. Here Ilka began to laugh. Leslie buttoned his coat and said, "I'm sorry, but I have to go on over. Ilka, Shlomo, please, I leave for Washington tomorrow, early, to talk to the Superfund people. While I'm there I want to get a Scream Project funded. Ilka? Ilka, what is it?" But Ilka was helplessly giggling and could not answer him. Leslie said, "What I need is for you two to please sit down, here and now, and come up with a formulation I can take with me to present to Arts and Humanities."

The Superfund granted Concordance an allowance, for scream disposal, and the dismembered stage of the New Theatre was loaded onto a flatbed truck and driven west. The population along Route 90 and all the way down to Arizona came out into the street, eyes squeezed together, heads pulled back and down into shoulders. They buried the thing fifteen feet under, well away from the highway, and let the desert howl.

Lazar Malkin
Enters Heaven

Steve Stern

MY FATHER-IN-LAW, Lazar Malkin, may he rest in peace, refused to die. This was in keeping with his lifelong stubbornness. Of course there were those who said that he'd passed away already and come back again, as if death were another of his so-called peddling trips, from which he always returned with a sackful of crazy gifts.

There were those in our neighborhood who joked that he'd been dead for years before his end. And there was more than a little truth in this. Hadn't he been declared clinically kaput not once but twice on the operating table? Over the years they'd extracted more of his internal organs than it seemed possible to do without. And what with his wooden leg, his empty left eye socket concealed by a gabardine patch, his missing teeth, and sparse white hair, there was hardly enough of old Lazar left in this world to constitute a human being.

"Papa," my wife, Sophie, once asked him, just after the first of his miraculous recoveries, "what was it like to be dead?" She was sometimes untactful, my Sophie, and in this she took after her father—whose child she was by one of his unholy alliances. (Typically obstinate, he had always refused to marry.)

Lazar had looked at her with his good eye, which, despite being set in a face like last week's roast, was usually wet and amused.

"Why ask me?" he wondered, refusing to take the question seriously. "Ask Alabaster the cobbler, who ain't left his shop in fifty years. He makes shoes, you'd think he's building coffins. Ask Petrofsky whose lunch counter serves nobody but ghosts. Ask Gruber the shammes or Milstein the tinsmith. Ask your husband, who is as good as wearing his sewing machine around his neck..."

I protested that he was being unfair, though we both knew that he wasn't. The neighborhood, which was called the Pinch, had been dead since the War. Life and business had moved east, leaving us with our shops falling down around our ears. Myself and the others, we kidded ourselves that North Main Street would come back. Our children would come back again. The ready-made industry, we kept insisting, was just a passing fancy; people would return to quality. So who needed luftmenschen like Lazar to remind us that we were deceived?

"The Pinch ain't the world," he would inform us, before setting off on one of his mysterious peddling expeditions. He would haul himself into the cab of his corroded relic of a truck piled with shmattes and tools got on credit from a local wholesale outfit. Then he would sputter off in some random direction for points unknown.

Weeks later he would return, his pockets as empty as the bed of his truck. But he always brought back souvenirs in his burlap sack, which he prized like the kid in the story who swapped a cow for a handful of beans.

"I want you to have this," he would say to Mr. Alabaster or Gruber or Schloss or myself. Then he would give us a harp made out of a crocodile's tail; he would give us a Negro's toe, a root that looked like a little man, a contraption called a go-devil, a singletree, the uses of which he had no idea. "This will make you wise," he told us. "This will make you amorous. This came from Itta Bena and this from Nankipoo"—as if they were places as far away as China, which for all we knew they were.

"Don't thank me," he would say, like he thought we might be speechless with gratitude. Then he would borrow a few bucks and limp away to whatever hole in the wall he was staying in.

Most of my neighbors got rid of Lazar's fetishes and elixirs, complaining that it made them nervous to have them around. I was likewise inclined, but in deference to my wife I kept them. Rather than leave them lying around the apartment, however, I tossed them into the storage shed behind my shop.

No one knew how old Lazar really was, though it was generally agreed that he was far past the age when it was still dignified to be alive. None of us, after all, was a spring chicken anymore. We were worn out from the years of trying to supplement our pensions with the occasional alteration or the sale of a pair of shoelaces. If our time should be near, nobody was complaining. Funerals were anyhow the most festive occasions we had in the Pinch. We would make a day of it, traveling in a long entourage out to the cemetery, then back-to North Main for a feast at the home of the bereaved. You might say that death was very popular in our neighborhood. So it aggravated us that Lazar, who preceded us by a whole generation, should persist in hanging around.

He made certain that most of what we knew about him was hearsay. It was his nature to be mysterious. Even Sophie, his daughter by one of his several scandals, knew only the rumors.

As to the many versions of his past, she would tell me to take my pick. "I would rather not, if you don't mind," I said. The idea of Lazar Malkin as a figure of romance was a little more than I could handle. But that never stopped Sophie from regaling me by telling stories of her father the way another woman might sing to herself.

He lost his eye as a young man, when he refused to get out of the way of a rampaging Cossack in his village of Podolsk. Walking away from Kamchatka, where he'd been sent for refusing to be drafted into the army of the Czar, the frostbite turned to gangrene and he lost his leg. Or was it the other way around? He was dismembered by a Cossack, snowblinded in one eye for good? . . . What did it matter? The only moral I got out of the tales of Lazar's mishegoss was that every time he refused to do what was sensible, there was a little less of him left to refuse with.

It puzzled me that Sophie could continue to have such affection for the old kocker. Hadn't he ruined her mother, among others, at a time when women did not go so willingly to their ruin? Of course, the living proofs of his wickedness were gone now. His old mistresses had long since passed on, and it was assumed there were no offspring other than Sophie. Though sometimes I was haunted by the thought of the surrounding countryside populated by the children of Lazar Malkin.

So what was the attraction? Did the ladies think he was some pirate with his eye patch and clunking artificial leg? That one I still find hard to swallow. Or maybe they thought that with him it didn't count. Because he refused to settle down to any particular life, it was as if he had no legitimate life at all. None worth considering in any case. And I cursed myself for the time I took to think about him, an old fool responsible for making my wife a bastard though who could think of Sophie in such a light?

"You're a sick man, Lazar," I told him, meaning in more ways than one. "See a doctor."

"I never felt better, I'll dance on your grave," he insisted, asking me incidentally did I have a little change to spare.

I admit that this did not sit well with me, the idea of his hobbling a jig on my headstone. Lie down already and die, I thought, God forgive me. But from the way he'd been lingering in the neighborhood lately, postponing his journeys, it was apparent to whoever noticed that something was wrong. His unshaven face was the gray of dirty sheets, and his wizened stick of a frame was shrinking visibly. His odor, no longer merely the ripe stench of the unwashed, had about it a musty smell of decay. Despite my imploring, he refused to see a physician, though it wasn't like he hadn't been in the hospital before. (Didn't I have a bundle of his unpaid bills to prove it?) So maybe this time he knew that for what he had there wasn't a cure.

When I didn't see him for a while, I supposed that, regardless of the pain he was in, he had gone off on another of his peddling trips.

"Your father needs a doctor," I informed Sophie over dinner one night.

"He won't go," she said, wagging her chins like what can you do with such a man. "So I invited him to come stay with us."

She offered me more kreplach, as if my wide-open mouth meant that I must still be hungry. I was thinking of the times he'd sat at our table in the vile, moth-eaten overcoat he wore in all seasons. I was thinking of the dubious mementos he left us with.

"Don't worry," said my good wife, "he won't stay in the apartment . . ."

"Thank God."

". . . But he asked if he could have the shed out back."

"I won't have it!" I shouted, putting my foot down. "I won't have him making a flophouse out of my storehouse."

"Julius," said Sophie in her watch-your-blood-pressure tone of voice, "he's been out there a week already."

I went down to the little brick shed behind the shop. The truth was that I seldom used it—only to dump the odd bolt of material and the broken sewing machines that I was too attached to to throw away. And Lazar's gifts. Though I could see through the window that an oil lamp was burning beneath a halo of mosquitoes, there was no answer to my knock. Entering anyway, I saw cobwebs, mouse droppings, the usual junk—but no Lazar.

Then I was aware of him propped in a chair in a corner, his burlap sack and a few greasy dishes at his feet. It took me so long to notice because I was not used to seeing him sit still. Always he was hopping from his real leg to his phony, being a nuisance, telling us we ought to get out and see more of the world. Now with his leg unhitched and lying across some skeins of mildewed cloth, I could have mistaken him for one of my discarded manikins.

"Lazar," I said, "in hospitals they at least have beds."

"Who sleeps?" he wanted to know, his voice straining up from his hollow chest. This was as much as admitting his frailty. Shocked out of my aggravation, I proceeded to worry.

"You can't live in here," I told him, thinking that no one would confuse this with living. "Pardon my saying so, but it stinks like Gehinom." I had observed the coffee tin he was using for a slop jar.

"A couple of days," he managed in a pathetic attempt to recover his native chutzpah, "and I'll be back on my feet again. I'll hit the road." When he coughed, there was dust, like when you beat a rug.

I looked over at one of the feet that he hoped to be back on and groaned. It might have been another of his curiosities, taking its place alongside of the boar's tusk and the cypress knee.

"Lazar," I implored, astonished at my presumption, "go to heaven already. Your organs and limbs are waiting there for a happy reunion. What do you want to hang around this miserable place anyway?" I made a gesture intended to take in more than the shed, which included the whole of the dilapidated Pinch with its empty shops and abandoned synagogue. Then I understood that for Lazar my gesture had included even more. It took in the high roads to luka and Yazoo City, where the shwartzers swapped him moonshine for a yard of calico.

"Heaven," he said in a whisper that was half a shout, turning his head to spit on the floor. "Heaven is wasted on the dead. Anyway, I like it here."

Feeling that my aggravation had returned, I started to leave.

"Julius," he called to me, reaching into the sack at his feet, extracting with his withered fingers I don't know what—some disgusting composition of feathers and bones and hair. "Julius," he wheezed in all sincerity, "I have something for you."

What can you do with such a man?

I went back the following afternoon with Dr. Seligman. Lazar told the doctor don't touch him, and the doctor shrugged like he didn't need to dirty his hands.

"Malkin," he said, "this isn't becoming. You can't borrow time the way you borrow gelt."

Seligman was something of a neighborhood philosopher. Outside the shed he assured me that the old man was past worrying about. "If he thinks he can play hide-and-go-seek with death, then let him. It doesn't hurt anybody but himself." He had such a way of putting things, Seligman.

"But Doc," I said, still not comforted, "it ain't in *your* backyard that he's playing his farkokte game."

It didn't help, now that the word was out, that my so-called friends and neighbors treated me like I was confining old Lazar against his will. For years they'd wished him out of their hair, and now they behaved as if they actually missed him. Nothing was the same since he failed to turn up at odd hours in their shops, leaving them with some ugly doll made from corn husks or a rabbit's foot.

"You think I like it," I asked them, "that the old fortz won't get it over with?" Then they looked at me like it wasn't nice to take his name in vain.

Meanwhile Sophie continued to carry her noodle puddings and bowls of chicken broth out to the shed. She was furtive in this activity, as if she was harboring an outlaw, and sometimes I thought she enjoyed the intrigue. More often than not, however, she brought back her plates with the food untouched.

I still looked in on him every couple of-days, though it made me nauseous. It spoiled my constitution, the sight of him practically decomposing.

"You're sitting shivah for yourself, that's what," I accused him, holding my nose. When he bothered to communicate, it was only in grunts.

I complained to Sophie: "I was worried a flophouse, but charnel house is more like it."

"Shah!" she said, like it mattered whether the old so-and-so could hear us. "Soon he'll be himself again." I couldn't believe my ears.

"Petrofsky," I confided at his lunch counter the next day, "my wife's as crazy as Lazar. She thinks he's going to get well."

"So why you got to bury him before his time?"

Petrofsky wasn't the only one to express this sentiment. It was contagious. Alabaster, Ridblatt, Schloss, they were all in the act, all of them suddenly defenders of my undying father-in-law. If I so much as opened my mouth to kvetch about the old man, they told me hush up, they spat against the evil eye. "But only yesterday you said it's unnatural he should live so long," I protested.

"Doc," I told Seligman in the office where he sat in front of a standing skeleton, "the whole street's gone crazy. They think that maybe a one-legged corpse can dance again."

The doctor looked a little nervous himself, like somebody might be listening. He took off his nickel-rimmed spectacles to speak.

"Maybe they think that if the angel of death can pass over Lazar, he can pass over the whole neighborhood."

"Forgive me, Doctor, but you're crazy too. Since when is everyone so excited to preserve our picturesque community? And anyway, wouldn't your angel look first in an open grave, which after all is what the Pinch has become." Then I was angry with myself for having stooped to speaking in riddles, too.

But in the end I began to succumb to the general contagion. I was afraid for Lazar, I told myself, though—who was I kidding?—like the rest, I was afraid for myself.

"Sophie," I confessed to my wife, who had been treating me like a stranger lately, "I wish that old Lazar was out peddling again." Without him out wandering in the boondocks beyond our neighborhood, returning with his cockamamie gifts, it was like there wasn't a "beyond" anymore. The Pinch, for better or worse, was all there was. This I tried to explain to my Sophie, who squeezed my hand like I was her Julius again.

Each time I looked in on him, it was harder to distinguish the immobile Lazar from the rest of the dust and drek. I described this to Seligman, expecting medical opinion, and got only that it put him in mind of the story of the golem—dormant and moldering in a synagogue attic these six hundred years.

Then there was a new development. There were bits of cloth

sticking out of the old man's nostrils and ears, and he refused to open his mouth at all.

"It's to keep his soul from escaping," Sophie told me, mussing my hair as if any ninny could see that. I groaned and rested my head in my hands, trying not to imagine what other orifices he might have plugged up.

After that I didn't visit him anymore. I learned to ignore Sophie, with her kerchief over her face against the smell, going to and fro with the food he refused to eat. I was satisfied it was impossible that he should still be alive, which fact made it easier to forget about him for periods of time.

This was also the tack that my friends and neighbors seemed to be taking. On the subject of Lazar Malkin we had all become deaf and dumb. It was like he was a secret we shared, holding our breaths lest someone should find us out.

Meanwhile on North Main Street it was business (or lack of same) as usual.

Of course I wasn't sleeping so well. In the middle of the night I remembered that, among the items and artifacts stored away in my shed, there was my still breathing father-in-law. This always gave an unpleasant jolt to my system. Then I would get out of bed and make what I called my cocktail—some antacid and a shpritz of soda water. It was summer and the rooms above the shop were an oven, so I would go out to the open back porch for air. I would sip my medicine, looking down at the yard and the shed where Lazar's lamp had not been kindled for a while.

On one such night, however, I observed that the lamp was burning again. What's more, I detected movement through the little window. Who knew but some miracle had taken place and Lazar was up again? Shivering despite the heat, I grabbed my bathrobe and went down to investigate.

I tiptoed out to the shed, pressed my nose against the filthy windowpane, and told myself that I didn't see what I saw. But while I bit the heel of my hand to keep from crying out loud, he wouldn't go away—the stoop-shouldered man in his middle years, his face sad and creased like the seat of someone's baggy pants. He was wearing a rumpled blue serge suit, its coat a few sizes large to accommodate the hump on his back. Because it fidgeted and twitched, I thought at first that the hump must be alive; then I understood that it was a hidden pair of wings.

So this was he, Malach ha-Mohves, the Angel of Death. I admit to being somewhat disappointed. Such a sight should have been forbidden me, it should have struck me blind and left me gibbering in awe. But all I could feel for the angel's presence was my profoundest sympathy. The poor shnook, he obviously had his work cut out for him. From the way he massaged his temples with the tips of his fingers, his complexion a little bilious (from the smell?), I guessed that he'd been at it for a while. He looked like he'd come a long way expecting more cooperation than this.

"For the last time, Malkin," I could hear him saying, his tone quite similar in its aggravation to the one I'd used with Lazar myself, "are you or aren't you going to give up the ghost?"

In his corner old Lazar was nothing, a heap of dust, his moldy overcoat and eye patch the only indications that he was supposed to resemble a man.

"What are you playing, you ain't at home?" the angel went on. "You're at home. So who do you think you're fooling?"

But no matter how much the angel sighed like he didn't have all night, like the jig was already up, Lazar Malkin kept mum. For this I gave thanks and wondered how, in my moment of weakness, I had been on the side of the angel.

"Awright, awright," the angel was saying, bending his head to squeeze the bridge of his nose. The flame of the lamp leaped with every tired syllable he uttered. "So it ain't vested in me, the authority to take from you what you won't give. So what. I got my orders to bring you back. And if you don't come dead, I take you alive."

There was a stirring in Lazar's corner. Keep still, you fool, I wanted to say. But bony fingers had already emerged from his coat sleeves; they were snatching the plugs of cloth from his ears. The angel leaned forward as if Lazar had spoken, but I could hear nothing—oh, maybe a squeak like a rusty hinge. Then I heard it again.

"Nu?" was what Lazar had said.

The angel began to repeat the part about taking him back, but before he could finish, Lazar interrupted. "Take me where?"

"Where else?" said the angel. "To paradise, of course." There was a tremor in the corner which produced a commotion of moths.

"Don't make me laugh," the old man replied, actually coughing the distant relation of a chortle. "There ain't no such place."

The angel: "I beg your pardon?"

"You heard me," said Lazar, his voice become amazingly clear.

"Okay," said the angel, trying hard not to seem offended. "We're even. In paradise they'll never believe you're for real."

Where he got the strength then I don't know—unless it was born from the pain that he'd kept to himself all those weeks—but Lazar began to get up. Spider webs came apart and bugs abandoned him like he was sprouting out of the ground. Risen to his foot, he cried out, "There ain't no world but this!"

The flame leaped, the windowpane rattled.

This was apparently the final straw. The angel shook his melancholy head, mourning the loss of his patience. He removed his coat, revealing a sweat-stained shirt and a pitiful pair of wings no larger than a chicken's.

"Understand, this is not my style," he protested, folding his coat, approaching what was left of my father-in-law.

Lazar dropped back into the chair, which collapsed beneath him. When the angel attempted to pull him erect, he struggled.

I worried a moment that the old man might crumble to pieces in the angel's embrace. But he was substantial enough to shriek bloody murder, and not too proud to offer bribes: "I got for you a nice feather headdress . . ."

He flopped about and kicked as the angel stuffed him head first into his own empty burlap peddler's sack.

Then the world-weary angel manhandled Lazar—whose muffled voice was still trying to bargain from inside his sack—across the cluttered shed. And hefting his armload, the angel of death battered open the back door, then carried his burden, still kicking, over the threshold.

I threw up the window sash and opened my mouth to shout. But I never found my tongue. Because that was when, before the door slammed behind them, I got a glimpse of kingdom come.

It looked exactly like the yard in back of the shop, only—how should I explain it?—sensitive. It was the same brick wall with glass embedded on top, the same ashes and rusty tin cans, but they were tender and ticklish to look at. Intimate like (excuse me) flesh beneath underwear. For the split second that the door stayed open, I felt that I was turned inside-out, and what I saw was glowing under my skin in place of my kishkes and heart.

Wiping my eyes, I hurried into the shed and opened the back door. What met me was a wall, some ashes and cans, some unruly weeds and vines, the rear of the derelict coffee factory, the rotten wooden porches of the tenements of our dreary neighborhood. Then I remembered—slapping my forehead, stepping gingerly into the yard—that the shed had never had a back door.

Climbing the stairs to our apartment, I had to laugh out loud.

"Sophie!" I shouted to my wife—who, without waking, told me where to find the bicarbonate of soda. "Sophie," I cried, "set a place at the table for your father. He'll be coming back with God only knows what souvenirs."

Mr. Mitochondria

Aryeh Lev Stollman

WE WERE HAVING BREAKFAST on the spring day before the locusts arrived. My family lived on the outskirts of Beersheba in one of those large white boxlike structures that bloomed in the sands of the Negev in the fifties and sixties. My parents, emigrants from Canada, had lovingly planted the yard with flowering succulents, brilliant desert varieties that filled their winter-bred souls with wonder and upon which they bestowed allegorical names. Outside the kitchen lay heavy rolls of transparent plastic between the purple pinnacles of Sarah's Handmaiden and the waxy crimson blossoms of Job's Wife. For the last several days, the radio and newspapers were full of terrifying reports on the desert grasshopper, "the largest infestation of the century," swarming over the Arabian Peninsula to the east, and ready to migrate across the Red Sea.

Adar, nine at the time, had spent several afternoons after school drawing all the plants in his sketchbook "so when they get killed, we can remember them." When he said this, Mother covered her ears with her hands. "Oh, God, please don't be so morbid. They're my special babies! I couldn't bear to lose a single one." Under each meticulous depiction of fleshy trunk, flower, and seed, Adar wrote the species's Latin name. To the side he drew a hovering, glowering figure, six-winged and brandishing a fiery staff—the threatened plant's guardian angel. "See, Tishrei," Adar said, pointing to one of the figures, "they all have curly red hair like you."

That morning, as usual, Father was preoccupied with his whole grain cereal, weighing exactly 55 grams, 180 calories, of organically grown cracked wheat and bulgar, and measuring exactly 250 milliliters of nonfat milk, 9.2 grams of protein. Father, who had always been perfectly healthy and lean, had recently begun to mistrust the innate brilliance of human physiology. He now stood guard against its errors, discounting the experience of his own well-functioning kidneys in keeping his bodily fluids and electrolytes balanced, or the wisdom of his liver and pancreas to metabolize the varying amounts and types of amino acids and sugars that a normal person might chance to take in from day to day. "Honey, you really ought to try and have more faith," Mother would say. "Faith keeps our atoms from flying apart and has restored us in this wilderness." Father answered with a half-smile, "Kayla, I have faith, but it's not an antidote to reality."

That morning as Adar came into the kitchen, Father put down the graduated cup he used to measure his milk. Adar looked less like a child than like a miniature man, a small, skinny replica of our father with the same smooth black hair and the same pale gray eyes. "Alien eyes," Mother called them, "windows to the alien soul."

"Well, Adar, I had a chance to read your report last night." Father held up the draft of Adar's entry into the National Science Institute's contest for schoolchildren. "It's outstanding. And your research proposal is brilliant. After all, imagination is the secret to all great discoveries. You're going to win." After a long pause Father continued solemnly, "I'm proud of you, Adar. You're a prodigy."

"A prodigy? Where? In my kitchen?" Mother, in a narrow white caftan and sandals, stood by the stove, her red hair tied in a long ponytail. After moving to the desert Mother still practiced the cuisine of her snowy Toronto childhood. Holding a skillet, she flipped a blueberry pancake high into the air, her intense gaze never leaving the revolving spotted disc. "A prodigy? That's quite a heavy label!" Adar was hurt at this implied negation of his new status. He stared at his lap. The pancake completed its brief parabolic flight and landed in the skillet, raw side down, with a faint sizzle.

Mother, eventually, if not instantly, sensitive to the effects of her words, made a clumsy retreat. "Of course, he's prodigiously smart." She slid the pancake onto Adar's dish. "The women of the planet Ichalob are extremely jealous of me"—Mother had been working on her epic trilogy, *The Ichalob Chronicles*— "despite the fact that the mothers are preoccupied, what with all the upsetting prophecies emanating from their moons, and their children being killed fighting the Uranites. Well, no matter what anyone says, I wouldn't trade in my children for all the particle transformers in Galaxy Five."

Father looked at her, alarmed. "What are you talking about?"

"Talking about? The particle transformers? It's just something I made up."

Father took a long breath, looked at us with his pale gray eyes, the eyes that Adar shared. "What I was trying to say, Kayla, is that you should not dismiss the fact that Adar might be more than *very smart*. The boy has something extra in him. An undeveloped, an *unconventional* genius. I don't know why I overlooked this before. He sees things differently. It should be encouraged."

Mother rolled her eyes, then leaned over Adar. "Why aren't you eating your pancake?"

"I can't. It's made with squished insects. Their purple blood is leaking out."

"You've eaten plenty of blueberries in plenty of pancakes before."

"I'm fasting so the locusts won't come."

Mother took away Adar's plate. "Well, I suppose we should all be fasting as the people of Nineveh did, or Queen Esther when trouble was brewing. God does appreciate a fast, but I have the feeling it's already too late and the locusts will eat everything and you'll be starving to death."

My brother and I were named for the lunar months in which we were born: Tishrei, for the autumn month when the world was created and is repeatedly judged, and Adar, for the last month of the rainy season, when God is especially gracious to His People, the month before Spring waves her fertile wand across the land.

Adar was clearly very smart, but to be a real live prodigy one had to accomplish some incredible feat at an extremely young, postfetal age. Like the Sage of Vilna, who as an infant recited the correct blessing for milk at his mother's breast. That was a prodigy. Or John Stuart Mill, who read the Greek classics at three. Adar was no John Stuart Mill. He was no little Mozart composing *Eine kleine Nachtmusik*.

Father was a researcher at an experimental nuclear station in the desert. Mother often told the story of their "great migration" from Canada to this faraway and unlikely scientific outpost. While Father was still a postdoctoral fellow in Toronto and already married to Mother, he wrote his first monograph, *Theoretical*

Deuterium Fusion in Enhanced Magnetic Fields. Soon after its publication, he was approached by emissaries from the Negev Nuclear Authority, who were scouting the world for new scientific talent.

"They courted your father more persistently and, I might add, more romantically than he courted me. They made extravagant predictions, 'You will help shape the destiny of your people and ensure the survival of their children.' And they made a wonderful promise, music to any scientist's ears: 'You can do whatever research you want.' They took both of us on a secret trip halfway across the world to see the desert and the facility, to help us think things over. I was still very sad then and I suddenly felt like I had traveled to another planet. That's when I had my first vision of Ichalob. And I understood even then that despite appearances, Ichalob was not a lifeless world. You know, it had very lush botanical life during its watery epoch that endured into the imperial desert age as well. But anyway it was a good thing that I became so inspired to write my trilogy, because otherwise I would have gone crazy."

Father rarely discussed his work, and when he did, only in the vaguest terms. "I'm working hard on this new project," or, "My experiments are going very well," he might tell Mother on those frequent nights when he came home late. We were led to understand that Father's work was very important and of a secret, restricted nature. Sometimes we were allowed to visit him at the low-rise outer buildings of the research facility. There he had an office filled with bulky computer equipment and large blackboards covered with the endless and incomprehensible chatter of equations. We were never allowed in the domed complex that housed the nuclear reactor. "I'm sorry, I'd like to, but it's not a tourist attraction."

In contrast to the secretive Negev Nuclear Authority, the National Science Institute was open to the public and a source of great pride and prestige to the country. The Institute, with its yearly contest, sought to encourage creative thinking from schoolchildren in the realm of research. Adar's entry, "Mitochondria, the Powerhouses of the Cell: How We Should Study Them Better," was, per the contest instructions, part science report and part proposal for innovative research. Mitochondria, the microscopic organelles that dwell within all living cells, are, in reality, ancient bacteria, tiny specks of life that invaded our ancestral cells and made their home there. In exchange for lodging they provide energy for life processes. Father acted as if Adar had discovered mitochondria himself instead of having gleaned known facts from the encyclopedia and the many scientific journals and magazines that filled huge bookcases throughout our house. Adar, in his own words, had proposed an original avenue for cellular research that impressed Father, and, as it turned out, the National Science Institute as well: "We should study the mitochondria of the locusts that are coming, because they travel very far and need lots of energy so they must have many mitochondria. It would be like a human person walking a million miles after eating only a sandwich. It may be important to wear gloves when touching the insects in case they are poisonous or have contagious and fatal diseases." Adar submitted several drawings of a migratory locust he had copied from the encyclopedia with small arrows pointing to the hypermetabolic wing muscles.

"You know, Tishrei," Adar said in the bedroom the night of his elevation to prodigyhood, the night before the locusts arrived, "it's creepy to think we have these parasites in our cells and would die without them. Maybe someone could destroy the mitochondria in the locusts and they would all die." There was a faint and nervous quaver in his voice. "And, you know what else, Tishrei, you only inherit them from your mother, never your father. Mitochondria have their own separate DNA."

"How do you know? Did you ever see one? It's just a theory."

"It's not a theory, Tishrei. It's a scientific fact. I read it."

"It's a sci-en-tif-ic faaact! It's a sci-en-tif-ic faaact! I read it! I read it! 'I'm so smart! I'm a prodigy!'"

Adar was on the verge of tears. "Don't be jealous, Tishrei. I never said that. You're two years older. You're smarter than me."

Just then Mother, the source of all our mitochondria, came into the room. "What's going on? I thought I heard talking!"

"Hi, Mom," Adar said, trying to sound calm.

Mother walked toward the window. "Why aren't you asleep? Are you too hot? It's already cool outside, so I've turned off the air-conditioner. I'll open this window some more. Tomorrow we have to get up extra early—we have a lot of work to do." She hesitated at the doorway. "You know, maybe we should read something together to prepare us." She came back a moment later and began reading from the Book of Yo'el. "'That which the cutting locust has left, the swarming locust has eaten; and that which the hopping locust has left, the destroying locust has eaten.'"

Adar suddenly grabbed her arm. "Mom, please stop reading. I'm tired."

"Oh, I'm sorry. You must be exhausted."

She stayed awhile longer to say the bedtime prayers: "On my right is Michoel, on my left Gavriel, before me Uriel, and behind me Refael."

After she left the room Adar called out softly as he always did when he was very frightened, "Tishrei, look at me. Okay? Watch me until I fall asleep. Okay? Please."

Next morning our father woke everyone up before sunrise.

"Mother Nature is on the march!"

On the radio we heard that the locusts had begun crossing the Red Sea at twenty kilometers per hour. Schools were closed in the southern half of the country and the population was urged to remain indoors. The air force was on alert, ready to spray the invading clouds of insects with tons of insecticides. The radio explained how the pilots would have to fly around and then above the swarms in order to avoid clogging their engines with locusts. The government warned that the spraying would only decrease but not eliminate the terrible pest. At first Adar would not come out of the house until Father reassured him that the locusts would not arrive for several hours. In the cool dawn light Mother handed out kerchiefs to wear around our mouths and noses to prevent inhalation of the insecticides, even though the spraying had not yet begun. We looked like bandits from a western. We placed dozens of tall metal stakes at equal intervals in the ground, and Father hammered them in for supports. We spread the thin clear plastic above the plants, tying the edges of the material to the stakes with string. The yard resembled a great tabernacle.

"It's like a wedding canopy for plants," Father said, taking hold of Mother. They drew close and danced awkwardly for a few moments, brushing against the covered blue flowers of Joseph Is Not. Mother began singing "The Voice of the Bridegroom, the Voice of the Bride." Father laughed. I thought Mother was laughing, too, but then I realized she had begun crying. She seemed to me as delicate and vulnerable as any of the wonders in our garden. Father broke off from dancing. He smoothed her hair back from her face. "Everything will be fine, Kayla. Like you say, we need to have faith. We'd better finish now. I almost knocked something over. And I still have to go to the lab."

Mother had stopped crying. "You shouldn't have to be driving in the open today with them spraying chemicals. You should be indoors. You're the one who's become so health-conscious."

"I'm in the middle of a project. I can't just stop. Besides, I'm sorry to inform you, all these precautions are useless. They'll be spraying the stuff for miles and way up in the air. It will be everywhere. Like strontium ninety."

Adar turned pale. He pulled the fingers of one small hand with the other. "Is there really strontium ninety in this desert? I thought it was only in America. It gives you cancer and makes your bones fall apart!"

"I was just kidding. Don't worry."

"What about all the insect poisons, Dad? They're nerve poisons, aren't they? Mom says—"

"You and your mother worry too much. The spray quickly dissipates. The wind will blow it all out to sea in a day."

Father began walking toward the car, removing the kerchief from his face.

After Father drove off, we went indoors. "'Worry too much!'" Mother said. "As if I didn't have reason. If I had better sense and hadn't been so preoccupied with the goings-on on Ichalob, I would have taken us back to Toronto until this plague was over! Well, maybe I'll get some new ideas for *The Ichalob Chronicles*."

Mother went haphazardly around the house, closing windows. "Please, leave them shut. I don't want any contaminated air in here. I don't want to be poisoned."

"We'll run out of oxygen!" Adar said. Even though we were indoors, he would not take his kerchief off his mouth and nose.

"Don't be silly. Besides we can still leave the central air-conditioning on. It has a new filter. Now I'd better get some real work done. The slave Queen of Ichalob and her retinue are in secret revolt against the evil King and have declared a solemn fast to ensure its success. They are going to destroy the particle transformer by releasing millions of scientifically created pseudoseraphs from their force-field clouds. The children must be saved!" As she closed her writing room door behind her we could still hear her: "Yes, thank God, *all* the children will be saved."

Adar went to his desk and looked over his drawings of the garden plants with their Latin names and their guardian angels. He fussed over each and every one of them, adding some details here, a bit of color there. He even drew additional guardian angels, larger and more ominous than the previous. Finally he said he was tired. "I'm going to take a nap, Tishrei."

"I'm tired, too, Adar, but you know I can't fall back asleep in the daytime. And the house is so stuffy even with the air-conditioning on. I wish we could open a window. Dad says it doesn't matter, and it's still cool outside. Mom likes to exaggerate everything."

"I have to go to sleep now, Tishrei. I'm really tired." Only then did Adar take off his kerchief.

In the early afternoon the sky on the eastern horizon darkened with thick approaching clouds, as it did before a terrible desert storm.

"Look, Tishrei!" Adar shouted. An insect had landed on the sill of the living room picture window. The creature's hind legs were brown-green and jointed like a frog's, its translucent wings vibrating. Adar ran back to the bedroom to get his magnifying glass.

Suddenly he began screaming. "The window's open!"

Mother came running from her studio. "What's happening! Adar! Adar! Where are you?"

Adar came back into the living room, crying and trembling. "You left the window open! You left the window open!"

Mother tried to calm him down. "It's all right, Adar. It's all right. I must have overlooked it. I thought I shut the window in your room. I'm sorry. I thought I shut it." She went into the bedroom and came back. "It was hardly open. Now it's closed. Please stop crying."

Adar began whispering to himself, "She left the window open. It was open the whole time. She left the window open in our room."

After Adar calmed down, he held the magnifying glass near the locust that still clung to the windowsill. We all crouched down and took turns watching the exhausted locust move its head slowly back and forth, looking at us with one, then the other black-green polyhedral eye. "Oh, it looks so sad and lonely," Mother said. She smiled nervously. "I guess its friends, our other little guests, will arrive soon enough to keep it company. I wish your father were home for the party."

"It looks sick," Adar said. "It can barely move."

"Maybe he's just resting," Mother said. "He's been traveling a long time. He's come a very long distance."

"It's dying," Adar said. "It's dying."

We heard planes flying overhead. Mother said, "They've just started spraying. See, Adar, we closed the window just in time." The sky overhead was now a starless, moonless night. A light pitter-patter began on the plastic canopies over the garden and on the roof of our house. The noise quickly grew in intensity like hail. All afternoon we heard the planes flying overhead and the locusts raining steadily from the sky. The fallen creatures covered the plastic tabernacles in the yard. They covered our neighbors' houses and they covered the road that led in one direction into town and in the other, over twenty kilometers away, to the research facility where Father worked. Soon the invaders covered all the windows of the house so we could barely look out. Mother got a spatula and went throughout the house banging at all the glass panes to frighten off the locusts, but this did not work. After a few hours the hail noise stopped but there was still the low, sad moaning of the locusts. On the radio we heard that the locusts that had fallen in the Negev would die within twenty-four hours. The vast majority of the invaders, however, moved on overhead in apocalyptic formations, each several miles long, threatening the lush settlements in the north and west. The government said that people and farms in the south had been relatively spared but the threat to the northern settlements was still great. The rabbinate had finally declared a fast, and prescribed psalms, prayers, and readings from the Bible.

In the late evening when Father returned, he skidded on the road in front of the house but then regained control of the car. "It happened three times on my way home," he later told us. "The roads are all slippery with locusts. They're like little capsules of grease."

He entered the screened-in porch. Mother met him there and helped him brush off the locusts that started clinging to him when he got out of the car. "At least they don't bite," he said. "They just tickle." Mother inspected his clothes one final time and with her fingers picked off a few remaining creatures from his shoulder, his zipper, and his cuff. "Okay, you're ready to come out of the decompression chamber. I will turn off the force field." And she led him into the house.

Overnight, while we slept, the great tabernacle protecting the garden collapsed under the sighing weight of the locusts. In the morning my parents went outside to try and salvage what they could but the task was near impossible. Piles of locusts were everywhere, on the collapsed plastic sheets, on the ground, on the house. Under the twisted plastic, most of the plants were severely damaged, their fleshy bodies ruptured, their flowered branches fragmented. Mother began crying uncontrollably. "My little babies," she kept saying. "Oh, God, my poor little babies."

Adar watched from the protection of the screen porch. Adar started crying, too. Father began telling Mother that he would plant everything again. "Every single one, Kayla. Every single one." He put out his hand to caress her shoulder but she shrugged him off.

"My little babies! My special babies! I should sit shiva!" With both hands she pulled on the collar of her caftan, rending it.

Suddenly Father's face turned red. His eyes became dark. In a low choking voice that carried over to the porch he rebuked her. "Kayla . . . Even to say such a thing! They're *plants* . . . Have you already forgotten? We sat shiva for a real boy . . . Kayla . . . you will not sit shiva for plants."

I was so shocked that for a moment I could not catch my breath.

Mother headed toward the house, heedlessly trodding over the crunching mounds of insects. She passed through the screen porch. As she entered the house, Adar, still crying, reached up and tried to pat down her torn collar. With an absentminded look, she pushed him away and continued through the living room.

Adar watched as the door of her writing room closed behind her. He stopped crying.

At lunchtime Adar went over to Father, who had stayed home. "My bones hurt. I'm achy."

Father checked his temperature. It was normal. "I don't know what's the matter with you, Adar. Maybe there's been too much excitement." Father went to get Mother, who had not yet come out of her writing room. When she came out she acted as if nothing had happened, as if her special babies had not died, as if she had not been rebuked by Father. As if she had never mourned a real child.

"Well, eveything's been topsy-turvy in Galaxy Five. Now let's see what's happening on Earth." She touched Adar's forehead with her lips. "Hmm, I'm not sure." She took his temperature again with a thermometer. It was normal. "Well, you're lucky. I bet the locusts all have a temperature!"

The next morning Adar woke up screaming. "Tishrei, I can't move my right side. I can't move my right side!" His cries woke my parents in their bedroom. A moment later they came running. When they saw Adar they became terrified. Adar was moaning. "Oh, my God," Mother kept saying. "Oh, my God." Father lifted Adar out of bed. His right arm and leg stretched out from his body, they floated out in the bedroom air as if weighing no more than feathers. It seemed as if he might drift out of Father's arms and become a ghost. My parents covered him in a blanket and went out to drive him to the hospital.

Mother and Father stayed overnight in the hospital with Adar. The next morning they all came home. Father carried Adar from the car to the house wrapped in a light blanket.

"I've been poisoned, Tishrei. I almost died, Tishrei," Adar whispered as Father carried him through the living room to the bedroom. My parents stared at each other for a long moment. They were pale and exhausted as if they had not slept in weeks. Mother's eyes began blinking and twitching, something that had never happened before. She stood aside trembling while Father put Adar in bed. She glanced at the floor, at her hands, out a window. She did not speak.

Adar's convalescence was brief. The doctors prescribed a regimen of exercises that Mother and Father did with him several times every day. They stretched out the joints of his arm or his leg, coaxing the paralyzed limb to move.

At the same time Father began the task of replanting and renaming the garden. He ordered plants from nurseries across the country and even took several days off from his research to make sorties into the wilderness. One afternoon, a week after the locusts arrived, Father brought home two strange waist-high specimens. They were almost identical. We had never seen such beautiful plants before.

"I found them near each other in a rock formation. It was hard to dig them out. Look at the shape of their flowers."

Mother watched as Father transplanted the shallow roots into our soil. Father looked up and smiled at Mother. "It looks like they came from Ichalob, Kayla."

She didn't answer.

"It looks like these plants came from Ichalob," Father repeated, still smiling. "They're highly evolved."

"I really wouldn't know anymore." She turned away and went back into the house.

The following day Adar fully recovered the use of his right hand. He sat in his wheelchair in the yard and copied the new succulents in his sketchbook. He drew the graceful weeping branches and the tiny yellow flowers of Elisha's Cure.

The following week Adar was able to walk normally again.

"I'm real lucky I got better from all that nerve poison," he said one night at bedtime. "I could have died or been paralyzed. It's still in my system but I adjusted. You never really get rid of it completely, Tishrei. That's the scary part. You could die at any time."

In the beginning of the summer, Adar received a letter from the National Science Institute. He had, as Father predicted, won first prize in the elementary school category. That afternoon, as a surprise, Mother baked an oval, cell-shaped chocolate cake.

In the evening after dinner she brought it quietly out to the table. On top, in white icing, she had written, "Congratulations Mr. Mitochondria!"

Adar climbed up and knelt on his chair. He stared at the cake. "Who is Mr. Mitochondria?"

My parents hesitated and looked at each other. A new uncertainty had overtaken them.

"You are," Father finally said.

"Yes, of course, you are, Adar," Mother repeated. "The one and only." And then she added carefully, slowly, as if she had been practicing for a very long time. "Tishrei would have been so proud of you."

"Yes. Tishrei would be very proud of you," Father said.

Adar smiled. "Really? He would?"

"Of course he would."

Adar leaned forward before the great celebration of the cake. Mother handed him a knife. "Please, Adar, do the honors. It's your cake."

Father said, "Yes. It's your cake, Adar."

"Okay."

Adar stretched out his right hand to cut the first piece. In the strange healing grace of that moment, a faint tremor, a slight vibration moved up his arm.

My parents did not seem to notice this.

I thought I might fall over but I didn't.

I just knelt there, leaning forward, staring at my cake, my right arm outstretched.

From that moment onward, I no longer needed to keep imagining my lost brother.

"Oh, Adar," I heard my parents say to me. They both spoke in the exact same voice, in the exact same breath. My mother and father had suddenly become indistinguishable to me. "Oh, Adar," they said to me and I realized they were crying. "Oh, Adar, don't you know? We are all so proud of you."

Where Writers Matter
An Afterword

David G. Roskies

THIS COMMUNITY OF WRITERS that we've welcomed you into—is it virtual or real? By rehearsing how this anthology came into being, we might arrive at an answer.

I grew up in a world where writers—poets, playwrights, novelists, and literary critics—mattered. For one thing, our home was a salon for Yiddish writers. Soon after escaping to Canada, in the Fall of 1940, my mother began to organize soirées to raise money for the publication of new books by any one of our own poets, prose writers, and Judaic scholars. She also hosted some of the great Yiddish writers who came to town, whether from New York or Tel Aviv. It was by invitation only, with an elegant spread of Mrs. Gaon's apple strudel and chocolate nut cake and catered party sandwiches. My chosen spot was beneath the piano, where I vowed that someday I too would sit in this august assembly and read from my Yiddish work.

Montreal could also boast—and still does—a Jewish Public Library, which not only housed the great books of the Jewish imagination, but also played host to its living practitioners and interpreters. And should you have missed so-and-so's lecture at the Library; should his latest book have been taken out by another borrower, you could always buy a copy at Kalles's Book Store on Park Avenue, later on Queen Mary Road. As a card-carrying member of the Yiddish intelligentsia, Hertz Kalles was happy to recommend additional books by the same author or on some related subject. He introduced me to Primo Levi's *Survival in Auschwitz* when I was fourteen years old. Finally, to ensure that a native-born generation of Jews would someday avail themselves of these treasures, Montreal had a network of Jewish day schools, where a *lerer* was someone you addressed only in Yiddish or Hebrew. In their spare time, our *lerers* wrote and reviewed books. Some of them were fêted by my mother.

Ever since then, I've been looking for a home to replace the one I had known in Montreal. Footloose in New York City during the mid-Sixties, I discovered that East Broadway was still in business, and the Yiddish diehards who worked for the daily press were bemused by a sixteen-year-old Yiddish literary hopeful. "You show some journalistic talent," was I. B. Singer's comment on my first Yiddish story. Volf Younin, with his Russian cap and flaboyant scarf, once took me to the Garden Cafeteria next to the Forward building and introduced me to all the guys. But when I finally moved to New York for good, in the summer of 1975, that whole generation of writers was dying out and the most I could do on occasion was to deliver a eulogy. Hearing me speak Yiddish was supposed to alleviate the sorrow.

I found the ambiance at the Hungarian Pastry Shop on Amsterdam and 111th to be appropriately bohemian, and for the price of a mug of coffee I could sit there all day with my new writer friends, who would throw in a Yiddish word here and there for my benefit. How these brief encounters made me long for the Old Café Royale on Second Avenue, where in the Twenties and Thirties (so the story went) each group of writers had had its own reserved table! Gone was the Garden Cafeteria where the cashier not only recognized every writer who walked in, but also tore into him for his latest op-ed piece in the Yiddish press. Gone, in fact, were all the cafeterias.

Writers, I sadly discovered, had no permanent home here in America, did not thrive within a communal setting, because ... because they did not want to. What they craved instead was seclusion, a remote setting, to be left alone, to rub shoulders with the rest of us only on state occasions, or to preside as high priests over some cultic happening.

At best, they found temporary homes within two secluded settings: in writer's colonies and creative writing workshops. At a writer's colony they mattered to each other. Here they were encouraged to imbibe the fresh air, to enjoy the camaraderie, or simply to hole themselves up for the duration of their tenure and to write. At creative writing programs, of which there were over three hundred in this country, writers mattered primarily to their students, young hopefuls who were apprenticing under acknowledged masters, even while their tuition provided the masters with a pension plan, health benefits, and other mundane amenities.

If writers felt most at home within such acommunal or anticommunal settings as a writer's colony or creative writing program, they did make an occasional appearance at discrete public fora. Each year the 92nd Street Y would feature a select group of Jewish poets to take part in its prestigious poetry series; or for the price of admission to a contemporary Jewish play you might exchange words with the playwright at an exclusive after-theater discussion; or better yet, for no money at all you might even hear a celebrated Jewish author deliver a keynote address at an academic conference on the state of contemporary Jewish culture. Alas, because these were state occasions, discrete and short-lived, the search for a *Jewish* home where writers still mattered was doomed from the start. I was tilting at windmills, trying to catch the moon in a barrel, chasing my tail.

Until the day in the summer of 1999 when I was on my way to the last meeting of the season of the Adult Education Committee at Ansche Chesed, our friendly neighborhood synagogue. Suddenly it dawned to me that the whole summer lay ahead and there was to be absolutely no programming until after the High Holidays, four-and-a-half months away. Wasn't there something we could do in the slack season that would be educational and fun? What about arranging a series of readings on the roof? Once, someone I knew had rented the roof of Ansche Chesed to throw a book party, had served drinks and done a presentation. A perfect setting for summer in the Big Apple.

The Committee greeted my suggestion with great enthusiasm. It was decided to go for Mondays, the one night of the week when the theaters are dark, and to schedule seven consecutive readings. I volunteered to line up the writers, seeing this as an opportunity to bone up on contemporary Jewish writing, for even though a full professor of literature ought to own the whole field, I am your all-too-typical academic mandarin, who reads within narrow limits, and insofar as American Jewish fiction was concerned, I was at least a decade behind the times. Fortunately, I had a deep throat, my writer-friend Melvin Bukiet, who taught creative writing at Sarah Lawrence and ran the KGB Bar on East 4th Street. There wasn't a Jewish writer on the eastern seaboard whom Melvin didn't know.

I was a quick study. I learned from Melvin that an audience could listen for no more than half an hour at a stretch; that you therefore needed two writers to pair up each time, preferably two writers who already knew and liked one another; that the guest writers expected to have unlimited access to the bar; that we had to provide an adequate sound system. He gave me sixteen names and a few of their phone numbers.

That night the phone rang at 11:30. It was Melvin. He had just been out for a walk when he had a brainstorm: to name the series "Scribblers on the Roof."

I set to work. My years in a Yiddish youth movement had taught me that in order to get people to appear gratis you had to lay on the charm. So I wrote out a spiel to recite over the phone. Nothing prepared me for the response. Of the first fourteen phone calls I made, all fourteen writers agreed on the spot and thanked me for the opportunity to launch such an exciting new series.

So the writers were ready and willing to read. But were there readers equally eager to hear? I won't keep you in suspense. Scribblers on the Roof was the most spectacular adult education program ever held at Ansche Chesed. With a zero budget for publicity we had to rely on a flyer and public announcements in the press. By the seventh program, it was standing room only. Almost everyone paid the five dollars suggested contribution and the Adult Education Committee made a handsome profit. We could have kept going all summer.

On the roof, surrounded by water towers and the Manhattan skyline, most of the writers read works that were drawn either from personal memory, or from the contemporary scene. For the most part, it was a literature in the city and of the city. And that is also why it mattered.

A place where writers mattered, therefore, was a place where culture was accessible, cumulative, and communal. Some people, of course, came by Ansche Chesed only in the summer, only on nights when the theaters were dark. But the building itself was open at other times as well, for other kinds of learning, reading, hearing, talking, singing, and debating.

Ten years ago, a program like Scribblers on the Roof could not have been organized. But today there is a hunger for meaning, for intimacy, for celebration, for crossing boundaries. Out of that hunger comes a remarkable flowering of Jewish writing, here, in Canada, in Israel, in Latin America, in France, and in Germany. For the first time in over a century there is even a Russian-Jewish literary diaspora, some of whose writers have already adopted English as their primary language.

To read through this anthology, then, is to conjure up a dynamic New World place where writers matter—except that there is never a threat of rain.

Biographical Notes on the Authors

PEARL ABRAHAM is the author of the novels *The Seventh Beggar* (2005), *Giving Up America* (1998), and *The Romance Reader* (1995), and the editor of the Dutch anthology *Een Sterke Vrouw: Jewish Heroines in Literature* (2000). Recent stories appeared in *Epoch*, the *Forward,* and *Brooklyn Noir*. "Hasidic Noir" won the 2005 Private-Eye Writers of America's Shamus award for best short story. Her essays, interviews, and reviews have appeared in the *Forward, Michigan Quarterly*, and *Who We Are*. Her paper, "Trust the Tale: The Modernity of Nachman of Bratslav," delivered at the 2003 MLA conference, can be read at www.pearlabraham.com. Abraham has taught at various schools, including New York University and the MFA program at the University of Houston. She lives in New York City.

JONATHAN AMES is the author of six books, including *Wake Up, Sir!* and *I Love You More Than You Know*. He is the winner of a Guggenheim Fellowship and is a recurring guest on *The Late Show* with David Letterman.

MAX APPLE's stories have appeared in various magazines since 1972. His books of fiction and nonfiction are *The Oranging of America and Other Short Stories*, *Zip, Free Agents, The Propheteers, Roomates* and *I Love Gootie*.

MELVIN JULES BUKIET is the author of seven books of fiction and the editor of three anthologies. He lives in Manhattan, where bad things never happen.

JANICE EIDUS has twice won the O. Henry Prize for her short stories, as well as a Redbook Prize and a Pushcart Prize. Her new novel, *The War of the Rosens*, is about an iconoclastic Jewish family in the Bronx. Her work has appeared in such anthologies as *The Oxford Book of Jewish Stories*, as well as in such magazines as *Tikkun* and the *Forward*. Eidus writes frequently about issues of Jewish identity—sometimes with humor, always with affection. She's been invited to speak at such venues as The Jewish Museum, The Berman Center for Jewish Studies at Lehigh University, and Hebrew Union College. She's also the author of the short story collections *The Celibacy Club* and *Vito Loves Geraldine*, and the novels, *Urban Bliss* and *Faithful Rebecca*.

MYRA GOLDBERG teaches writing at Sarah Lawrence College. She is the author of *Whistling*, a collection of stories, and *Rosalind: A Family Romance*, a novel. Her recent publications include a story in NPR's publication, *Hanukah Lights*, and in *Shock and Awe: War on Words*, an anthology. She is writing a mystery on a piece looted from the Baghdad Museum during the current war. She lives in New York City.

DARA HORN was born in New Jersey in 1977, and is completing her doctorate in Hebrew and Yiddish literature at Harvard University. Her first novel, *In the Image*, received the National Jewish Book Award, the Edward Lewis Wallant Award, and the Reform Judaism Prize for Fiction. Her second novel, *The World to Come*, was published in 2006. She lives with her husband and daughter in New York City.

KEN KALFUS lived in Moscow, Russia, from 1994 to 1998. While there, he wrote the story in this volume, "Pu-239." He is the author of four books, *Thirst* (1998), *Pu-239 and Other Russian Fantasies* (1999), *The Commissariat of Enlightenment* (2003), and *A Disorder Peculiar to the Country* (2006). A film adaptation of "Pu-239" is in production for a 2006 release.

BINNIE KIRSHENBAUM is the author of two story collections, *Married Life* and *History on a Personal Note*, and five novels, *On Mermaid Avenue, Pure Poetry, A Disturbance in One Place, Hester Among the Ruins*, and *An Almost Perfect Moment*. She is a professor at Columbia University, Graduate School of the Arts.

JONATHAN LEVI is the author of the novel *A Guide for the Perplexed* (1992). His articles and short stories have appeared in the *Los Angeles Times, The Nation, GQ, Terra Nova*, and other magazines and newpapers. He has written operas with the composers Mel Marvin and Bruce Saylor, most recently libretti for *Guest from the Future* and *Buwalsky: A Road Opera* with Marvin, which had their premieres in 2004. A founding editor of *Granta* magazine, Levi was also the first Director of the Fisher Center for the Performing Arts at Bard College.

MARY MORRIS is the author of many books, including six novels—among them, *Revenge, Acts of God, The Night Sky*, and *House Arrest*—three collections of short stories, including *The Lifeguard*, and three travel memoirs, including *Nothing to Declare: Memoirs of a Woman Traveling Alone* and *Angels & Aliens: A Journey West*. She has also co-edited with her husband, Larry O'Connor, *Maiden Voyages*, an anthology of the travel literature of women. Her numerous short stories and travel essays have appeared in such places as *The Paris Review*, the *New York Times, Travel and Leisure*, and *Vogue*. Her work has been translated into more than ten languages. A new travel memoir, *The River Queen*, will be published in 2007. The recipient of the Rome Prize in Literature from the American Academy of Arts and Letters, Morris lives in Brooklyn with her husband and daughter.

CYNTHIA OZICK writes fiction and essays. Her most recent novel, *Heir to the Glimmering World*, was on the short list for the International Man-Booker Prize, and was a candidate for the Prix Medici in France. Of her essay collections, *Fame & Folly* was a finalist for the 1996 Pulitzer Prize and *Quarrel & Quandary* won the 2001 National Book Critics Circle Award for nonfiction. Among numerous other awards, she has received four O. Henry First Prizes, a Rea Award for the Short Story, and a Lannan Foundation Award for fiction. *The Din in the Head*, her fifth essay collection, will be published in 2006.

JON PAPERNICK is the author of the story collection, *The Ascent of Eli Israel*. His fiction has appeared in *Exile, The Reading Room, Night Train Magazine, Nerve.com*, and has been anthologized in *Lost Tribe: Jewish Fiction from the Edge*. Papernick has taught writing at Pratt Institute, Boston University, Brandeis University, Bar Ilan University, and continues to teach for Grub Street Writers in Boston. He recently completed a novel, and lives outside Boston with his wife.

SONIA PILCER was born in Augsburg, Germany, and lives in New York. She has published five novels, most recently *The Holocaust Kid*, which she adapted as a theatrical play for Shakespeare and Co. in Lenox, Massachusetts. Universal Studios bought the film rights to her first novel, *Teen Angel*, and she wrote the screenplay with Garry Marshall. Her other books include *Maiden Rites, Little Darlings*, and *I-LAND: Manhattan Monologues*, produced as a play in New York and Los Angeles. Pilcer teaches fiction and memoir writing at Berkshire Community College and at the Writer's Voice in New York City.

JONATHAN ROSEN's most recent novel, *Joy Comes in the Morning*, has recently been published in paperback. A chapter of that novel is in this book. He is also the author of the novel *Eve's Apple* and of *The Talmud and the Internet: A Journey Between Worlds*. His essays have appeared in the *New York Times*, the *New Yorker*, and many other publications. He is the editorial director of Nextbook. He lives in New York City with his wife and two children.

NORMA ROSEN has published both fiction and nonfiction. Her books are *Joy to Levine!, Green, Touching Evil, At the Center, John* and *Anzia: An American Romance, Accidents of Influence: Writing as a Woman and a Jew in America*, and *Biblical Women Unbound: Counter-tales*. A dramatic reading of her play, "The Miracle of Dora Wakin's Art," was given at the 92nd Street Y. Her short fiction and essays have appeared in a variety of magazines, including the *New Yorker, Commentary, Ms., Midstream, Hadassah, Lilith*, the *New York Times Magazine*, and the *New York Times Book Review*. She has received numerous grants and awards for her writing and has taught at Harvard, Yale, University of Pennsylvania, Hofstra, The New School for Social Research, Barnard, Columbia, and New York University.

LUCY ROSENTHAL is the author of the novel *The Ticket Out* and editor of *The Eloquent Short Story: Varieties of Narration, Great American Love Stories*, and *World Treasury of Love Stories*. She is on the writing faculty of Sarah Lawrence College and has taught in the creative writing programs of Columbia and New York University.

DAVID G. ROSKIES was educated at Brandeis and the Hebrew University, and is the Sol and Evelyn Henkind Professor of Yiddish Literature at the Jewish Theological Seminary. A former Guggenheim recipient, Mr. Roskies was also awarded the Ralph Waldo Emerson Prize from Phi Beta Kappa for his book *Against the Apocalypse*. Mr. Roskies lives with his wife and son on the Upper West Side of Manhattan. Other times, he resides in Old Katamon, Jerusalem.

LYNNE SHARON SCHWARTZ is the author of nineteen books, most recently *The Writing on the Wall*, a novel dealing with the aftermath of the 9/11 attacks. Her other works include the novels *Disturbances in the Field* and *Leaving Brooklyn*, as well as several short story collections; translations from Italian; the memoir, *Ruined by Reading*; and a collection of poetry, *In Solitary*. She lives in New York City.

LORE SEGAL is a novelist, essayist and writer of children's books. One of her novels, *Her First American*, was recently reissued.

STEVE STERN is the author of several works of fiction, including *Lazar Malkin Enters Heaven*, which won the Edward Lewis Wallant Award for Jewish American Fiction, and *The Wedding Jester*, which won the National Jewish Book Award. His most recent book is a novel, *The Angel of Forgetfulness*.

ARYEH LEV STOLLMAN's first novel, *The Far Euphrates*, was a *Los Angeles Times Book Review* Recommended Book of the Year, an American Library Association Notable Book, a National Book Critics Circle Notable Book, and winner of a Lambda Literary Award. It has recently been translated into Hebrew. His second novel, *The Illuminated Soul*, was a winner of *Hadassah Magazine's* 2003 Harold U. Ribalow Prize for Fiction. "Mr.

Mitochondria" appears in Stollman's story collection *The Dialogues of Time and Entropy*. Dr. Stollman is a neuroradiologist at Mount Sinai Hospital in Manhattan.

Acknowledgments

The publisher and the editors wish to thank the following authors and publishers, who so generously contributed to this volume:

Pearl Abraham: "The Seven Fat Brides." From *The Seventh Beggar* by Pearl Abraham. Copyright © 2005 by Pearl Abraham. Used by permission of Riverhead Books, an imprint of Penguin Group (USA) Inc.

Jonathan Ames: "Looking for the Answers." Copyright © 1989 by Jonathan Ames. From the novel *I Pass Like Night* (originally published by William Morrow, 1989; reissued by Washington Square Press, 1999). By permission of the author.

Max Apple: "The Eighth Day. " Copyright © 1983 by Max Apple. Originally published in *Ploughshares* and included in *Free Agents* (Harper and Row, 1984). Reprinted by permission of the author.

Janice Eidus: "Elvis, Axl, and Me. " Copyright © 1997 by Janice Eidus. From *The Celibacy Club* (City Lights Books, 1997). Also appeared in *Mondo Elvis* (St Martin's Press). Reprinted by permission of the author.

Myra Goldberg: "Gifts. " Copyright© 1993 by Myra Goldberg. Originally appeared in *A Shout in the Street* and included in *Whistling and Other Stories* (Zoland Books, 1993). Reprinted by permission of the author.

Dara Horn: "Readers Digest. " From *The World to Come: A Novel* by Dara Horn. Copyright © 2006 by Dara Horn. Used by permission of W. W. Norton & Company, Inc.

Ken Kalfus: "Pu-239. " Copyright © 1999 by Ken Kalfus. First appeared in *Harper's Magazine*. Included in *Pu-239 and Other Russian Fantasies* published by Milkweed Editions, 1999. By permission of the author.